Amber Luna
My Bright
Light

Kaitlyn Marquart

Praise for
Amber Luna My Bright Light
Awarded the 2025 Moonbeam Children's Book Award
Bronze Medal for Pre-Teen Mature Issues, and the Literary
Titan Gold Book award.

"Amber's voice is sharp and funny but tinged with loneliness as she deals with a toxic ex–best friend and the relentless gaze of social media. Mari's chapters are softer but heavy, weighted by her struggles with faith, belonging, and a private pain she hides from even her closest friend. Both perspectives weave together into a portrait of adolescence that's as tender as it is raw, capturing the ways we protect ourselves, sometimes at the expense of connection." –**Literary Titan, Starred Review**

"Young or old, this Kaitlyn Marquart novel, *Amber Luna My Bright Light,* will fill your heart with a new appreciation of your talents and inner strengths… It's so well written that the pages practically glow." –**Judy Hannigan, Award-winning Author of *Lost in Prosperity***

"*Amber Luna My Bright Light* is an honest and deeply moving debut. I recommend this story to anyone who's ever felt trapped, confused, and in search of their own light."
–Dorothy Deene, Award-winning Author of *Gravity of Lies*

Published independently by Kaitlyn Marquart
Copyright © 2025 Kaitlyn Marquart, Syracuse, NY
Cover Design: Moon Photograph by Ashley Duff, with design edits by the Author
Author photo: by Ashley Duff

LCCN: 2025906083
Hardcover ISBN: 979-8-218-64943-2
Paperback ISBN: 979-8-218-64670-7
eBook ISBN: 979-8-9990353-1-8

Connect with the author at
Website: kaitlynmarquartwrites.com
Social platforms:
Instagram: @kaitlyn_marquart_author
Facebook: Kaitlyn Marquart

Emily Dickinson's poem **"Hope is the thing with feathers"** appears in this book and is in the public domain.

This book contains **brief, non-detailed mentions** of self-harm and childhood abuse. These topics are referenced **without graphic description or explicit detail**, but they are acknowledged as part of the character's experience. **Please read with care.**
If you or someone you know is struggling, you're not alone. Talking to a trusted friend or adult can help. Support is always available:
National Suicide & Crisis Lifeline (US) - call or text 988
Suicide Crisis Helpline (CA) – call or text 988
Crisis Text Line (US) - Text HELLO to

For Kristy

Chapter 1

AMBER

My eighth-grade art project, a painting on canvas, hangs above my desk where only I can see it.

It features the silhouette of a girl stepping across the night sky, reaching for the crescent moon. Carefree and determined, she believes she's capable of anything. It's supposed to be a self-portrait. But she's nothing like me.

There was a time when I did feel like her, before I learned that even though other people's opinions *aren't* supposed to matter, they *do* when you're in middle school. Painting was the one thing I felt confident about, but after what happened to my sixth-grade painting, I learned the hard way that putting myself out there is a *big* mistake.

"Amber! Have you seen my planner?" Mom shouts from upstairs.

"I'll look," though honestly, I'm tempted to say, "Ask Google," since that's how she usually responds to most of my questions—especially if it's about my math homework.

Chances are Mom's planner is in the craziest place I can think of, so I open the dishwasher (*oh, come on, you don't really think it will be in there, do you?*) I check the medicine cabinet and the shelf above the coffee maker. I open the freezer and—*hallelujah!* "Found it!"

"I don't know what I'd do without you," Mom says as she shuffles into the kitchen with her empty coffee mug, wet hair tied up in a messy bun, and socks that don't quite match. "Anything exciting happening at school today?"

"Is there ever?" I ask, rolling my eyes. The last week of school is always a joke. Even the teachers have thrown in the towel at this point. "We're watching movies or documentaries in every class today *and* tomorrow."

"Documentaries aren't so bad, are they? And look on the bright side—only five more days until Camp Evergreen!" Mom has been counting down the days, and suddenly, documentaries don't sound nearly as bad as spending a week in the wilderness.

It's not that I'm *not* looking forward to camp—I am. A break from keeping up appearances and the nonstop notifications from social media actually sounds kind of nice. It's just... Camp Evergreen is *Mom's* thing. She hasn't stopped talking about it since the registration brochure arrived in the mail last month. She went to Camp Evergreen when she was my age and swears it changed her life. Somehow, I doubt it will have the same effect on me.

Sleeping in the wilderness with a million flying insects and going an entire week without Wi-Fi or my phone doesn't exactly sound like a good time. And even though I know she won't force me to go if I say I don't want to, the last thing I want is to disappoint her.

"My keys were just here," Mom mumbles, looking around frantically. We're going to be late, as usual, but I miraculously spot her keys in the fruit bowl. I snatch them out from under the apples and dangle them in front of her. "You're a lifesaver," she says as her "time to go" alarm goes off.

It used to be an obnoxious—*beep, beep, beep*—sound, until I showed her you can use any song from your iTunes playlist. Now we leave the house with *Eye of the Tiger* at full volume and images of Rocky Balboa punching the air to get us pumped for the day.

On the way to the middle school, we listen to Mom's usual station, *Y94-FM, the '80s to Now,* and sing along with one of her favorite Celine Dion songs. I would never admit to anyone that I know all the words to *My Heart Will Go On*, but with Mom, I belt it out at the top of my lungs.

As we pull up to the student drop-off circle, we finish our car ride karaoke before anyone can see us waving our arms and clutching our chests like Celine would on stage. When the car comes to a complete stop, I open the passenger door, and Mom, as she does every day, reminds me, "Remember who you are!"

I roll my eyes. It gets a little old being told to remember who you are when you're a teenager still trying to figure that out.

Making my way to the side entrance, the school resource officer greets me with an uninterested nod as she flirts with the PE teacher. Whatever happened to teachers looking like they could be our grandparents? This man gives Chris Hemsworth a run for his money.

As I take the first step up the stairs, I hear, "Amber, no granny skirt today?"

Granny skirt? What the actual heck?

Ignoring them, I continue toward my locker, but another random insult is thrown at me. Jared, from my Science class, says, "Looks like you forgot your walker!"

"Nice one, dude." His friend gives him a high five.

What is everyone talking about? I keep my head down and pick up the pace, making a beeline for the girls' bathroom instead of my locker.

I push the door open and step inside, where two girls I don't know have their phones out taking selfies. They look at me and laugh. One of them says, "You're Amber, right? The girl in Miranda's Instagram post!" I stare back at her dumbly. "You haven't seen it yet? Oops. My bad."

That's when I see the bright red writing on the bathroom mirror:

AMBER BROWN AGE 82
LOOKING FOR A HOT GRANDPA
TO SWEEP ME OFF MY FEET
CALL ME #607-357-1932

I try to play it cool, but I'm mortified. Their phones are pointed directly at me. I try to move past them quickly, but one of them steps into my path. I throw my hands up to cover my face and accidentally knock the phone from her hand.

"Not cool!" she screams, scrambling for her phone. She wipes it with her shirt and inspects the screen for cracks. "You're lucky it didn't break. Come on," she says to her friend. "Let's get out of here. It's starting to smell like old people."

I quickly move past the row of sinks and lower myself to the ground with my phone in both hands. I swipe the screen and immediately see the Instagram notification: *"miranda.thebest1* has tagged you in a post."

My stomach feels like it did when Mom convinced me to get on that awful pirate ship ride at the county carnival last year. Tapping the notification, I hold my breath and wait for the post to load.

I blink once, twice, then keep my eyes shut for a few seconds longer. I beg the Universe, *please, don't let me see that photo when I open my eyes again. Don't let it be real.*

My heart is pounding in my ears, and my hands are shaking. Opening my eyes, I see the photo of the two of us at her family's lake house in the Adirondacks from the summer between fourth and fifth grade. Miranda is showing off her flattering, hot pink two-piece with her gorgeous smile, as usual. And then there's me, leaning forward awkwardly—which only helps the camera make me look ten pounds heavier—wearing a horrendous black swimsuit with polka dots and a little granny-style skirt attached.

But there's something else. She's used some stupid filter called "Age Yourself Twenty Years," and it makes me look like the Wicked Witch of the West. Meanwhile, she's glowing like Anne Hathaway. *Dang it.* How is it possible we used to be best friends?

That stupid swimsuit. The day before leaving with Miranda for the lake house that year, I was a wreck when I realized that no matter how hard I tried, I couldn't squeeze into my favorite neon orange bathing suit from the previous two summers. It was the beginning of my "pudgy phase," and Mom tried to console me by blaming puberty; I blamed too many sleepover snacks.

To make matters worse, I was caught between junior and women's sizes, where the smallest women's size is slightly too big, while the largest junior size isn't quite right either. Realizing you no longer fit in junior clothing when you're still very much a kid, and not yet a woman, is a real blow to the ego.

After hours at the mall, Mom and I ended up in the women's swimsuit section at Macy's, and that's where we found that polka-dot monstrosity. It was the only one that somehow managed to fit every part of my strangely proportioned body. I hated it, but I was tired of shopping, my feet hurt, and I was hungry. Miranda was picking me up the next morning, so it was that or nothing. I caved.

Wearing that polka dot suit in front of my best friend at her family's lake house without anyone looking took a lot of courage. But now the whole world is looking. I can't let this go. I *have* to say something to Miranda:

> hey miranda u know the
> pic of us in ADK u posted to
> ur insta pls take it down.

Her response comes in the form of three never-ending bouncing dots. *Hit send already.* Instead of torturing myself by watching them dance, I return to Instagram, remove my tag (emo_nemo19), and see dozens of comments. Some are from people I don't know, but a *lot* of them are from people at school. Like Parker, the captain of the football team, and Renata from Algebra.

> @Parkerboy458>>bro, my grandma had that same bathing suit did she let u borrow it
> @Dollypartsthesea04>>miranda looking lit who the guy next to you
> @WizardWizeWoman>>OMG is that amber she hasn't changed a bit still a girl of style i see LOL
> @SnapbackDragon05>>poor ugly duckling oh wait OMG is that amber wow sorry amber didn't realize

I can't believe this is happening. How could she? Why? Everyone has seen it! A text from Miranda pops up at the top of my screen: stop being so extra.

Anger propels me from the ground. I tear a paper towel from the dispenser, run it under water, and begin to wipe away the message and my phone number on the mirror, scrubbing as hard as I can. The letters and numbers, written with lipstick, just smear and make an awful mess. *Well, it might be a mess, but it's a mess you can't read.*

My heart is racing, so I take two quick breaths in and let them out slowly, the way Mom taught me. I toss the towel into the trash, stomp it down aggressively with my foot, and my leg gets stuck in the dang bin. Wrenching my leg out, I lose my balance and crash to the ground, taking the trash can down with me.

At the same instant, the bathroom door swings open. Kirsten, from the track team, appears and stops to pull out her phone. Pointing it directly at me, she laughs. *Great. Another Instagram post of me for everyone to laugh at.* I put the trash bin upright and pick up the paper towels that escaped during the crash.

"You look frazzled today, Amber. You good?" Kirsten asks, laughing and recording my humiliation.

I turn away immediately as the first hot tears gather in my eyes. I'm angry at Miranda— and myself— for letting this get to me. I scold myself and wipe the tears from my face.

Leaving the girls' room, I put my head down and charge forward to my locker just as Pete, my neighbor from up the street, rounds the corner and runs into me. He mumbles incoherently and keeps walking like nothing happened.

I raise my voice loud enough for the entire hallway to hear: "It's okay, I'm fine. Thanks for asking," I say, sarcasm dripping from my lips. The giant earmuff headphones glued to Pete's head keep him from hearing my speech, and no one around is bothered by me either. *Whatever.* I will not let this ruin my last week of middle school. I've survived the last three years; what's another two days?

Chapter 2

MARI

Yellow caution tape surrounds a rusty backhoe taking a break from digging up the ground for the temple that's about to be built. The murdered forest with scattered branches piled on each other like wounded soldiers on the battlefield is a sad sight. The irony of destroying God's creations "to build a temple in His name" is not lost on me.

After the hour-long drive, Dad parks, and I get out to stretch. I'm so stiff, I wonder if I'm a thirteen-year-old trapped inside a seventy-year-old's body. Looking out over the construction site, I watch the others from the church youth group happily working despite the early June heat. There's laughter and upbeat chatter as the younger boys find ways to make the chore a game.

"Go long," one boy shouts as he hurls a leafless branch into the air like a track-and-field javelin. His buddy, a few yards away, drops his pile of brush. "Nice catch!"

Usually, I can match the energy of the people around me, but lately, it's impossible. I can't just put on a happy face and pretend everything is fine. Everything is not fine.

"Mari!" Rachel waves at me from the edge of the forest. "Over here!" She bends at the waist and disappears into the brush for just a second. She reemerges with her arms full of branches.

I trudge through the field toward her, cramming my hands into a pair of crusty old work gloves.

"So? How did it go with Aaron?" she asks.

"Nothing has happened yet," I say, turning away from her to pick up branches. Rachel is my best friend, but I still worry she'll laugh at me and maybe even feel sorry for me if I tell her the truth about what *really* happened.

I expect her to press me for more, but she continues to work quietly instead. Somehow, her *not* asking more questions makes me second-guess myself. Maybe she'll understand and help me feel better about it.

"I wrote him a letter," I say carefully, unsure how she'll respond.

"Oh. I thought you were going to call him," Rachel says as she works, but then stops abruptly. "Wait. What *kind* of letter? Not like a declaration of *love*, right?" she asks thoughtfully.

I'm already dripping with sweat, and now the heat of humiliation makes my cheeks burn as I remember watching Aaron, my kindergarten best friend, open my letter and read it out loud to all of his friends: *Something happened to me the first time I saw you at the beginning of middle school. I'm not sure, but maybe it's love? Do you feel it, too?*

They laughed at him, but he laughed along with them before tearing up the letter and throwing it away. Looking right at me, he yelled to his friends, "She's a crazy freak."

"It wasn't anything serious," I lie. "I just said I hoped we could maybe hang out more."

"Oh, well, that's not that bad. Did he write back?" Rachel asks, a glimmer of hope in her voice.

She's a hopeless romantic, so I don't have the heart to tell her that the story doesn't have a happy fairytale ending. "He just said he missed our time as kids, too, and that we should hang out soon."

"That's great, Mari! Oh my gosh, that's so sweet!" She claps her hands in quick succession and hops three times; it's the most girlish thing I've ever seen her do. "I can't wait to hear all about you two getting together!"

"I'll let you know." Another lie because there won't be anything to tell. I wish I could be honest with Rachel. But if I tell her about the heaviness that drags me down or how much I hate myself—how sure I am that everyone else does too— she'll give me a preachy lecture and quote the Young Women's Motto from the Mormon church we belong to: "We are daughters of our Heavenly Father, who loves us, and we love him… we strive to live the Young Woman values… faith, hope, divine nature, individual worth…" blah, blah, blah.

I struggle to live up to all of the church's strict rules and expectations—to believe I'm a child of God who's worthy of love. It doesn't seem to be too hard for Rachel (or my older sister, Laura, for that matter), so why is it so hard for me?

Most of the church's expectations align with generally good values, but some feel extreme, such as the strict dress code that forbids tank tops, short skirts, and "revealing attire." That might seem reasonable, but at five feet tall, finding modest shorts or skirts that don't make me look like an Oompa Loompa is impossible.

And the Sabbath Day must be kept holy—meaning family time, scriptures, and rest—no mall trips or birthday parties. Not that it matters. After my hundredth, "I can't on Sundays," people stopped inviting me, probably thinking it was just an excuse. But if I did make it up, that would be lying—and that's *definitely* against the rules. I wonder if lying to yourself is against the rules, too.

I want to believe—it would make things a lot easier—but I'm not convinced. When others share their unwavering certainty that God is real, tears sting my eyes. But I've always wondered if crying is just contagious, and I'm not immune. (Being an empath in a spiritual world isn't for the faint of heart.)

The truth is, the tears spilling over aren't because I feel the Holy Spirit and believe—they're from guilt and shame. Because I know I don't belong. I'm an impostor. There's no lonelier place for someone filled with doubt than being surrounded by people who are certain of everything.

I was baptized into the church at age eight and promised a fresh start—my sins washed away and the Holy Spirit as my constant companion and guide. The Holy Spirit assigned to me must have gotten lost because my only constant companion is the monster that haunts my dreams: "I told you not to tell anyone. Now look what you've done."

There are things that happened to me before I turned eight that I wish I could forget—but baptism doesn't promise a cleansing of memories.

After returning home from working at the temple construction site, I take a quick shower and change into fresh clothes. I don't feel any cleaner. There's no soap strong enough for that.

The sun has had enough for one day and sinks low on the horizon. The moon takes its post, casting a gentle glow over the hundred apple trees surrounding our house, tucked away at the end of our driveway, two-tenths of a mile off the main road.

When I was five years old, I remember coming to this house with Dad to buy apples from Mr. Wagner, the previous owner. "I'm not getting any younger," Mr. Wagner said to Dad as he loaded our family's van with a bushel of Cortland apples. "I hate to leave this place, but after sixty years, it's time. Goin' on the market next month."

"Is that so?" I remember Dad's eyes lighting up at Mr. Wagner's news.

"Yup, yup," Mr. Wagner continued. "Patricia and I bought the farm right after we got hitched. Lost her, oh, let's see." He paused to count the years, disappointed that he didn't know offhand. "Goodness gracious, it's been seven years already without my Patty."

"That's a long time," Dad said, trying to be respectful of Mr. Wagner's misfortune while trying to contain his excitement.

A few months later, shortly before my sixth birthday, Mr. Wagner sold the farm to Dad. Aaron's family had just moved, so leaving the neighborhood behind wasn't hard. I was excited about living in the country, like Fern Arable from my favorite book, *Charlotte's Web*. Mom used to read it to me and Laura at night before homework and studying took the place of bedtime stories.

I thought leaving the neighborhood meant escaping the monster—the neighbor—that hurt me. But he followed me, a stowaway in a box labeled *DO NOT OPEN*, shoved to the back of my new bedroom closet.

I remember Dad hanging a wooden swing from the giant oak in the backyard the minute we moved into the farmhouse. I also remember being glad I knew how to ride a bike; otherwise, walking to the end of our ridiculously long driveway to catch the school bus would have been miserable without my lilac-colored banana-seat bicycle.

I miss that bicycle. One Friday after school in fourth grade, I rode it through the orchards and ditched it in the tall grass to climb an apple tree in the Empire orchard. I sat up there for hours, thinking and making up songs, singing to myself.

It was getting dark when Dad came around with the tractor and offered me a ride back to the house. I didn't think the bike would grow legs and walk away overnight, so I decided to leave it and come back for it the next day.

What I didn't know was that Mom and Dad had given permission to the highway department to excavate a few acres of our open land. They needed dirt fill for a project across town, and in exchange for the dirt, they would fill the hole with water, creating a beautiful pond that would irrigate the orchards. The work crew arrived early the next day to begin digging the hole.

I'm sure my lilac banana-seat bicycle still exists—carried away by six-wheeled dump trucks and buried under layers of dirt and gravel next to the 481 South off-ramp. Rusting in the dark, still waiting to be found—like me.

Chapter 3

AMBER

"I forgot to ask you how school was today," Mom says as she stuffs her purse into the infant seat of the grocery cart and searches for her glasses. *Should I tell her they're on top of her head?*

"Just another Monday," I say, scrolling through my Instagram feed. I'm not about to tell Mom about Miranda's stupid post. That would mean I'd have to relive it. *Immediately, no.* And I don't want to upset her.

"But the *last* Monday of *middle* school!" she points out before discovering her glasses on top of her head—where she always puts them. *I knew she'd find them.*

As we approach the first aisle, I can sense Mom's jitters. She gets a little overwhelmed because the pasta shelves are full of *choices*: different shapes and sizes, made with whole wheat or enriched white flour, gluten-free, spinach- or squash-flavored, locally made or imported from Italy. Mom takes a deep breath, consults her list, and confidently reaches for the two boxes she decided on *before* seeing all the choices. "What do you think?" she asks. "We can have fettuccine Alfredo with broccoli, or I can make chicken riggies."

Mom isn't keen on making decisions, but she's always giving *me* choices about *everything*—and that's not an exaggeration. She would never let me do anything dangerous or reckless, of course, but I can't think of a time when I *didn't* decide something for myself.

I was ten when I caught on to it and decided to test the waters. First, I admitted I didn't want to play soccer anymore. Mom said, "If soccer isn't fun for you, it's up to you if you want to try something different." After a few more tests, I got brave and asked if I could dye a few strips of my hair bright blue: "How fun!" she said and dropped everything to take me to the beauty supply store.

By the time my thirteenth birthday came last year, I knew there was something I *one hundred percent* wanted. Even though blue hair wasn't exactly one of my best choices, it didn't take *too* much courage for me to ask if I could get a small nose ring. "It's your face," she said, though I noticed some hesitation before she agreed.

The pattern has always been the same—Mom lets me choose. But sometimes I want to tell her I'm tired of always having a choice. *Just decide, Mom.* I know I can't say this to her, so instead, I say, "We haven't had chicken riggies in a while." I continue my Instagram scroll and stop to double-tap a photo of

Prince Harry and Meghan Markle from their royal wedding last month.

"Perfect." Mom checks *pasta* off her list and sticks the pen back into her ponytail. I don't know why she doesn't use the Notes app on her phone. I rarely see her with her phone, except when she takes a call or looks up a recipe. (Aside from being my mom, cooking is her favorite thing in the whole world). She's obsessed with watching her favorite cooking competition show, "MasterChef," featuring Gordon Ramsay on Netflix.

Mom crosses the aisle in search of marinara, but before I can tag along to offer moral support, I hear, "Amber!" Miranda's haughty voice cuts through the clanking of shopping carts and the scanning of items at the checkout. "I love your outfit!" she says, oozing with over-the-top flattery as she looks me up and down.

My striped pink and purple knee-high socks coordinate with a pink shirt starring a girl in a powder blue tutu riding a unicorn with a rainbow mane. The shirt's caption: "Never Underestimate the Power of a Girl."

"Still rocking that bold style, we all know and love, I see!" Her laugh borders on mocking.

I force a smile as Mom returns with her arms full of bottled marinara—more than any chicken riggies recipe could *possibly* need. I don't have the guts or the energy to say anything other than, "Hi, Miranda," and then focus on organizing the items in our cart to hide the tension between us.

"Ms. Brown!" Miranda gushes. "You look amazing!"

Mom doesn't miss a beat. "Hi, Miranda. Thank you!" she says, searching for her pencil (*yes, the one she always sticks in her ponytail but can never find*). She finds it and frees it from her hair. "Good grief," she laughs. "If it's not a pencil, it's my glasses—or the car keys. Right, Amber?"

"Mmhmm," I manage before turning my attention to the all-important mission of finding the freshest bag of tortilla chips, which are most definitely on the top shelf, all the way at the back.

"It's been forever, Miranda. How have you been?"

Ugh, Mom. Why would you ask her that? I'm sure she's frickin' fantastic.

"Thank you for asking! I'm *marvelous!*"

Same thing. Meticulous Miranda is always marvelous. And who says 'marvelous,' anyway? Miranda does.

"I just ran my personal best of the season at last weekend's track meet," Miranda boasts, needlessly smoothing her perfectly straight hair with absolutely *zero* frizz or split ends. She's the only one who looks the same in real life as she does in her Instagram photos. I swear, she doesn't need a single filter. It's so unfair.

"That's wonderful, Miranda," Mom says before making her way down the aisle (*leaving me in the lurch*) to compare jars of olives. Suffering through relish tray selections with Mom is usually unbearable, but I'd rather be doing that than dealing with Miranda.

"And Kirsten, you remember her, right?" Miranda continues as I climb down from the shelf and toss the tortilla chips into the cart. "She finished dead last, the poor thing. She's trying so hard. But some girls got it," she leans in closer and whispers, "some just, ya know, don't."

I bite my lip and then my tongue. Every muscle in my face tightens, and all I can do is grunt. Poor Kirsten. She doesn't know what's coming. Miranda will eventually grow bored with her, just like she does with everyone else. She only keeps people around as long as they make her look better.

I organize the shopping cart—again—as Miranda buries her nose in her phone, which is dinging nonstop. *Looking for another way to humiliate her next victim on social media, no doubt.* Tapping at the keyboard with lightning-fast thumbs, she stops and laughs at something. "O-M-G. Some people shouldn't even bother," she sneers, rolling her eyes. *Is she talking about me? No, I'm sure she isn't.* But with Miranda, you never know.

The snare drum rolling in my chest won't quit, but Mom, returning with an assortment of pickles and olives, gives me hope she'll offer a way out of this awkward situation. "It was good to see you, Miranda," Mom says, saving the day. "Congrats on your personal best."

"Thanks. It was lovely to see you as well, Ms. Brown," Miranda says in her best adult voice. "Enjoy the rest of your night!"

Finally, she turns to leave. *Hallelujah.* I let out an exasperated sigh. My shoulders, so tense they had been touching my earlobes, settle back down to where they belong. I hate myself for not standing up to Miranda. She had no right to do what she did, and there's no way she didn't know how humiliated I'd be.

"That was nice, wasn't it?" Mom asks, oblivious to the fact that Miranda and I haven't been friends since the beginning of middle school. I didn't tell her because I didn't want her to make a big deal about it. I knew she'd be upset, and I didn't want her to worry. Besides, I knew she'd probably try to fix things between me and Miranda. I know she means well, but Mom doesn't understand that people change and that some friendships just aren't worth saving. At least *Miranda* has made that very clear.

Despite Mom's best efforts to stay optimistic and hope that I'll believe in the goodness of people, she doesn't realize I already know the truth about the world—like how the people who should stay are the ones that leave, and that putting yourself out there, showing your true colors, is the same as painting a target on your back, inviting the scavengers to attack and pick you apart. I know how much it would hurt her if I told her I know these things, so I don't. She's always trying to protect me, but she doesn't know—I'm the one protecting her.

Chapter 4

MARI

"Mari! The phone is for you!" Laura shouts upstairs. "It's Rachel!"

I drag myself to the phone in the hallway and pick up. "Hey, Rachel."

"So? Did you talk to your parents about Aaron?"

"I didn't bother bringing it up," I say, having to keep up the lie for her sake. "They aren't going to let me go out with him anyway. You know the rules."

"I know." Rachel grimly quotes the church's Strength of Youth Manual, which outlines all the reasons why dating before the age of sixteen can lead to trouble. "How many days until you're sixteen?" she asks. There's a pause as she does the math. "It's only seven hundred twenty-one more days."

Only? I'm having enough trouble making it through *one* day.

"Right. Hey, Rachel. I have to go. Laura needs the phone."

"Okay, see you tomorrow at church!"

I put the phone back on the receiver in the hallway and return to my room, where I sit at my desk and pull my journal from the top drawer. I flip on the lamp and begin to write:

Tomorrow is church, and I don't know how much more I can take. Unless I wake up with strep throat and a fever that puts me on my deathbed, I'll have no choice but to go. There's still one more week of Seminary to suffer through, too. Getting up at five a.m. to go to bible study on school days is absolute torture. I don't understand how Laura managed to complete four years of it—willingly and cheerfully. But she's good at everything she does and doesn't ever seem to do anything wrong. The only time I even get noticed is when I do something wrong. Like when I dyed my hair purple last month. I thought Mom and Dad were going to kill me. They said, "Stripping the natural color from the beautiful hair our Heavenly Father gave you and dying it purple is not how you treat your body like a temple." I can only imagine what they'll say when they find out I've pierced my belly button and that I cut myself.

I lay my head down on the desk, reminiscing about the time in first grade when I went with Aaron and his family to Myrtle Beach—before our friendship became a thing of the past.

We were fishing for minnows at the shores of the Atlantic Ocean, and I was frustrated after he filled a second pail with the tiny fish before I could catch even *one*. It's one of my earliest memories of feeling like I could never measure up. It wouldn't be the last.

Criticizing my fishing methods, as if he were a fishing pro-master, he said, "You gotta have a little more finesse."

"Finesse? Where'd you learn that word, dummy?" I snapped, embarrassed and angry that he was showing off.

"Everyone knows the word *finesse*, Mari."

"Only because of that stupid shampoo commercial, I bet." I began singing the ridiculous jingle: "No matter what your hair goes through, no matter what life throws at you..." striking silly poses, like the models on TV. I concluded my performance by dramatically flipping my hair and exclaiming, "Finesse your hair to beautiful!"

If only healthy hair could solve everyone's problems.

What was I thinking when I wrote that ridiculous love letter? I feel so stupid. I can't do anything right. Whenever I believe I've got something figured out, it never goes the way I hoped. I was so sure about Aaron—and look how that turned out.

I stand and cross the room to my bed. On my nightstand, littered with balled up papers and gum wrappers, is the small jewelry box where I keep most of my sharps. My fingers tremble as I lift the lid and reach inside. When I touch the blade of the broken pencil sharpener, a strange, inexplicable relief washes over me. But why am I drawn to hurting myself when one of the reasons I'm so lost is because someone else hurt me first? I know I can't carve out the pain. Logically, I know I'm only making it worse, but at least for a moment, I'm in control.

The Mormon Tabernacle Choir singing "How Great Thou Art" wakes me. This can only mean one thing: it's Sunday.

The familiar dread of having to dress for church anchors itself in the pit of my stomach. Anger—one emotion that hasn't decided to abandon me—is the only thing that makes me sit up and throw the covers back. I glare at the clothes hanging in my closet. Everything in my Sunday wardrobe is uncomfortable and makes me self-conscious, and Mom insists we wear tights and a stupid slip under our skirts that never stays put. I have to bobby pin it to the top of my tights to keep it from sliding off my waist, because God forbid anyone see the lacy hem sticking out from beneath my awkward-length skirt.

I spend the entire three hours of church adjusting it, not daring to breathe, move, or sit still for too long. It's all I can think about when I'm not avoiding eye contact with the person at the front of the room speaking about Jesus Christ, his love, and redeeming grace.

By the time we get home around one-thirty in the afternoon, I'm starving. The minute we pull into the driveway, I jump out of the minivan, ditch my Sunday dress shoes by the door, and run up the stairs faster than a firefighter answering an emergency call.

I shed my skirt and control-top tights with the annoying slip attached, finally able to breathe again. I throw on a thin cotton T-shirt from last year's marching band season and a pair of gym shorts before returning to the kitchen for lunch.

I open the fridge and search through bottles of salad dressing, two days' worth of leftovers, and half a dozen containers of lemon yogurt—Laura's favorite—before finally finding my favorite, green olives, and a block of cream cheese. Opening the pantry, I grab the club crackers and don't waste any time making my usual Sunday lunch: two-bite cream cheese and green olive club cracker sandwiches.

Still dressed in her Sunday best, Laura asks, "How can you eat those things?" as she points at the jar of olives. She takes a lemon yogurt from the fridge and a spoon from the drawer. Peeling the lid off the single-serve container, she changes the subject before I can tell her to mind her own business. "Isn't it exciting we're going to have a temple only an hour from home?" she asks, leaning against the kitchen counter.

I shove a two-bite olive cracker sandwich in my mouth and dramatically point to my mouth, so she knows I can't respond. Talking with a mouthful of food is strictly prohibited in our house.

Laura goes on and on about the temple as Mom comes through the kitchen, holding a Sunday School lesson manual.

"Sister Campbell asked if I would teach her Sunday School classes for the next two weeks while she's out of town."

"What are the lessons?" Laura asks, genuinely interested.

Mom places the manual on the counter in front of us and goes to the sink to fill a glass with tap water. "She bookmarked the manual. I haven't opened it yet. Take a look," she says to Laura.

Obediently, Laura opens the manual and reads the lesson title out loud. I don't hear her because my attention is on the pink bookmark she has strategically placed next to my lunch plate. The words from the church's Young Women's motto—faith, divine nature, individual worth, knowledge, choice and accountability, good works, and integrity—loop together in cursive, creating a continuous border that frames a portrait of Jesus Christ. He's standing with his arms open, waiting to hug the first person who could use one. I can't help but notice the complacent expression on his face. He never looks very happy in any of the sketches or paintings I've seen of him. For a second, I wonder if he wasn't convinced of his purpose either.

As Mom and Laura move to the sofa in the living room to discuss lesson plans, I tiptoe up the stairs, holding my breath, and only let it out once I've closed my bedroom door. I collapse on my bed and stare at the jewelry box on my nightstand. Cutting has become an addiction—one I can't keep myself from giving in to. Sometimes, it makes me sick thinking about it, but when I do it, I'm making a choice. No one is making me do it, and no one can stop me.

I pull the sheets over my head, feeling tired and hopeless. Through my open window, I hear Laura playing her favorite hymn, *Come, Come Ye Saints*, on the piano. There isn't a Mormon on earth who doesn't know all the words: "…And should we die before our journey's through, happy day, all is well. We then are free from toil and sorrow, too…"

I've tried writing in my journal—all of these dark thoughts and feelings—but the words that circle in my mind crash into each other like branches of a tree during a fierce thunderstorm. The only words that survive the collision frighten me. I'm afraid that if I *do* write them down, they will take me hostage. I doubt anyone will pay the ransom to get me back.

She cringes at her reflection—barefoot, half-dressed—
heat creeping up her neck. No one's watching, but
shame and self-hatred still cling to her.
"Here, try this one," Mom calls, tossing a flannel shirt
over the dressing room door. It's hideous, but she slips
her arms into the sleeves.
"This one is adorable! You'll love it," Laura swoons,
flinging a pink turtleneck with tiny strawberries
stitched along the hem.
More clothes rain down. Too many. Too fast.
"Try this! And this! Oh, this one is perfect!"

The layers pile up, suffocating.

"No more! Stop! I can't—"

Silence. Regret grips her. She should have kept her mouth shut.

"Mari! Laura! Your father is home. Dinner time," Mom calls upstairs, waking me from a horrible dream. I must have been asleep for at least three hours. I whip my sheets back and force myself up. My stomach growls as I head downstairs, with Laura five steps ahead of me, as usual.

Settling into our unassigned-but-always-the-same dinner table seats, Mom sets a piping-hot casserole dish next to a basket of fresh-baked dinner rolls. The smell is heavenly, and my mouth waters instantly. Reaching for a warm pillow of bread, my eye catches a small pamphlet in the middle of the table:

Camp Evergreen: Summer Camp for Teens!
Registration Information Enclosed!

I send up a silent prayer: *please, God, let it be for Laura, not me.*

Dad asks, "Who would like to offer the blessing on the food?"

"I'll do it!" Laura cheerfully volunteers. She begins her prayer the way all Mormons do: "Dear Heavenly Father, we thank Thee for this day and for all of our many blessings…"

I don't pray often, especially since I'm unsure if I believe in God. But when I do, I imagine God crossing his arms and turning away, saying, "Hmph. You don't believe in me, so why should I listen to you?" Can't say I blame him.

"We offer this prayer in the name of Jesus Christ, amen."

"Amen," everyone echoes, except for me.

"Hand me your plate, Mari," Mom says, one hand extended to accept my plate, the other holding a spoonful of tuna noodle casserole. "How hungry are you? One scoop or two?" Mom asks, already plopping a second scoop onto my plate.

"What did you learn in Sunday school today, girls?" Dad asks.

Laura says, "Today was wonderful. Sister Campbell's lesson was about eternal marriage in the Temple, and she shared with us her own Temple Marriage to Brother Campbell. It was so beautiful."

"What about you, Mari? Did you enjoy Sister Campbell's lesson?" Dad asks as he dips his butter knife into the tub of Country Crock, taking only a thin layer of the yellow spread for his dinner roll.

"Sure." I shrug, then take a bite of my buttered dinner roll. Dad doesn't seem satisfied with my answer, but since I'm following *his* rule about not talking with a mouthful of food, he lets the insufficient answer slide.

What I want to say is how ridiculous it is to be thinking about marriage when I can't even date a boy yet. How can I even think about the future when I'm still trying to figure out what I believe and where I belong—*here* and *now*? They don't understand how hard it is to be uncertain about everything. I want to tell them that I'm not sure if the church is the right place for me. Instead, I sit in silence, listening to them talk about futures I can't imagine myself being a part of.

hapter 5

AMBER

Before school, I pop a bagel into the toaster, then reach into my pajama pants pocket for my phone. *Dang it. I left it on my nightstand.*

Annoyed with myself, I plop down on a kitchen chair and stare at the extensive photo collage of every professional school photo taken of me from preschool through eighth grade this past year.

In the center of the collage, there's a cross-stitch Grandma made with my newborn stats: **Amber Luna, born July 19, 2004 — 6 lbs. 7 oz., 19 in.** Off to the right, there's a photo of Mom and Grandma holding me as a toddler with another cross-stitch below it that reads: "It takes a village." I find it ironic since my dad left when I was only seventeen months old. It's not something that's talked about; it's just something I know. There aren't any photos of *him* hanging on the walls.

The first time I was bothered by the vacant position left by my dad (*can you imagine? Now Hiring: Full-Time Dad: Apply Within*), I was in kindergarten. The fifth graders at my elementary school created posters to advertise and invite students to a Family Fun Night. They hung them all over the school, featuring the slogan, "Bring your mom! Bring your dad! Even your brothers and sisters can join us for Family Fun Night!"

When Mom and I arrived at the school for Fun Night, another parent, Mrs. Carrie, introduced herself to us and asked Mom if she could help in the cafeteria. "This is Miranda," Mrs. Carrie said, introducing me to her daughter before she and Mom left to report for PTA duties.

"I already know your name," Miranda said brightly, beaming with pride. "It's Amber, and you have Mrs. Candella. I see you in the cafeteria, but we can't sit together because we have to sit with our own kindergarten classes. I think that's just silly."

I was envious of her sparkling red dress with silver flowers stitched along the hem and her matching sparkly red shoes. I wore a basic blue shirt, boring black leggings, and simple white slip-on shoes from Walmart. Her hair was styled in the most intricate French braid, while mine was tied loosely in a sloppy ponytail, making me look like I had just woken up from a nap. But Miranda was friendly, and how I looked didn't seem to bother her. Now, I realize it probably didn't bother her because it made her look *that much* better.

Miranda and I went off to explore the Fun Night activities and games in the gymnasium. On our right, Eva's dad was supervising bobbing for apples. At the next table, Miranda's dad called out bingo numbers, and even Joseph's dad, a doctor who usually misses school activities, was helping kids with archery games in the farthest corner, away from all the other activities (you had to be a fifth grader to play that one).

On the left side of the gymnasium, my neighbor, Pete, was helping his dad show the kids how to assemble birdhouses with popsicle sticks, while Sydney's dad managed the dessert prize wheel he had built himself. It was only a dollar to spin the wheel, and everyone was guaranteed a prize. There were at least six large tables filled with plates of brownies, cookies, and cupcakes.

Before I could suggest to Miranda spinning the dessert wheel first, she insisted we start on the right and work our way around. I didn't speak up because something about her told me she was not one to argue with.

I followed her obediently to the right, but my eyes kept darting to the dessert wheel. It would be our last stop, and all I could think about were the peanut butter cookies and red velvet cupcakes. I couldn't help but worry that they'd be gone by the time we got there.

Finally, the dessert wheel was our next stop. As we approached the table, Miranda asked, "Where's *your* dad?"

It was an odd question; one I had never been asked before. Suddenly, I felt uncomfortable, like everyone was watching me. At the time, I didn't have a word for the unfamiliar sensation that made me feel like fireworks were exploding in my belly. I think it was the first time I realized I was different.

Later, as we were driving home, I asked Mom, "Where's my dad?"

She turned the radio down, adjusted her seat belt, and searched the glove box for a napkin to blow her nose. "Gosh, these darn allergies," she said, rolling the window up. "I wish I had an answer for you, Amber, but I don't know."

Grandma probably knew the answer. She always had the answers to my questions. If she didn't, we'd go to the library to find books on every subject under the sun. After preschool ended, Grandma and I made a long list of questions for our next trip to the library.

But we never went. She passed away that weekend, just before the Fourth of July. I remember sitting with Mom, watching the town's fireworks light up the sky, feeling sad instead of excited.

It bothered me for a long time—not knowing where my dad was—but what bothered me even more after Fun Night was the way I felt like a rag doll next to Miranda, all floppy and forgettable. If I wanted her to be my friend, I knew I had to step up my game, and the best place to start was my appearance.

I started wearing outlandish outfits with bright colors, quirky patterned knee-high socks, and funny animal shirts with silly slogans like "Messy Hair. Don't Care." Giant hairbows, faux fur vests, and oversized character earrings, nearly as big as my face, made it impossible to miss me.

Miranda thought my style was fun. "Better think twice before you make fun of my *best friend!*" she said, after I was teased about my wacky wardrobe the first day I tried it out. The bold look quickly became my signature style, sending a clear message: *stare or make fun if you dare.* Miranda and I were inseparable after that.

Countless sleepovers and summer weekends were spent together, swimming from sunrise to sunset at her family's Adirondack lake house, plus monthly trips to the movies at Hollywood Theatre—also known as the "cheap seats"—where they only cleaned the floors weekly, and the ancient seats creaked every time you reached for more popcorn.

We went apple picking every fall, froze our butts off at the outdoor ice rink in winter, and hiked at Green Lakes State Park year-round. These were rituals—entirely out of the question to miss even *one* of them. Those were the good old days—*before middle school ruined everything.*

Chapter 6

MARI

I plod through the last week of school like a toddler taking its first steps; calculating every move, feeling off balance, landing flat on my butt once or twice. Seminary is done for the year, but Mom still needs to get to work on time, so I arrive at school early and make my way down the corridor leading to the music wing. It's the only place where I feel safe and can be myself, even if I'm not sure who that is.

Both doors to the band room are shut and locked. I peer inside the windows, but the room is gray. The sun, low in the sky, doesn't cast enough light to reveal the blue color of the chairs set in perfect formation. The music stands, not cooperating with the perfectly placed chairs, are turned in all directions like they don't belong.

Removing my black JanSport backpack and setting it on the ground, I lean against the tiled wall and slide myself down to a crouch. I unzip the small front pocket of my bag and pull out a compact mirror, the only mirror I don't avoid entirely, along with my black eyeliner. Mom and Dad disapprove of the makeup I use to darken my eyes, and I have to wipe it off on the afternoon bus ride home.

After applying the eyeliner, I glance at my reflection, just long enough to make sure I didn't miss a spot—not long enough to *look* at myself. Tucking the mirror and eyeliner away, I pull out my journal and pick up where I left off:

...people just don't understand, but anyway, it's finally the last day of school. Not that it really means anything. Mom and Dad signed me up for some camp for teens. I tried praying to God—begged that it was for Laura—but no luck. It doesn't sound like fun at all. Sleeping in the middle of the woods, boating, hiking, and swimming? That means bathing suits. Yikes. But once again, the decision has been made for me. I'm going. I'll have "such a wonderful time," Mom said. The good news is that it's a regular camp for teens and not a church camp—

"Morning, Mari!" I jump at Mr. Shepherd's greeting.

"Morning, Mr. Shepherd."

"You sound a little down in the dumps. Everything okay?"

I shrug. "Sure."

"I'll grab my horn, and we can practice together. Or is it too early for your chops?" he teases.

"Really? I've been up since five a.m. It's not too early."

I follow Mr. Shepherd into the band room and put my backpack on the nearest chair. I'm the only one who plays the

French horn in the middle school concert band, and it's also Mr. Shepherd's primary instrument. I think it's a pretty cool coincidence.

As he fiddles with the keys again to enter his office, I find my horn stored on the instrument cubbies in the back of the room. I open the case and stare at the golden tubes, twisting and turning, overlapping like interstate bridges stacked on top of each other. Usually, my horn glistens and shimmers in the light, sending a thrill through me. But today, it stares back at me, dull and lifeless.

Mr. Shepherd pulls up a chair and adjusts a music stand, his French horn in hand. "How about some chromatic scales? Those are always fun."

"Sure, why not?" For the remaining twenty-five minutes before the first bell, we play our hearts out. For the last seventeen minutes, I forget about the razor hidden in my backpack.

Later at lunch, I find a spot at the corner table closest to the theatre stage. It's the only one that offers a buffer of several empty seats between me and the next group of kids laughing and enjoying their Lunchables and snack-sized bags of Cool Ranch Doritos.

Mr. Shepherd is the monitor for my lunch period and makes his way to me as I sip a carton of skim milk and nibble on pretzels.

"That looks tasty," he says sarcastically. "Not very hungry today, are we?"

"Not really," I say, shrugging.

"You about ready for the upcoming marching band season?"

He's been pretty good about not bringing it up after I told him last year I may not return. "I still haven't decided," is the safest response I can come up with.

"Okay, okay. I won't pressure you, but—Mr. Edwards!" he shouts, turning his attention to the boys at the end of my table. "Don't even *think* about launching that cosmic brownie!" He shoots a stern look at Brian (the kid poised to toss the brownie), then turns back to me. Finishing his sentence, he says, "First marching band practice is in three weeks! I hope you'll decide to come!"

"I'll think about it."

"Fair enough," he says, before catching Brian in the act of nailing his buddy with a spit wad. "Duty calls, Mari. See ya later."

It was the music that drew me into the marching band. I had always loved it, but last year, things were different. I had to drag myself from my room to make it to weekly practices on time. It used to be exciting, especially during the competitions—the suspense and thrill of being announced as first- or second-place winners would rush through my entire body. There was a time when I had friends to share the nail-biting anticipation of those moments with, but that was not the case last year—or this year.

At the final competition of the season, I stood at attention in my uniform, my mind wandering, just wanting it to be over. The PA system crackled faintly, then fell silent, the pause stretching uncomfortably long. Finally, a man's voice boomed over the loudspeakers: "In third place, with a score of 90.1, West Evansport Marching Band!"

After finishing dead last, I glanced at my bandmates, their faces marked with obvious horror and disappointment. But I stood there, expressionless and numb. I didn't care at all.

One of the dads rang a cowbell wildly out in the stands, like he does at every competition. The smiling faces of cheering parents were encouraging, but they weren't mine. Mom and Laura were touring college campuses out west, and Dad couldn't make it; his flight home from a work conference hadn't even landed yet. The emotions and tears that would normally overwhelm me stayed locked away—the key, long gone.

After everyone hung up their uniforms and stowed their instruments, they were all picked up, leaving only me. Watching the road, I desperately hoped to see the family's minivan round the corner. I heard the main door of the school bang shut, then another, slightly softer bang, as Mr. Shepherd pulled at the handle to ensure the door was locked. There's nothing more mortifying than being the last kid left waiting on the curb for a ride home. The last thing I needed was his pity. My embarrassment burned a hole in the bench I was sitting on.

"Mari! You're still here? Don't you know it's past my bedtime?" Mr. Shepherd asked teasingly.

My heart sank a little. I could only imagine how inconvenient it must be to wait with kids whose parents are always late.

I responded as cheerfully as I could, "Sorry about that, Mr. Shepherd. You know my parents are always late."

Taking a seat next to me on the bench, he said, "You know I'm just kidding. It's not a problem. And look on the bright side: since you're the last one here, you get a sneak peek at next year's band show." He reached into his leather messenger bag and pulled out a small cassette player. "I know, I'm a dinosaur—still using cassette tapes. Have a listen," he said, pushing a large block button.

A piano introduced a simple melody, soft and slow. Soon after, the woodwinds joined with a beautiful counter-melody that normally would make my arms prickle with goosebumps. Then, the brass section entered, commanding the spotlight and taking center stage. Despite taking a back seat to the brass, the piano and woodwinds still played their part, knowing that without them, the music wouldn't be the same.

The percussion transformed the piece, sharing the spotlight instead of stealing it and moving the music forward. Together, the instruments reached an unimaginably powerful peak, but it was only the first movement. There was more to come.

I remember closing my eyes, begging the music to consume me—to overpower the darkness I didn't have the strength to pull myself out of. As the music ended on the most glorious chord, the cymbals crashed with such velocity, making it clear: "Pay attention, folks. This is the big finish!"

Mr. Shepherd pressed another button to stop the recording. "What do you think?"

"It's amazing," I said quietly.

"I was thinking you could play the piano part at the beginning before grabbing your horn to march on the field."

I had cringed at the idea. He didn't know I stopped playing piano long ago. "I don't know about next year," I said, not wanting to go into the details.

"That's too bad. Is there any reason why you're on the fence about it?"

There was no easy answer, and I didn't know how much I wanted to tell him. How could I commit to something months away when I wasn't sure I could get through one day?

The family minivan I had so desperately wished for earlier finally turned into the school driveway, saving me from having to answer his question. Relieved, I quickly stood up. Dad zoomed up alongside the curb and waved frantically through the window. As I opened the door, he addressed Mr. Shepherd. "Sorry about that, Captain. My flight was delayed, and baggage claim was a nightmare. Thanks for waiting with Mari."

"It was no trouble at all. The kids did great tonight, and I'm proud of them!"

I shut the passenger door, and through the open window, Mr. Shepherd said, "Great Job, Mari. You're a good egg." He says this all the time, and I picture Veruca Salt from Willy Wonka & the Chocolate Factory being sent down the garbage chute when the *Egg-dicator* decided she was a *rotten* egg.

Pulling away from the curb, Dad turned on his left blinker, even though there was no one around who cared which direction he was going. Always one for following the rules. "So, did you bring home the gold?" he asked enthusiastically.

"Not this time. A little disappointing, but…" I let the *but* hang in the air. I was too tired to continue. I just wanted to go home and go to bed.

Dad reached for the volume knob on the radio and turned it up when he recognized one of his favorite Beatles songs — *Eleanor Rigby.* He sang about the sad old woman who died, "buried along with her name." Only the pastor came to pay his respects — but that was his job.

Now, sitting alone in the noisy school cafeteria, I continue sipping my carton of skim milk. I glance at the empty chair across from me when Eleanor Rigby appears, her eyes filled with sadness and pity. "You'll end up like me if you don't learn to use your voice, Mari."

I look down at my lap. "I don't know how."

"You know the poster that hangs in the school lobby with that quote by Theodore Roosevelt?" she asks. "What does it say?"

"Nothing worth having comes easy," I mumble, picking at my fingernails.

"That's right."

"But how do you know if what you *think* you want is worth risking everything to have it?"

There's no response. When I look up, Eleanor is gone. It's just me, alone and still unsure.

I swear it feels like an eternity before the last bell rings, and I make a beeline for the exit.

As I board the bus, Mr. Franklin, who has been my bus driver for as long as I can remember, greets me kindly: "Afternoon, Mari. You survived middle school!"

"Just barely, Mr. Franklin," I reply, slumping into a seat in the second row.

He's a friendly man with a round face and a perfectly groomed snow-white beard. I'll never forget boarding the bus years ago, on the last day before winter recess, and being greeted by the jolliest-looking Santa Claus I had ever seen. Mr. Franklin was dressed in the most authentic Santa Claus suit, nailing the entire ensemble, right down to a pair of shiny black patent leather boots and crisp white gloves. He made sure the magic of Santa Claus never faded, even for us middle school students all these years later.

Looking out the bus window, I watch a group of boys from the lacrosse team walking down the path like a herd of young billy goats, bleating and bumping into each other, spitting in the grass, and laughing together. I wonder what that would be like. Not bleating like a goat or spitting in the grass, of course, but having a herd. A pack. Friends gathered around me on all sides so that no matter what, I felt safe, accepted, and part of something.

Mr. Franklin reaches for the lever to pull the bus doors closed. I let out a sigh of relief. I pull out the makeup remover wipes from my bag and erase the darkness from my eyes, then lean my head against the window as I feel the bus lurch forward. The engine rumbles and coughs as it gains speed, taking me away from West Evansport Middle School one last time. I don't look back.

 hapter 7

AMBER

The taunting at school slowed down only a little today. Literally everyone has seen Miranda's post and my granny swimsuit. At least I only had to suffer through a half day of school, and I'm glad to be home now. But not even my bedroom is safe. Social media's superpower is that it can move through walls. Nothing can stop it, and it refuses to be ignored.

I set my phone to *Do Not Disturb* and gather my willpower to leave it on my desk, where I won't be tempted to check for notifications. The blazing sun threatens to roast me, so I take the box fan out of the window and close the curtains.

Plopping myself on the bed, I look at the funny posters hanging on the walls. The Minions from *Despicable Me* chanting, "Ba-Ba-Ba-Banana," and Grumpy Cat with the caption, "Not today," don't give me the usual urge to laugh. Not even a little.

My bedroom used to be Mom's when she was my age. We moved into Grandma's house after she died, and I once asked Mom if it was weird living in her childhood home, now raising her own child. "It's not like I lived here my *whole* childhood, she said. "I was in ninth grade when we moved into this house. And after all the remodeling we've done, the house hardly resembles the one I remember."

The bedroom walls used to be *Crayola Grass Green*, but a few years ago, Mom decided it was time for me to pick my own color. After applying two coats of white primer to one wall, we painted four large squares spaced several inches apart in two shades of purple, a bright blue reminiscent of the forgetful fish from *Finding Nemo*, and a warm yellow, *Dreaming of Honey*, which reminded me of Rapunzel's hair from the movie *Tangled*.

"I can't decide. Which color do you think I should go with, Mom?"

She shook her head and smiled, "Oh, no. I am *not* deciding. *You* are. Whichever one makes *you* feel happy."

After taking my Disney Princesses and Monster High Doll posters off the wall, we spent an entire weekend erasing the green and watched as the *Dreaming of Honey* paint transformed the room right before our eyes.

Years later, I almost feel guilty about all the posters taped and tacked to the walls, leaving hardly any of the beautiful color visible. But that was another thing Mom insisted on. "Amber, it's *your* room. Holes can be patched, sanded, and painted. Life is too short to have blank walls."

Over time, dozens of photos of me and Miranda, each one representing our countless adventures together, filled the blank spaces between posters of *One Direction*, Jack and Sally from *The Nightmare Before Christmas*, and Snoopy napping on top of his little red house.

Class photos dot the walls from second through fifth grade when we had the same teachers. Some have stickers on a few people's faces—mostly the boys who had a crush on Miranda, who we thought were gross.

But the world *ended* the week before sixth grade. We compared schedules and were devastated to see we didn't have a single class together—not even lunch!

"We can still hang out, Amber. It will be fine," Miranda said in her usual optimistic way.

I quickly realized that her promise was just a pipe dream. Her AP classes meant she was buried under a mountain of homework every school night, and she was always busy with sports on the weekends. The one time we passed each other in the halls, I lit up with excitement and waved wildly like a buffoon. She ignored me. I told myself she didn't see me.

Later that week, I saw her in the lobby with her new friends. She was doing all the talking, and they were gobbling up every word—laughing, gawking, and covering their mouths.

"No, she didn't. Are you serious?" one of them squealed as I approached their circle.

They could have been talking about anyone, but Miranda confirmed my worst fear: "I told her it was cool, but honestly, I was thinking, *O-M-G, Amber, you're not seriously going to go dressed like that, are you?*"

I froze, heartbroken and humiliated. Desperate for a quick escape, I turned to leave, but I tripped, and the books in my hands scattered across the lobby floor. The commotion drew the attention of Miranda's new pose, and rather than lend a hand, they laughed and turned their backs on me.

Sitting on my bed, my posters seem to be laughing at me, too: "Lam tos nopa tu ods migo!" the Minions say in their gibberish. *She was never your true friend.*

Hurt stabs my ribs, overshadowing the humiliation and anger I initially felt about Miranda's Instagram stunt. I know we drifted, but drifting is different than demolishing. Middle school is hard enough without losing your best friend at the same time.

Was our friendship not as important to her as it was to me? Did she just feel sorry for me? Was that always the case? Am I really so pathetic that I never realized it until now?

The Minions, who can't seem to mind their own business, chime in again: "Unami Google." *Ask Google.* Google never has the answers to the questions that actually matter.

Besides, I already know the answers *without* Google's help. I *was* her dopey sidekick. I was *never* good enough for her in the first place, and everyone knew it. I was just the last to figure it out.

I've tried to make new friends, but everything feels superficial. I can't count on any of them the way I used to count on Miranda, and everyone is already paired up with a best friend, someone they've known forever. I feel like the extra bolt that comes with the *Assembly Required* DIY furniture: I'm here, just in case.

Screaming into my pillow before throwing it across the room, I lunge from my bed, tearing every photo of Miranda and me off the walls. Shoving them into the trash under my desk, I realize, once and for all, that there's no hope our friendship will ever be what it was before. I think to myself, *it took you long enough to figure that out.*

"Dinner!" Mom calls from the kitchen.

She always makes me a plate of dinner looking like a MasterChef entrée. She also likes to properly introduce me to my meal, as if I'm meeting one of her clients.

As I take my seat at the table, Mom sets a plate in front of me and, as predicted, begins describing the dish like a MasterChef contestant: "Here we have a deconstructed meatloaf, consisting of one part ground beef, and one part ground turkey, dressed in caramelized Spanish onions."

Pausing to settle into her seat, she proudly continues, "In addition to the slightly mashed red potatoes, the meatloaf features fresh mustard seeds, chopped garlic, and shredded carrots, all grown in my very own patio garden."

"It looks delicious, Mom," I say as I push the pile of meat on top of my mashed potatoes. She whipped the potatoes to perfection, piped them onto my plate, and added a sprig of fresh parsley. It really is a beautiful dinner, so I feel awful vandalizing her work of art. I should know better. I stop immediately.

"Everything okay, Amber?" she asks, concerned. "I remembered to leave out the black pepper in the potatoes."

I pull out my phone to see if there are more notifications from Instagram, but surprisingly, there are none.

"No phones at the table, Amber," Mom gently scolds.

"I know. Sorry," I say, putting it away. "And yes, Mom. I'm fine." I lie as I shove a spoonful of creamy potatoes into my mouth to fend off any more questions; Mom doesn't believe in talking with a mouthful.

"I can't believe tomorrow's your last day of *middle* school," Mom says, placing a hand on her heart. "My Baby Burrito, growing up so fast," she says, wiping an imaginary tear from her eye.

Baby Burrito. The nickname always takes me back. I used to wrap myself tightly in my pink baby blanket to fall asleep at night. I'd refuse to budge when Mom tried to wake me for school in the morning. She'd scoop me up, blanket and all, and nibble at my ears. "This is the most delicious baby burrito I've ever had," she'd say. I'd squirm away from her kisses and laugh as she unwrapped me.

I miss those mornings — starting the day with kisses from Mom and a healthy round of giggles.

"Have you got your outfits planned for camp yet?" Mom asks, and I nod politely. "I loved Camp Evergreen so much," she says, staring off into the distance, lost in her memories of summer camp. "I can't believe it's been *twenty years* since my first year!"

"Sure, Mom. Camp will be great."

"The great outdoors and all that fresh air will be good for you!"

I quickly spoon more potatoes into my mouth, not wanting to say my thoughts out loud: *No amount of fresh air will fix anything.*

I open my eyes and instinctively reach over to my nightstand, where my phone remains sleeping. Tapping the screen to wake it, I punch in my passcode and scan the colorful icons on the screen, lit up like an arcade game. My eyes dart around the home screen from one red notification bubble to the next, each one looming over the icons like Pennywise's balloon, tempting me to lose myself if I take the bait. The Instagram icon mocks me, "Fifty notifications await you, freak."

I pull the covers over my head and hear Mom's voice describing one of her MasterChef entrées: "Today I have made for you *Tears of a Humiliated Teenager Soup*, simmered in organic body odor broth, combined with *everyone ditches you eventually* and *nothing you do is good enough*, served with blanched *you can't hide from the truth* on the side."

At least it's finally the last day of eighth grade. *Hallelujah.*

I take a deep breath, sit up, and start planning my outfit. At the beginning of middle school, I considered ditching my wacky wardrobe, especially after Miranda mocked me. But I don't know; I just couldn't do it. Besides, it's the only thing that has ever made me—me. There's no point changing it up now. Maybe if it's wild enough, everyone will forget about my granny bathing suit fashion faux pas.

I pull on a pair of red shorts and a black shirt featuring Jack Skellington dressed as Father Christmas. I rummage through my sock drawer, searching for my bright red, knee-high candy cane socks. I stop when I see the ones with Zero from *The Nightmare Before Christmas* dancing with mischievous jack-o-lanterns, grinning back at me like they know something I don't.

The Pumpkin King pretending to be Father Christmas is brilliant—but also kind of sad. Jack tries so hard to be something he's not—something he thinks everyone will love—but it's just not who he is. I know how that feels, so I give in to Jack's wish to be Father Christmas and reach for the candy cane socks.

I accessorize with a pair of dangly jingle bell earrings and a hair clip featuring a miniature Santa hat. At the last second, I slide on a pair of bright green, fingerless fishnet gloves that stretch to my elbows because—why not? Normally, I'd congratulate myself on another amazing ensemble, but not today. I look in the mirror and remember that my wacky style is just a strategic move to keep anyone from guessing the truth: I'm not as confident as I look.

"Amber!" Mom calls from the kitchen. "We're going to be late for your last day of school!"

I turn away from the mirror and grab my phone. "We're always late, Mom. Coming!"

"You want a snack to go?" Mom asks, opening the snack cabinet as I walk into the kitchen. "I couldn't decide between granola bars or those little bags of chocolate chip muffins—and then I saw they had those pita chips and remembered you liked those too, so I bought all three." She pulls the snacks from the cabinet, displaying the choices on the counter.

In addition to always having trouble making choices, Mom is very particular about reading the labels on every item she buys. She's trying to protect me from "harmful ingredients and unnecessary fillers," as she often points out, especially when she talks about "America's broken food system."

I wish I could tell her that there are scarier things out there than high-fructose corn syrup and Red No. 40. It isn't the preservatives that make me feel inadequate. If she could find a snack labeled "Trust Your Friends to Be True and Stick

Around: 45 grams per serving" or something made with "100% *Real* Confidence and Nothing Artificial," I'd tell her to buy the whole shelf. She should probably also grab a twelve-pack of bottles labeled "Stop Comparing Yourself to Others" to help me wash all those snacks down.

"Last day!" Mom cheers as *Eye of the Tiger* alerts us it's time to go. She hastily grabs her coffee mug, leaving a mess on the counter. "Keys. Keys. Keys."

Not again. "Did you check the fridge?" I tease. But Mom figures I could be right, and despite it being the most absurd suggestion ever, she opens the fridge door.

"Ah-ha!" she shouts triumphantly, pulling her lanyard from the shelf next to the Coffee-mate creamer. *Seriously?*

"Hallelujah," I say as I wipe up the coffee dribbles she has left on the counter.

The drive to school passes in slow motion. My stomach is doing cartwheels, and there's a good chance I'll have to make Mom pull over so I can throw up. As the drop-off circle comes into view, my head begins to pound. The car stops, and I open the door on autopilot. I know Mom is saying her usual "remember who you are" mantra, but all I can hear is the swooshing in my ears.

"Oh, look, guys! It's Granny!" I hear in the stairwell. "I thought I smelled mothballs."

Whatever. I block them out and head straight to the art room.

Turning the corner, I'm thrown into chaos. The hallway to the art room is packed with students signing yearbooks, chatting about summer plans, cleaning out their lockers, and tossing loose papers everywhere. They're not even trying to make it into the trash bins the custodians have strategically placed along the halls, knowing the last-day-of-school-clean-out is always messy.

I almost make it to the art room when, ahead of me, Jenna from my English class stumbles. Her overloaded, unzipped backpack slips from her shoulder, sending a cascade of papers across the floor. A few students glance over but keep walking, stepping around the mess.

I stop to help, scooping up some of the scattered pages. Jenna's cheeks are crimson, and she wipes her eyes before quickly ducking her head. "You don't have to help, Amber. I've got it."

"It's fine. I don't mind," I say, handing her two notebooks and her school planner. I look around, noticing that, for once, there aren't any phones directed at us to capture Jenna's humiliation. "Your secret's safe with me, Jenna."

She manages a small laugh, her shoulders relaxing slightly. She zips her bag this time and heaves it onto her back, securing the straps on both shoulders. "Thanks," she mumbles before hurrying off and disappearing into the crowd.

Pushing my way through the madness, I reach the art room and step through the open door. It's dark and empty. *Hallelujah.*

Flipping on the lights, I breathe in the comforting smell of acrylic paint and pencil shavings. Unexpectedly, the fruity aromas of Mr. Sketch watercolor markers linger in the air. High-top chairs, the kind I always need a running start to climb into (I'm only four feet eight inches), are tucked neatly under long wooden tables, streaked with dried smears of paint—the scars from battles with novice artists who seemed to get more paint on the furniture than on their paper or canvas.

I grab the basic painting supplies from the back of the room and head straight to my usual spot—the furthest table from the teacher's desk, where the most natural light streams in from the only window. Tuning out the bickering and shouting of students in the hallway, I hop (literally, I jump) up into the chair and introduce myself to the canvas just like Mom introduces her entrées.

Hello, Blank Canvas. I'm Amber Luna Brown, an average thirteen-year-old, locally grown and hand-picked a little too early—I still have some growing to do. Today, I will bring you to life using a palette of deep violet, Paddington blue, and peony pink paint. I have selected one fan and one flat brush, each made in the USA from synthetic nylon. For the finer details that will really make this painting shine, I have also selected a delicate round brush, perfect for adding dimension and depth.

Dimension and depth to what, though? Even after carefully choosing the colors only a minute ago, my vision of what to paint seems to have gone out the window—well, more accurately, the art room door I foolishly left open. My vision is out in the halls with the students and their obnoxious hollering and immature mudslinging. I can't think of a time when I wanted to paint and couldn't tune out the world, but today, I just can't.

Hey Granny, where's your walker? It smells like old people.

Then, the memory of my sixth-grade painting forces itself into my mind. The art teacher had clutched her chest and gasped when she first laid eyes on it. "Amber, this is spectacular! The details, the light—it's stunning!" She dabbed her eyes with a cloth from her apron dotted with dried paint. "Who's the woman picking the apples?"

"My grandma," I said, keeping my emotions in check and fighting the tears pounding at the door. *Don't answer. Don't let them in,* I told myself.

"Your grandma is beautiful," she said with a sniffle, then, with a dramatic flourish, declared, "I must display this in the school's front lobby!"

I remember thinking, *Oh no. Seriously?* But I couldn't stop her. A few days later, my painting was hanging in the front lobby as expected. What I didn't expect was the googly eyes plastered to Grandma's face and the thick black mustache scribbled above her lip.

Everyone pointed. They stared. They laughed. They didn't notice my broken heart or the tears that wet my face. None of them knew or understood how special that painting was to me. None of them cared.

Dipping the flat brush into the paint, I push the taunting from my mind and wipe away an angry tear. I touch the brush to the stretched fabric of the canvas, its cracks and lines visible up close. I watch the pale pink paint cling to the surface as the ridges and imperfections of the canvas fade away. No matter how beautiful the completed masterpiece is, I know what lies beneath it: the flaws, the plainness. The secret the canvas keeps is that you can hide behind anything—even brightly colored outfits and larger-than-life accessories. Everyone has something to hide.

The hallway hustle slows, and the vicious voices fade as the first block bell blares through the intercom, signaling that classes can begin. I keep my eye on the door, still hoping, not exactly expecting, that my vision will return. There's nothing, only the thought—*some girls got it; some just, ya know, don't.*

Chapter 8

MARI

At family dinner, Laura goes on and on about her day at work, which doesn't leave time for anyone to ask me any questions. It's fine because I don't have funny anecdotes to share like Laura does.

"Oh my gosh, it was so funny," Laura begins excitedly. "In the break room, one of my coworkers was talking about the apartment he might be moving into this summer. He said, 'It's a two-bedroom place with one and a half baths and a decent yard.' Then my other coworker looked confused and said, 'How do you have half a bathtub?' We were *all* confused, but finally, we realized—he didn't know what a half bath *was*. He thought the bathroom had a bathtub cut in half! We couldn't stop laughing."

Mom and Dad laugh as if Robin Williams himself has just delivered the punchline. I stare at my plate.

Finally, we're excused from the dinner table, and as I wash my dish, Mom asks, "Have you finished packing for camp, Mari? We leave tomorrow at six a.m. sharp."

"Bright-eyed and bushy-tailed!" Laura chimes in.

Ignoring Laura and her obnoxious positivity, I lie and tell Mom I'm almost done.

It takes every ounce of what precious energy I have left to keep myself from running to the safety of my bedroom. Closing the door behind me, I look around my messy room—a "pigsty," Mom calls it. My nightstand is filled with papers ripped from spiral-bound notebooks, bubblegum wrappers rolled up in tight little balls tucked between stacks of old homework assignments graded with red Cs and Ds, and three or four different novels, since I can never decide what to read before bed.

There aren't any posters on the walls, unlike most teenagers, because Dad doesn't want tape stripping the paint or tack holes ruining the drywall, especially now, since they've been talking about putting the farmhouse up for sale. The last two apple seasons weren't profitable because Mother Nature took a toll on the orchards.

Last autumn, I remember my parents standing on the back porch, shaking their heads in disbelief as they watched the hailstorm that wiped out most of the apples. It broke my heart. I know how hard they worked.

My clean laundry, piled in the basket in the corner of the room, seems to be staring me down. I know I should fold and put it away, but I don't have the energy. Instead, I sit at my desk and press play on my CD player. The theme song from *Indiana Jones* fills the room. Surprisingly, it was Laura who gave me this great CD, *The Movie Scores of John Williams*, for Christmas last year. I say *surprisingly* because Laura usually gets me something that she knows there's a good chance I won't want and will eventually let her keep.

Last year, she got me wool slipper socks, knowing full well my feet are always too hot. The year before that, she gave me the ugliest striped sweater that I had ever laid eyes on. Of course, I noticed that everyone her age was wearing the same style, but it didn't quite fit me, so I let her keep it.

Speaking of ugly clothes, I guess I had better pack for stupid Camp Evergreen. I force myself up and walk to the closet. I reach for the string to turn on the light, and the dreaded question, "What should I wear?" makes me nauseous.

I search through the closet but can only find things that used to be Laura's, mixed in with sweaters and blouses I've been given for birthdays and Christmas over the years — things I wouldn't be caught dead in.

I give up the search and grab my suitcase from the back, buried under a pile of extra blankets. Tossing it on the bed, I look at the laundry basket I've been avoiding and decide to dump the clean clothes directly into the suitcase. It's a mound of black cotton with no color — unless gray counts. I close the suitcase, zip it shut, then toss it on the floor at the foot of my bed.

I swear I hear my feather pillow calling me by name—"Mari, come lay your head down, just for a bit." I look over at the digital display on the radio alarm clock and see the bright blue block numbers 8-1-5 glowing. I crawl into bed and gather the blankets all around me. The temperature dropped when the sun set, so the fan in the window draws in a cool breeze along with the scent of charcoal grills and bug spray, the official smells of summer.

I lay there, my mind blank for once. The music of John Williams—*Flying Theme* from *E.T.*—drifts through the room, attempting to console me. I wait for the usual rush—the chills, the goosebumps, the racing heart, that weightlessness that makes me feel like I'm floating—but it doesn't come. The fire that music used to ignite in me is lost, like a candle whose wick is too short and won't light.

I've always wondered if the feelings music used to give me are the same feelings people at church have when they share their faith in God—their "spiritual experience." Before the darkness I feel now, music would take over like a full-blown infection—something I couldn't shake, even if I wanted to. It was my escape, my anchor. Now, it just feels like another thing—this part of me—that's lost. I can't remember who I am without it, and worse, I may never get it back.

When my eyes become heavy, the clock's blue digital numbers change from 8-5-9 to 9-0-0, and the next track begins. The Imperial March (also known as Darth Vader's Theme) from Star Wars becomes the ominous soundtrack to my dream.

The skeletal fingers on the wheel make it clear that it's the monster—the nice old man in the neighborhood whom no one suspected would hurt a fly—driving the car. Swerving and darting around cars on the crowded highway, the constant change of direction makes it impossible for her to find her center of gravity.

The monster fiddles with the radio knob; a piano sonata fights its way through the crackling static. Terror and panic pound through her veins the same way his fist pounds the radio display.

"Please stop," she begs.

"It's fine, Mari. Everything is fine. This is completely normal, but you can't tell anyone. They'll blame you if you do," he says in a strangely soothing tone. "This is just between you and me. You're special."

She looks out the car window and down at the road, watching the broken white lines—like Morse code— sending a silent message, a plea for help, vanishing into the asphalt.

Without warning, the car slows its momentum.

She turns to look at the man in the driver's seat.

It's empty.

Relief visits briefly as she realizes she can get away.

She leans over to unfasten the seat belt.

She tries to release the buckle, but it refuses to budge.

She's trapped—panic returns.

The monster's laughter resonates through the car radio: "I warned you not to tell anyone. Now look what you've done."

# Chapter 9

AMBER

It doesn't take long for me to pack for camp. After closing my duffle bag, I toss it on the ground at the foot of my bed. Something tethered to a mile-long, tangled cord falls out of the side pocket. *What the actual heck?* As I reach down to pick it up, I have a vague memory of Mom finding this—this *thing*, slightly bigger than a Nintendo Switch, when we were looking for a pair of ice skates in the attic. (I hated having to rent the bulky hockey skates at the rink, especially since Miranda always had those beautiful white skates like the professional figure skaters wore).

I turn the device over in my hands, inspecting it like a TSA officer. I can't remember what she called it. *A Walk and Talk? No, I'm thinking of a walkie-talkie. Disco player? Got it.* It's a discman and it's clunky. How did people walk around carrying this thing? It's not like it could fit in your back pocket.

I push a button, and the top pops open. Inside, there's a CD with a list of songs I've never heard of written in Mom's handwriting. They're probably all mushy love songs like the ones she listens to on *Y94-FM*. I stuff the discman back in the bag, figuring that, without a phone or Wi-Fi at camp, it might be good to have it around as a last-ditch option to keep me from losing my mind.

I look out my bedroom window and see that it's Golden Hour—when the blue sky isn't willing to go to bed just yet, and the last of the muted orange glow of the sun kisses the treetops goodnight. Since Mom is working late, there's no five-star Michelin dinner tonight, which means it's the perfect opportunity for me to whip up a box of mac and cheese. I can already taste the gooey cheese melting away my problems.

Mom hates buying it, but every now and then, I'll sneak a box into the shopping cart. She'll roll her eyes at checkout as she catches me tossing the box on the conveyor belt. "Really, Amber? That stuff is so unhealthy. I can make macaroni and cheese from scratch, with Gouda and mozzarella, which tastes infinitely better and has far superior nutritional value than that processed cheese." Mom's recipe might be healthier and tastier, but she can't whip it up in ten minutes. She always gives in, anyway. Boxed mac & cheese is my one guilty pleasure, and she doesn't have the heart to take it from me. There are far more important battles for Mom to fight—and artificially flavored cheese is not at the top of the list.

Sitting on the sofa with a mixing bowl of unnaturally bright orange pasta in my lap, I flip through the Netflix shows for the third time. There's nothing to watch, and nothing new comes out until after I get back from camp. Giving up entirely, I shut off the TV and look around, not knowing what to do with myself.

I stand and cross the room to Mom's desk. She's clumsy, forgetful, always distracted, and typically leaves a trail of crumbs and spilled coffee wherever she goes, but when it comes to her desk and bookshelf, she's immaculate. Her workspace rivals the perfectly manicured pictures pinned to my Pinterest décor boards.

I look at her framed photos on display—my favorite being the one of Mom playing the piano, her back to the camera, with two young women standing to her left. One of them cradles me as a newborn, swaddled in my pink blanket, which I still sleep with almost fourteen years later.

A few more knick-knacks are nestled between the pictures, with every one of my clay art projects from elementary school dotting her desk. Her journal is placed perfectly in the center of the desk, with a beautiful fountain pen to the right. She spends just as much time with that pen and journal as she does playing the piano and watching MasterChef.

To the right is a table with a small lamp that turns on automatically every night at eight o'clock. It's dimly lit now and shines on several more photographs: one of me in my soccer uniform and one of Mom, eight months pregnant with me, receiving her diploma from the community college.

In between those, the People Magazine from February 1998 that Mom kept from when she was my age is displayed prominently. The cover features a beautiful photo of Michelle Kwan, a figure skater, with her arms extended and her leg raised elegantly behind her. In bold, capital letters, "YOU GO, GIRLS!" appears directly next to three more female figure skaters.

"A magazine with a cover story like that doesn't get shoved into a box," Mom said to my aunt when she came to visit. I flip through the pages and find the featured article about Michelle Kwan, who was still a teenager when she went to the Olympics that year.

I skim through the article, stopping to read the caption under a photo of Michelle laughing: *Kwan, removing her skates after a disappointing performance, yanked the laces, lost her grip, and punched herself in the face. With a slip of the hand, she had knocked some sense into herself.*

The poor girl. A heartbreaking and embarrassing moment in her career was broadcast on international television. I can relate, even if it is on a smaller scale, to having an embarrassing moment recorded and shared for everyone to see. But after her disappointing loss, she didn't let one embarrassing moment stop her from moving on and winning the World Championships later that year. *Yeah, well, I'm no Michelle Kwan.*

My phone buzzes in my pocket, but I ignore it. Everyone has moved on from my fashion fiasco by now, right? On second thought, what if someone posted another picture? I decide to take a quick peek, relieved when I see only my weekly screen-time report.

The shelves to the left of Mom's desk have no less than two hundred books. Lord almighty, the woman loves her books. There are three different copies of the *same* book: *Pride and Prejudice.* I've caught her reading each copy, cover to cover, multiple times. It's her favorite book, and I once asked her what made it so special. She said, "I just love how real it is. Elizabeth Bennet is so fiercely independent and sharp. I love that she knows herself so completely and believes she is whole, with or without a husband." That sure as heck makes sense coming from my *single* mom.

Toward the end of the second shelf, there's a book I've never noticed before. It's not exactly a book—more like a presentation portfolio—with 1998 handwritten on the spine. It's wedged between the wall and *Atlas Shrugged*, a thick hardcover, and I have to be very careful pulling it out of its place. Before I can free it from its tight spot, I hear Mom come through the front door.

"Amber? Are you down here? Can you help me for just a minute?"

"Yeah, Mom, I'm coming," I say, pushing the portfolio back into its place.

In the kitchen, Mom struggles to free her arms from a tote bag overflowing with paperwork, a lunch pail, her purse, and three grocery bags. She sets everything down with a huff, then spins in a slow circle, scanning the counters. "Where's my mug?" she mutters. "I swear I just had it." She pushes her glasses up her nose, adjusts her loose ponytail, and finally notices me. "There you are! I stopped at the store after work, and there are a few more bags I could use your help carrying in."

"Okay, I'm on it." I head to the door and call over my shoulder, "Your mug is sticking out of your lunch pail."

I hear Mom's sigh of relief and her usual, "What would I do without you?" as I head outside, where the glow of the moon creates shadow art. The black outline of the neighbor's fence, merging with the trees, creates a peculiar-looking shape that reminds me of a giant, winged bird. I shiver as porch lights illuminate, and the neighbor's cat crosses the street, heading home after his daily hunting excursion.

Except for the distant hum of traffic, it's quiet—too quiet—for the second day of summer vacation. There's not a soul in sight, not even a single bike abandoned in the driveway, as if the rider had made a crash landing when they arrived home just in time for dinner, having promised their mother they would.

Mom shouts from the front door mockingly, "Did you get lost?"

"No, I did not get lost," I reply, mimicking her tone. "I'm coming." Grabbing the three shopping bags from the back seat, I bump the door closed with my hip. "What do you have in these bags?" They're *heavy*."

"Filet Mignon was on sale, so I grabbed a few pounds," Mom answers with more excitement than anyone should have about reduced-price meat. "It's so quiet out here," Mom says as she holds the door open.

"I was just thinking the same thing," I say, clumsily tromping into the kitchen.

She takes the heaviest bag from my arm and says, "I've got some new recipes I want to try out. I figure while you're away at camp, I can experiment, and when you get back, I'll serve you the winning dish!"

I roll my eyes but smile regardless. To be honest, I admire her enthusiasm.

"Did you see the letter that came in the mail?" Mom asks as she

follows me to the kitchen, where I drop the remaining bags with a grunt. When I turn around, Mom is holding up a crisp white envelope in front of her face. The upper left corner says, "University of Visual Arts, 1218 Albany Street, Rochester, NY." I've never heard of it and wonder why it's addressed to me.

"Your art teacher called last week and told me to be on the lookout for an envelope like this." I take the fancy envelope from her, inspect the gold emblem in front of the University's name, and look again at mine in the center. Mom waits patiently, but the suspense is clearly too much for her. "Well? Open it already! See what it says!"

Turning the envelope over, I rip the top corner carelessly—

"Careful," Mom says. "You don't want to rip the paper inside." She's more excited about this envelope than she was about discounted meat.

Exaggerating slow and careful movements to open the envelope, I roll my eyes at the same time Mom rolls hers. "Today would be nice," she says.

"Okay, okay," I say, finally pulling the thick letterhead from the envelope. I read it out loud:

Dear Amber L. Brown,

It is an honor and a pleasure to inform you that you have been selected to submit your artwork to this year's Congressional Art Competition, hosted by the University of Visual Arts in Rochester, NY.

"How exciting!" Mom throws her arms around my neck and gives me a tight squeeze.

I'm at a loss for words since I can't think of anything to say that will match Mom's energy right now. Standing in my underwear in front of the whole school sounds far less intimidating than entering any of my artwork into this competition, surrounded by everyone else's amazing art. The only thing worse than being judged by people who *don't* have a clue is being judged by the ones who *do.*

"I'm so proud of you, Amber," she says, finally releasing me. She doesn't notice the look of dread on my face as she turns her attention to her discounted meat, waiting patiently to be put into the fridge.

She's busy unloading and saying all the usual motherly things: "You've got so much talent. I knew I wasn't being a biased mother." I fold the letter back into thirds and return it to the envelope. Disregarding Mom's instructions to be careful with the letter, I fold it twice more, cram it into my back pocket, and begin unloading the bags filled with snacks.

As I start restocking the snack cabinet, my nagging thoughts drown out Mom's voice. How can I even consider entering this competition? After what happened to my painting of Grandma? Fat chance. Besides, I already know everyone else's work will be way better than mine.

When I was Miranda's best friend, I was constantly reminded that I was only third or fourth best at anything since nothing ever comes easy to me. She had this idea for us to join the community soccer team together in fourth grade, and as usual, she was a natural.

As for me, if the coach didn't put me on the field just outside the goalie box, I was a benchwarmer—a sideline bartender—pouring drinks for my teammates and making sure they stayed hydrated during time outs. Miranda was always on the first-place podium while I watched from the sideline.

"Did you grab the duffle bag I pulled down from the attic for you to pack for camp?" Mom asks after we finish putting the groceries away.

"Yeah, I finished packing hours ago and already helped myself to dinner. There's some mac and *fake* cheese left if you want some," I say.

"How thoughtful of you, but here's the thing—I'd rather eat elephant poop."

"Eww. Gross, Mom."

"Hey, for some, it's a delicacy. Ever heard of elephant dung coffee?" She then clears her throat and, in her best French accent, declares, "Tout naturel!"

"Immediately no, Mom!"

"It's true! Ask Google!"

"Anyway," I say, trying to rid the image of elephant excretions from my mind. "Before you got home tonight, I was looking at the framed photos by your desk."

"Did you happen to dust them while you were at it?" Mom says as she reaches for the canister of coffee grounds.

"Dang it. I will next time," I say, but don't make any promises. "I also read that People Magazine article again, the one about Michelle Kwan and the 1998 Olympics."

"Oh, really?" Mom says. "I haven't read that article in forever. I used to read it once or twice a week to remind myself that no one is perfect." Then, as if I haven't heard her say it a thousand times before, she asks, "Did you know that Michelle Kwan was the crowd favorite, and everyone was so sure she'd win the gold medal that year?"

After pouring water into the coffee maker reservoir, she says, "I try to remember that it's not always about *being* the best at something—it's about *giving* your best at whatever you decide to do."

"Giving your best isn't always enough," I say cynically.

"It absolutely is, Amber. And you know what? It's not just things like art, music, or sports that people can be the best at. There are so many more talents and gifts that people have, and just because they don't always get the recognition they deserve or some kind of award, doesn't mean they aren't just as important as the other stuff," Mom says as she scoops coffee grounds into the filter basket. "Figuring out what those things are and discovering what makes us *who we are* takes curiosity and a lot of living and experiencing things—the good *and* the bad— and it doesn't happen overnight. You know what I think *you're* good at?"

"Judging your MasterChef entrées?" I respond smartly, with a sarcastic laugh.

"That's true," she says, "but what I was *going* to say is, besides your amazing painting talent, you are good at expressing yourself and not letting people's opinions get in the way of being yourself. You do what makes *you* happy, and I'm sure your friends at school admire that about you. I know I do. You're kind and thoughtful, and that's something people notice. That's a gift, you know."

Being myself and not letting people's opinions bother me? And what friends? So much for moms knowing everything.

Mom double-checks that she put water and coffee grounds in the coffee maker before turning off the light above the sink. I follow her out of the kitchen, knowing her next stop will be the piano, where she always plays a song or two before heading off to bed.

She switches on the piano light as I flop onto the sofa. She flips through the music book on the stand beneath the light and smiles when she decides to play Katy Perry's classic feel-good anthem, *"Firework."* Singing has never been her strong suit, but she belts out the words about letting your color burst.

I can't help but think about how my wardrobe is already bursting with color, a distraction from how insecure I feel. People look at me and assume confidence. No one realizes how carefully I've built this bright, bold cover.

Mom sings her favorite part about the lights inside of us burning brighter than the moon, igniting the Congressional Art Competition letter in my pocket. She's right: I don't usually care what people think of me, but when it comes to my art, it's different. It's not easy to put yourself on display and risk judgment—or *vandalism.*

I let out a dramatic yawn as Mom finishes the song. *Not exactly the thunderous applause she was hoping for.* "I should probably get to bed, especially with camp tomorrow," I say, rubbing my eyes.

"Yeah, it is getting late," she says, glancing at her small wristwatch. "Yikes! It's almost ten-thirty! We'll want to make sure you get to camp early and have plenty of time to get settled in before lunch is served at eleven-thirty." Leave it to Mom to remember the meal schedule. "Hopefully, the food isn't too dreadful."

"I'm sure it will be *normal* food, Mom. Probably nothing like your five-star Michelin entrées, but I'll survive," I say, standing from the sofa as she tucks the piano bench away.

"You're so sweet," Mom says as she walks toward me and kisses me on the forehead like always.

Once, when I was little, I had to remind her to give me my forehead kiss before bed, except it came out as, "Can I get a *horror-fed* kiss?"

"A horror-what?" Mom said, looking at me like I had grown a beard.

"A horror-fed kiss," I repeated, pointing to my forehead, not knowing why she was looking at me so strangely.

"Oh! A forehead kiss!" Mom looked relieved, and I remember her warm laugh. Funny how those little things stick in your brain. Like how I used to ask for blueberry kisses—mixing them up with raspberries.

Now, at the bottom of the stairwell, I call over my shoulder, "See you in the morning."

"Bright-eyed and bushy-tailed!"

I roll my eyes and remind her, "You're not a morning person, Mom. Good night."

"Good night, Baby Burrito."

Closing my bedroom door behind me, I remove the Congressional Art Competition letter from my pocket and stuff it under my mattress. I collapse on my bed and lie in the dark listening to the box fan: *mmhmm—click clack, mmhmm—click clack.*

I open Instagram *(listen, I know it doesn't make any sense, but I can't help myself)* and don't see anything unusual. There are a few photos of people from school already showing off the suntans they've worked on since spending the first days of summer vacation poolside or at the beach. I see a bunch of people posting selfies in their Stories with that "Age Yourself Twenty Years" filter Miranda used to humiliate me. I'll admit, some of them are funny, but others—well, let's hope for Joseph's sake that these filters have missed the mark.

The battery icon at the top of my screen warns me it's time to plug in. I reach for my charging cord, frayed and falling apart. The connector has been threatening to come undone for weeks, so I've wrapped it with duct tape. If I don't keep the phone at a *very* specific angle, it doesn't charge. I don't want to tell Mom because she has already bought two chargers for me this school year.

A few weeks ago, I must not have been careful enough because I overslept on a school day when my phone died overnight. I told Mom I forgot to plug it in, and she suggested I pull out my radio alarm clock so it wouldn't happen again.

Mom got me the radio alarm clock for my tenth birthday after I started asking for an iPhone. I wrote out a list of all the reasons I thought having a cell phone—an iPhone specifically—was a necessity. The first item I mentioned was that I could set alarms on an iPhone and wake up for school on my own.

Convincing, right? Apparently not. I didn't get the iPhone that year. Instead, I got the radio alarm clock. My list needed some work, and I ended up writing a full-blown persuasive essay for Mom prior to Christmas that year—
and before every birthday and Christmas after that. Several edits and drafts later, I submitted the final draft with a box of French macaroons a month before my twelfth birthday. Mom gave me an A+ and a new iPhone.

I pull the radio alarm clock forward from behind the bedside lamp and adjust the time to be a little earlier than my usual school day wake-up time. After making sure at least ten times that I've set the wake-up alarm for a.m. and not p.m., I settle back into my blankets. Within minutes, I'm asleep.

I swear I've just closed my eyes when the radio alarm clock begins its incessant chirping. "Time to get your lazy butt out of bed," it mocks. I ignore it as long as I can until I remember—today is the first day of Camp Evergreen.

I bolt upright, stop the alarm, and reach for my phone, relieved to see *100%* next to the battery icon. Throwing the covers back, I get out of bed, change out of my pajamas, and then rush to the bathroom. I brush my teeth vigorously and tie my hair back. Checking the mirror, I tell myself it's camp, not a beauty pageant, so it's good enough.

I take another look around the room, hoping I've got everything. I hate the feeling of forgetting something. I look at my phone, plugged in on my nightstand, and even though I know I'm not supposed to bring it to camp, the thought of going an entire week without it makes me nauseous. I make sure it's on *Do Not Disturb* before unplugging it and tucking it into my back pocket. *In case of emergency. Promise.*

I head downstairs and scrounge up a quick breakfast from the fridge. There are *four* different varieties of yogurt to choose from: Greek, coconut milk, whole milk, and reduced-fat, each of them in three flavors. *Seriously, Mom, having two flavors of yogurt is more than enough.* I grab the whole milk lemon yogurt and set it on the counter next to a trail of coffee dribbles—a clear indication that Mom is up and should appear any minute.

Right on time, which is to say ten minutes late, Mom charges into the kitchen with wet hair and makes her way to the coffee pot on the counter. "You grab your sleeping bag, and I'll take the duffle bag," she says, her eyes scanning the kitchen with concern.

"Looking for these?" I say, holding up her keys. This time, they were hanging from the paper towel holder.

"Lifesaver!" she exclaims, taking them from me.

After tossing my things in the trunk, our seat belts click in unison, and Mom puts the car in reverse. I'm still getting settled into my seat when she breaks out into song: "Hey-ho! Camp Evergreen! Hey-ho! Here we come!"

"Camp Evergreen or bust!" I echo her enthusiasm. Then, using my best Siri voice, I add, "You will reach your destination in two hours and fifteen minutes."

Mom laughs. "I know. I wish it were closer, too. Take a nap, and we'll be there in no time."

"A nap sounds like a great idea," I say, fluffing my pillow, grateful I didn't toss it in the trunk. Surrendering to sleep for the remainder of the car ride, I have the strangest dream about Mom.

A beat-up car comes to a stop in front of her. Three chickens greet her as she opens the passenger door. Fighting and clawing at each other, she pushes them aside as if having chickens ride in the front seat is as normal as having a golden retriever.

The car bumps along a dirt road, kicking up dust. They pull into a parking lot in front of a one-story building. The sign running nearly the entire length of the building reads, "Skate-O-Rama."

Mom jumps out of the car as one chicken escapes, hoping to join her. She scolds the chicken. "No, Corky. Chickens don't come to the roller rink."

Inside the deserted building, the hardwood floor gleams like a freshly waxed basketball court. A spotlight illuminates a piano at the center of the rink, spinning on a platform like it's inside a music box. Mom, wearing a sparkling baby-blue leotard with a satin skirt, plays the piano, yet there is no sound. Unexpectedly, she stops playing and begins gliding around the rink effortlessly, hand in hand with a handsome young boy. But a dark forest appears, separating them—an eerie sight of dead trees, knocked over by a brutal windstorm, lying in their graves, uncovered and exposed, left behind to decompose and rot alone.

A thick fog rolls through the lifeless forest, the limbs and branches still clinging to the trunks of the trees, refusing to let go.

"We're almost there," Mom says from the other side of the gloomy forest. "Amber?" She stands with her hands on her hips, becoming impatient. "Amber, we're here."

"Earth-to-Amber. Amber, wake up. We're here!" Wiping the drool from my mouth, I immediately act as though I've been awake the whole time. "Yeah, yeah, I'm awake."

"Uh-huh. That was an interesting dream you were having," Mom laughs, rolling down her window.

The open window welcomes the smell of—what *is that? Rotten eggs? No. Pine. Definitely pine.* Apparently, Mom left this minor detail out of her many discourses on Camp Evergreen.

The sky is clear, and things are relatively quiet for the first day. I didn't think we'd be early—*we're never early*—but I don't see any cars parked in the stone lot. I step out of the car and stretch, stifling a yawn.

I meet Mom at the back of the car where she's waiting patiently to hand me my duffle bag. "Everything looks exactly the same as I remember!" She says. I take my sleeping bag as Mom hands me my bag. Opening her arms wide, she invites me into one of her mama bear hugs. "Don't forget your sunscreen," she says before releasing me. "Have a good time and—" *we all know this next part—* "remember who you are!"

Then, as I turn away— "Amber, wait! Your pillow!"

I turn back as Mom grabs my pillow from the front seat. "That sure would have been a sad thing. I know it's bad enough that the cots are as stiff as a board! I put two pool floats in your bag for you to sleep on."

"Thanks," I say, taking the pillow from her.

Almost in a whisper, she says, "Love you, Baby Burrito."

"Love you too, Mom," I reply.

I set my things down behind a row of boulders lining a stone path in front of the camp office and look around. The office is dark, and the door is closed, so I take a walk to check out the beach. It's nothing fancy, but if I squint a little, and ignore the muddy parts, it kind of sparkles. Like it's trying to be a real beach. I like that about it.

As I reach the sandy shores of the beach, I remove my shoes and then my socks. The water is clear, and the view of a heavily wooded island in the distance is so beautiful that I *have* to get a picture. I scan the area to make sure no one's looking before pulling my phone from my back pocket.

With the lake as my backdrop, I snap a quick selfie. Moving closer to the water, I open Instagram (*I've got data—hallelujah!*) and find the Polaroid icon. I wonder if now that I'm older and look different, the "Age Yourself Twenty Years" filter will give me a different result than the one from Miranda's post. I hold the phone at the right angle, conjuring my best Anne Hathaway smile, and press the button. *My gawd, I look like my mother.* The tide suddenly rushes and swirls at my feet. Its icy temperature shocks me, and I stumble backward. My phone slips from my hand—*MY PHONE!*

I jump into the frigid water and frantically pull it from its inevitable watery grave. I shake it violently and use my shirt to wipe the screen—*as if that's going to do anything.* I jab at the screen, but it remains black. I press the power button on the side—still nothing.

Dang it.

Unexpectedly, a rumble of thunder echoes loudly. I look up at the blue sky, not a cloud in sight. *That's odd.* Then, out of the corner of my eye, I see a girl with purple hair in the parking lot shutting the door of a beat-up minivan—the impending storm?

A wave of nausea returns as I think about going a week without my phone. I realize this is bad—very bad. Unless the camp cook plans to serve white rice (which is highly unlikely), there's no way I'll be able to fix it anytime soon. And what will Mom say when I tell her I need more than just a new charger?

Feeling pretty miserable, I pull on my socks and sneakers and tell myself that, despite a rocky start, I will not let a broken phone ruin my first year at camp. I look across the lake and let the peaceful sounds of nature calm me. I'm sure Mom will understand. She knows everyone makes mistakes. Maybe she'll say, "Life is too short to cry over an iPhone." *Right?*

I take a deep breath, stand up, and start humming *Eye of the Tiger* as I punch the air the way Rocky would. Putting on my best game face, I shout, *"Hey-ho! Camp Evergreen! Hey-ho! Hey!"* and charge forward to sign in.

Chapter 10

MARI

Laura pokes me as we pull into the parking lot of Camp Evergreen. Just like arriving early for school, I'm not surprised I'm the first to show up before registration has opened. Mom remains buckled in the driver's seat and offers a quick goodbye. "You're going to have such a good time, Mari."

I jump out of the minivan and slam the door closed. The gravel crunches under the tires as Laura waves from the passenger seat. Mom is dropping her off an hour up the road from here, where she will be a counselor at another camp for at-risk teens. Last night, after dinner and before Laura and I retreated to our bedrooms, I asked her what "at-risk" teens meant exactly.

She paused in the doorway of her room and said thoughtfully, "There are so many kids out there who don't have a safe home or family that can take care of them. They've lost their way because, unlike me and you, no one has taught them the right way." I wanted to roll my eyes and make a snarky comment, but Laura's response wasn't smug, and I didn't want to be a jerk. "It's going to be a great opportunity to help these kids see their full potential," she said, "to figure out who they are, and to teach them that it's never too late to get on the right path."

Maybe I should be going to *that* camp.

This camp has the most revolting smell of rotten eggs and mildew. A shack at the top of the hill, nothing more than a dilapidated shed, has mismatched colored boards and leans precariously to one side. I have no idea how the sad building is still standing.

Down the hill, across from the shack, is a patch of dirt with weeds surrounding a small pond. A rusty sign, leaning at an angle, says in bold letters, "BEACH." I wouldn't call it that. You can't just throw dirt at the edge of a pond and call it a beach. Everyone labels things and sees what they want to see, but that doesn't always make it true.

At the water's edge, there's a girl dressed in all yellow, and I'm surprised I'm *not* the first one here, like I originally thought. Before I can look away, I watch as she waves her arms in the air like a maniac—probably fighting off a swarm of mosquitoes or horseflies.

Outside the camp office where campers need to report and sign in, a row of giant boulders lines a stone path. I drop my things on the ground and climb onto the furthest boulder from the closed door. I pull out my eyeliner, then apply it thickly under my eyes.

I can see the camp counselors moving about inside through the dirty glass window. The walls are thin, and I can hear their laughter and friendly chatter. There's nothing more obnoxious than *happy* morning people—*bright-eyed and bushy-tailed*—I say in my best Laura voice. Picking at my fingernails, I wish the counselors would hurry up and open the door. The sooner we get started, the sooner I can leave. I can't believe I have to spend an entire week at this prison camp.

The laughter, once muffled by the closed door, becomes crystal clear as a young man, probably in his late twenties, swings open the door and greets me with so much enthusiasm I wonder if he's for real. "Mornin', camper! I'm Adam, and you are?"

"Mari."

"Mari-rhymes-with-sorry, how the heck are ya this mornin'?" Adam asks in a Midwestern drawl.

"Fine." I don't offer anything more.

"Alrighty then! It's good to have ya here at our beautiful Camp Evergreen!" He spreads his arms wide and takes in a giant deep breath. He doesn't gag from the smell like I expect him to. "Come on into the office!" he says, waving me down from the boulder. "We'll get your bunk assignment taken care of and a map so you can start to take a look-see 'round! You're gonna love it here—fresh air and all. Nothing better than the great outdoors, am I right?" He's so gleeful, I think I might throw up in my mouth.

Sticking with the idea, *the sooner things get rolling, the sooner they can end*, I hop off the boulder and follow Adam into the office. He announces me as we walk through the door: "First camper has arrived, ladies! This is Mari!"

Behind a folding table, two women dressed in the same green Camp Evergreen T-shirt as Adam are fighting with papers flying around wildly from the gust of wind that the open door has invited in. Both women, with raccoon tan lines across their eyes, look up to greet me with smiles plastered on their faces.

"Good morning, darlin'! I'm Joanna." She's chewing a massive piece of pink bubble gum and stops to blow a bubble. It pops as she taps her sidekick on the shoulder. "And this is Sara. We're happy to have ya here. You can go ahead and sign your name on the clipboard—first name and last initial is good enough. And let's see here… ah, yes, we've got a map for ya, and a bunk assignment—bunk number sixteen. I'll just go ahead and circle it on your map for ya," she says, writing on the map like an author at a book signing event.

As I pick up the clipboard, Sara greets another camper who has come into the office behind me and gives him a similar speech about signing his name and assigning him his bunk. He looks over at me, pointing at the clipboard in my hand, and asks, "Are you all signed in?"

"Oh. Yeah, sure," I say clumsily, handing it over.

"I'm Pete."

"Mari."

Joanna takes the clipboard from Pete and says, "Okay, you guys are all set! You can go and get yourselves familiar with the grounds. Lunch is served at eleven-thirty daily at the mess hall on the hill. No matter where you're at in the camp, you can follow your nose to Ms. Wolcott's amazing cooking!"

Before I can turn to leave, Sara adds, "By the way, I absolutely love your hair. Purple is my favorite color!"

"Thanks," I say. I might not want to be here, but I do at least have good manners.

Turning away from the registration table at the same time as Pete, we walk awkwardly toward the exit. The girl from the "beach" steps through the door and looks at us as if she knows both of us somehow. I keep my head down and let my hair fall in front of my face.

There seems to be no avoiding this girl as she stands her ground inside the door. Her yellow T-shirt says, "Normal is boring," and matches her yellow knee-high socks. She looks pretty confident in her eye-grabbing get-up.

"Hey, Pete," she says, then immediately turns to me and introduces herself. "Hey, I'm Amber."

"Mari," I say, not really in the mood to make friends.

"Nice to meet you, Mari," she chirps. She seems nice enough but a little too eccentric for my taste. She compliments my hair (at least, I think she does. Something about being ironic? Or bionic? She's definitely a bit odd). Then she says, "I'll probably see you around after I check in," before finally moving away from the door, allowing me to pass.

A few more cars arrive, filling the empty parking spaces as kids and parents step out of their vehicles. Most of them must know each other from previous years at camp and are excited to be reunited. The familiar feeling of being alone and not belonging makes my heart sink. I shake it off and remind myself I probably won't be the only new kid. And besides, I'm not really interested in making friends.

I turn away from the parking lot and figure I should find bunk sixteen to unload my stuff. According to the map, it's located on the other side of the mess hall, up the hill, and to the right.

After crossing a huge field, I arrive at a trail leading into a small forest where a sign directs campers to the left for bunks one through eight and to the right for bunks nine through sixteen. At least bunk sixteen is the furthest away from everyone.

Campers laughing and talking off in the distance are muffled by the sounds of birds chirping, bugs buzzing, and the breeze rustling through the treetop canopy. Looking ahead, I see the first bunk on the right, number nine, and stop dead in my tracks.

A tent? I thought they were bunks—as in *cabins*. Dark green fabric hangs over a simple metal pole shaped like an A-frame. I approach the tent and peer inside. Two cots with mattresses— more like the floor mats Jane Fonda uses in Mom's aerobics video—are positioned on either side. *Two* cots mean I'll be assigned a bunkmate.

It's probably not a good time to test if God has changed his mind about listening to my prayers, but I give it a shot anyway. "Please, God. Don't put me with the biggest camp loser, or worse, the most popular camper," then quickly add, "or the camper who absolutely *loves* camp." Asking God to make sure no one else is assigned to bunk sixteen seems like a big stretch. I know that would be an absolute miracle, but I'm probably not deserving, so I don't bother adding that to my ridiculous prayer.

Letting the flap close on bunk number nine, I continue up the path, passing each bunk until finally reaching bunk sixteen. I throw my sleeping bag, pillow, and suitcase on the cot to the right. They land with a thud and absolutely no bounce. I flop onto the cot to test it out and nearly break my tailbone in the process. It's like a rock. I move to the cot on the left to see if it's the same, but there's no difference.

It doesn't matter. Even if they were luxury hotel quality, it wouldn't change anything. I don't want to be here. I'm never certain about anything, but I'm certain of this: it's going to be the longest week of my life.

Chapter 11

AMBER

Before entering the camp office, I stuff my waterlogged phone to the bottom of my duffle bag. I'm surprised when I see my neighbor, Pete, inside. He looks different somehow, but it's probably just because he doesn't have his giant earmuff headphones encapsulating his head.

The girl with purple hair, who was dropped off by the noisy minivan, is with him and looks strangely familiar. As they approach the door where I've stopped, I quickly say hello to Pete before introducing myself to the girl: "Hey, I'm Amber."

Both Pete and the girl look uncomfortable, and neither responds right away. Finally, the girl mumbles, "Mari." I can't decide if she's shy or miserable.

"Nice to meet you, Mari," I say, hoping she won't be a Debbie-Downer for too long. "I love your hair! I once dyed some of my hair blue, but it didn't look nearly as iconic as yours does. Anyway, I'll probably see you around after I check in."

"Yeah, sure," Mari says, walking out of the camp office, keeping her head down.

Pete looks at me like I've been speaking Pig Latin this whole time, and for an uncomfortable minute, I think he might not say anything at all. Finally, he acknowledges me with a formal nod that reminds me of Sheriff Woody from *Toy Story*, when he tips his hat and says, "Howdy, partner," then leaves without another word. I don't know him well, but that was just plain weird.

I continue to the registration table where two young women in their twenties are waiting to greet me. The camp's emblem, a bright pink flowering shrub—Mom called it a Starburst Bush—is stitched onto emerald fabric draped over the table. Off to the right, my eye catches another table crammed with paint bottles and brushes. If camp isn't as great as Mom says it is, at least I can sneak away to paint.

"Hello, dear. I'm Sara, and this," she says, placing an arm around the girl on her left, "is Joanna."

"Hi there! What's your name, darlin'?" Joanna asks.

"Amber."

"Hm," she says, scanning her list. "I'm not seeing an Amber."

"Well, that's a pickle," Sara says, peering over Joanna's shoulder. "Must have missed it when we transferred names from the registration forms."

"It looks like there was an odd number anyway," Joanna adds after counting the names, "which means there's definitely an available bunk for you. We'll just add you at the bottom. It's no problem."

"I'm sure your parents wouldn't just dump you off in the middle of the wilderness without registering you first, right?" Both women laugh.

Their shirts feature the same logo as the tablecloth: a silhouette of pine trees and a bright pink starburst bush with 1998 stamped below. I wonder why they're wearing shirts from twenty years ago. Maybe that's when the camp was established, but Mom never mentioned how long it's been around.

"Okay, here you go, darlin'. Your bunk number is circled," Joanna says, handing me a camp map. "You shouldn't have any trouble finding your way around! See you at eleven-thirty for lunch!"

I leave the camp office and approach the mess hall, where an obvious path leads to the bunks in the woods. Mom explained that the bunks are actually A-frame tents with canvas cloth covering a small plank platform. The bunks have just enough room for two cots and are intended solely for sleeping at night and changing in private.

Mom also told me that there are strict rules about not having food in the bunks. I mean, *duh,* it *is* the wilderness with wild animals lurking everywhere. Remembering her third year at camp, Mom said, "My bunkmate thought she was pretty tough and was one of those Rules-Don't-Apply-To-Me types. One afternoon, we returned from kayaking at the beach and discovered two raccoons inside our tent, munching on Doritos. Scared us half to death!"

I laugh out loud, remembering her story, as I enter the woods where the bunks are hidden. I'm on high alert for wild animals scurrying about, especially raccoons.

Mom and her bunkmate spent their last night at camp sleeping in the mess hall, afraid the raccoons might return. "It ended up being one of the best nights of the week," she said. "The camp cook, Ms. Wolcott, gave us full access to her secret stash of cheddar popcorn and Pizza Pringles to go with the most delicious root beer floats."

My mouth waters at the thought of an ice-cold root beer float as I arrive at my bunk. Pulling open the tent flap, I jump because I'm not expecting anyone else to be here yet.

"Oh! Hi!" I say to the girl with purple hair sitting on the cot to the left. "So, I guess we're bunkmates!

Chapter 12

MARI

Before I can decide which side to settle into, the tent flap whips open, and the girl from the camp office appears.

"Oh! Hi! So, I guess we're bunkmates!" she says cheerfully, but not as enthusiastically as the counselor who greeted me at registration.

"Looks like it," I reply, trying to remember if her name is Allison or Amanda or—

"Sorry, I was just waking up from my car ride nap this morning, so I can't remember your name," the girl admits.

"It's Mari. I can't remember your name either," I respond uneasily.

"No worries, I'm Amber," she says, looking at my belongings on the cot to the right, then back to me, sitting on the left.

Realizing it looks like I've taken ownership of the whole bunk, I quickly get to my feet and offer her the cot on the left. "Sorry, I was just seeing if both cots are as hard as a rock."

Amber laughs. "Yeah, my mom warned me they're pretty bad. She gave me a pool float to sleep on. I've got an extra you can use if you want."

"Um, sure. That would be cool. Thanks."

Amber finally steps inside the bunk and drops her things on the plank floor. Unzipping her duffle bag, she produces two brightly colored inflatable rafts like the ones you can buy at Walmart for less than three dollars. "Here ya go." She offers me the purple one, I'm guessing because of my purple hair. "Might as well blow them up before unrolling our sleeping bags."

The next ten minutes are spent blowing hot air into the pool floats and not having to suffer through girl talk. I thank God silently and remind him of my earlier prayer request about not getting the camper that *loves* Camp Evergreen. The absurd thought, "Don't hold your breath," pops into my head. Since I'm still blowing up my pool float, *holding my breath* definitely isn't an option.

After our floats are inflated, the only other reasonable excuse I can think of to avoid making small talk is needing to find the outhouse.

"It's just up that hill," she says, pointing to the right." I worry she's going to tag along, but she continues to unpack her things and unroll her sleeping bag.

After my trip to the outhouse, I notice another path leading to the left, away from our bunk. My curiosity—and wanting to avoid an awkward conversation with Amber—make me decide to scope things out.

I'm disappointed to find that the trail just leads back to the entrance of the woods, where the posted sign informs campers of the numbered bunks. Maybe the bunks are separated by gender, with girls to the right and boys to the left? I wonder if I'm allowed to follow the path leading to the first eight bunks. What's the worst thing that can happen—they kick me out of camp and send me home? I don't have that kind of luck.

As I head toward bunks one through eight, my suspicions are confirmed when a group of boys approaches me from that direction. One is Pete, the guy I met at registration this morning. Recognizing me, he gives a small wave. The others pay no attention. After acknowledging his wave with a nod, I immediately put my head down to avoid further contact.

Once they pass, I'm not sure why, but I look over my shoulder. At the same time, one of them glances back and locks eyes with me. Even from a distance, I can see his piercing blue eyes. Butterflies flutter in my chest. I'm so embarrassed to be caught looking that I quickly turn my head. I feel like such an idiot.

Since I don't want to continue wandering into the *boys-only* side, I start to turn back but notice a narrow, untouched trail hidden behind a row of prickly bushes. Cautiously pushing aside the branches, I disappear behind the curtain of spiky thorns.

After only a few minutes of easy walking, I reach the end of the path and come upon a beautiful freshwater pond. Flowering lily pads and a small waterfall cascading down from a large boulder, similar to the ones outside the camp office, make the sight before me seem surreal.

Camp wouldn't be so bad if I could spend the week *here*. I've entered a completely different world here, where the air is light and filled with the scent of pine mixed with a hint of fresh moss.

Closing my eyes, I take in the sounds of my newly discovered hideaway: the bubbling noise of fish mouths tapping the water's surface, the slow trickle of the waterfall, and the conversations of birds chirping at each other. They aren't exactly in sync but somehow make music—a beautiful symphony of sound. Still, I don't feel anything. I'm empty. I wish I could find those feelings again—the ones that music used to stir inside of me, back when playing the piano wasn't complicated and didn't send me to a time and place I'd give anything to forget.

Finding a soft patch of grass close to the water's edge, I begin the arduous task of removing my socks and high-top Chucks. It always takes forever to untie the laces and tug my feet from their grip, but they're my favorite shoes. They're the first pair of sneakers I can remember picking out for myself.

Before that, my dad always got stuck taking me back-to-school sneaker shopping. It usually wasn't too bad, except before fifth grade, when we spent hours at the mall, leaving store after store empty-handed. Nothing fit right, was poor quality (Dad said, "flimsy"), or the price was too high.

After striking out at Payless Shoes, I tried on a pair of clunky white New Balance sneakers at Finish Line. Sensing Dad's impatience, I muttered, "These aren't that bad," even though they were awful.

"Great! We'll take them," Dad said to the salesman before I could protest. And just like every year before, I ended up with sneakers I didn't like or choose for myself.

Finally winning the battle with my Chucks, all ten toes are free, and I cautiously dip them in the water. Being shaded by the forest, it's frigid, and I immediately withdraw. Scooching further away from the water, I find a row of small boulders, making for the perfect spot to lean my back against.

The waterfall trickling lulls me into a dreamy state, but I stop myself from slipping into sleep. That's when the voice—the images—invade. I open my eyes and shake my head to keep from falling further in, but my eyes fall heavy again and close.

Another flash, and I jolt awake. All I want is to close my eyes and not see the piano in the corner of the room, not hear the sounds of the neighborhood, not smell the old furniture, and not watch the dust dancing in the rays of sun breaking through the crack in the drawn curtains. I just want it all to stop.

The smell of something burning and the sound of a triangle from the percussion section pull me back to reality. It must be lunchtime already. I don't want to leave the freshwater pond, but my stomach growls in protest. I wish I hadn't refused the Pop-Tart Laura offered me this morning before arriving at camp.

Slipping my socks back on and forcing my feet into my high tops, I curse the sneakers again. They're just as tricky to get on my feet as they are to take off.

Venturing back to the main trail and leaving the forest, the mess hall comes into view. It doesn't look any less wrecked from this side than when I first arrived at camp. Campers are running up the hill for lunch, some in groups of two or three, a few on their own. Looking around, it appears I'll be the last one to arrive (late), and hopefully, there's not some embarrassing thing I have to do in front of the whole camp, like stand on one foot and *bawk* like a chicken, as punishment for being tardy.

As I enter the mess hall through the wide double doors, the room is an explosion of activity, and no one notices me. I let out a sigh of relief when I see it's the usual school cafeteria routine—grab a tray and utensils, wait your turn, let the cook slop a spoonful of this and a spoonful of that onto your tray, then make the walk of shame through the seating area to find a place to sit—knowing there's not a table of friends waiting to wave you over to join them.

I grab a metal tray and get in line behind the boys I saw near the bunks earlier. One of them is the boy with piercing blue eyes who caught me looking. His buddies, on either side of him, are talking about baseball and how they played together on an all-star team in Florida over spring break. He seems uninterested but nods politely and offers the occasional, "Yeah, that's cool, man."

I'm careful to maintain a good distance between us. I take baby steps to keep up with the moving line, trying desperately not to draw attention to myself. I think I'm doing all right until I'm bumped forcefully from behind.

My tray crashes to the ground as I fall forward, and the boy in front of me leaps aside to avoid being struck. The boy ahead of him—Eye Contact Boy—turns just in time to break my fall, catching me with his left arm as his other arm still balances a tray with two hot dogs.

The entire mess hall turns to see the ruckus, but most of their view is blocked by other campers already headed to their seats with trays full of food. Regardless, I'm humiliated.

Immediately righting myself and taking a drastic step away from the boy, I apologize and bend to retrieve my empty tray from the ground. "There's nothing to be sorry about. It wasn't your fault. Are you okay?" he asks.

"Yeah. I'm okay. Thanks," I mumble without looking up.

"It's all good," he says, turning to get a scoop of potato salad from the camp cook as if I didn't just fall into his arms like a helpless idiot.

Everyone must be feeling the same way, as they've already returned to their food and chatter. The boy behind me, who caused the fiasco, is shifting his weight from one foot to the other and hitting himself on the forehead. He's upset and repeating himself: "I'm sorry. I'm sorry. I didn't mean it."

Adam, the animated counselor who welcomed me this morning, appears beside him and begins to soothe him. "Hey, listen, Charlie. It's okay. Everything is fine. You said you were sorry, and look, Mari is okay."

Charlie stops hitting himself but continues his sidestep dance. "Okay. Good. I didn't mean it. I'm sorry, I didn't mean it."

"We know, Charlie. We know you didn't mean it. Now, let's get you some lunch." Adam directs Charlie's attention back to the food line, where the camp cook stands patiently waiting to serve him potato salad and a hot dog nestled inside a soft white bun.

At this point, I'm sweating profusely, but my heart rate is returning to normal as I turn to find a place to sit with my food. I opt for the seat furthest from the crowded tables.

Dressing my hot dog with a perfect squiggly line of yellow mustard, I watch Adam with Charlie as they settle into the seats at the other end of my table. A young lady joins them, and Charlie greets her. "Hi, Molly. I've got chips," he says, and is happy once again, excited to have his own snack-sized bag of Lay's. I didn't see chips and really wish I had.

Instead of pining over potato chips, I bite into my hot dog. Surprisingly, it's really good. Or maybe I'm just so hungry that even a warm tuna sandwich would impress me. That might be taking it a bit far. Still, something is better than nothing, and for now, I'm satisfied to sit alone and eat.

I glance at the clock hanging on the plank wall and count the hours I've survived so far. Three. It really *is* going to be the longest week of my life.

Chapter 13

AMBER

It might be my first year, but with all the stories Mom has told me about camp, I feel like I know this place like the back of my hand.

Sitting on the edge of my cot, I scan the camp map again, making sure nothing looks different from the one that came with the registration brochure.

Mari never made her way back after her trip to the outhouse. She must have gone exploring, so I decide I will, too. Leaving the map behind, I take the path from our bunk and head to the main campgrounds. Up ahead, I see two girls hanging a clothesline between two trees.

As I get closer, one of them waves enthusiastically. "Hi! I'm Jessica," she says, introducing herself like a politician running for office, "and this is Chelsea." The second girl gives a shy wave without a word.

"I'm Amber," I say, not stopping to chat. But before I can move on, Jessica says, "This must be your first year! I don't remember you from last year. Do you, Chelsea?" Chelsea gives a sheepish shrug.

"First year," I say, remembering how disappointed Mom was because even though I'd be thirteen by the first day of camp, I wouldn't be old enough by the official registration deadline.

Jessica finishes tying the line to the tree and says, "Chelsea and I can show you around the campgrounds if you want. There are a lot of things you might not notice if you go alone. We can show you all the hidden gems and shortcuts."

It's an offer I easily accept since it's almost lunchtime, and the thought of showing up to the mess hall alone gives me the jitters. There's nothing worse than walking into a crowded room of strangers and having to find a place to sit.

They join me on the trail, Jessica taking the lead. We walk to the main campgrounds, where several more campers arrive in the parking lot. Trunks and hatches are ajar as parents help kids unload sleeping bags, pillows, and backpacks. Parents shouting, "Don't forget your..." and "Have a good time..." overlap with others saying, "See you at the end of the week! Have fun!" Multiple conversations among campers throughout the grounds create an electrifying buzz, unlike the peaceful campgrounds I remember from this morning.

Jessica points discreetly to the beach where two boys are skipping rocks on the water and asks, "Do you see him? The one on the left."

"What about him?" I ask.

"That's Duke. He's the best-looking guy at camp. Well, at least he was last year. We'll have to see if any newcomers give him a run for his money," she says, blushing.

I'm not interested. *Boys. Who needs 'em?*

After making our way around the perimeter of the camp, Jessica and Chelsea show me where the blackberry bushes are. "They're just up over there at the entrance to the rock-climbing wall," Jessica says, pointing up the hill opposite the mess hall. "The bushes were so full last year, but by the end of the week, everyone had picked them clean. They're the *best* blackberries you'll ever have. Come on! Let's go pick some!" she says excitedly.

We trek up the hill, and by the time we reach the blackberry bushes, I'm sweating severely. *Remember—I'm a benchwarmer, not an athlete.*

After picking a section of the bush completely bare, a loud bell rings. "That's the mealtime bell," Jessica informs me. Her tone reminds me of Miranda, and obviously, she enjoys knowing everything, almost as much as making sure everyone else *knows* she does. "Ms. Wolcott rings it when meals are ready, and you can hear it from anywhere in the camp."

Ms. Wolcott is still the cook? She must be ancient!

Walking down the steep hill is obviously much easier than the ascent, and I'm grateful for the cool breeze that helps to dry my T-shirt. We step inside the mess hall, where the line for food is just beginning to form. After filling our trays with lunch, we have our pick of seats in the dining area.

"This table over here is good," Jessica says, taking a seat at the table closest to the mess hall door. "It has a perfect view of the entire room and the doors to see who's coming and going. Speaking of—who's the new girl with purple hair?" she asks as she watches Mari get in line behind Duke and his friends.

"Her name is Mari. She's nice," I say, taking a small bite of potato salad as Mom's voice pops into my head describing the side dish; *Classic American potato salad consisting of yellow fingerling potatoes, boiled and slightly mashed, blended with an array of seasonings, diced green peppers and onions, combined with a homemade creamy dressing, stone ground mustard seed paste, and spritzed with fresh squeezed lemon juice.* I would hate to hear Mom describe the process and ingredients of my perfectly flame-broiled hot dog.

"I don't know. It looks to me like she's trying too hard with the whole *look-at-me; I'm Punky Brewster with my purple hair and skater girl high tops* thing going on," Jessica scoffs.

As I swallow my potato salad, I wonder who the heck Punky Brewster is. I want to ask, but instead say, "Yeah, she's my bunkmate, actually."

"Oh, you poor thing," she says, her voice dripping with fake sympathy. "I mean, that's good. You can take her under your wing and maybe snap her out of the whole *I'm depressed and don't want to be here* attitude."

How am I going to survive a whole week with this Jessica girl? Shrugging my shoulders in response to her careless comments, I say, "Yeah. Maybe."

A crashing sound in the kitchen startles everyone. We turn to look and see a commotion in the food line and Mari in the arms of Duke.

"How convenient," Jessica says, rolling her eyes. "Falling into the arms of the best-looking guy at camp." She's obviously jealous.

We watch as Mari bends to pick up her food tray, the source of the crashing noise that caught everyone's attention. "Who's that?" I ask, referring to the boy behind Mari, who is being comforted by a camp counselor.

"That's Charlie. He has special needs. He's a hoot," Jessica says, taking a bite of her hot dog. "He has an aide who stays with him. Her name is Molly."

A few moments later, two camp counselors stand at the front of the mess hall, calling for everyone's attention. "Alrighty, everyone. Eyes on me!" one of them hollers. "Welcome, everyone! My name is Adam, and my sidekick here is Sam."

"Who are you calling sidekick?" Sam teases, gently pushing Adam aside to take the spotlight. "Hello, everyone! Welcome to Camp Evergreen! It's wonderful to see so many returning campers!"

A *whoop-whoop* comes from the back of the room. Everyone looks at the two boys sitting with Duke and my neighbor, Pete.

"Yes, hello, Josh and Eric. Welcome back! Camp wouldn't be the same without you two, our favorite camp clowns, am I right?" Adam teases.

Sam, not willing to share the spotlight, presses on with his welcome speech. "Where are all of our new campers? If it's your first time at Camp Evergreen, stand up so we can see your faces and give you a proper Camp Evergreen Welcome!"

Several kids scattered throughout the mess hall sheepishly stand, including me. Some get to their feet with encouragement from their neighbor; others don't seem bothered by the attention. I look around at all the new kids and spot Mari, still seated, looking distracted by something.

"All right, everybody! On three!" Adam counts down, "One, two, three! Hey-ho! Camp Evergreen! Hey-ho! Hey!"

Laughter and applause explode after the Welcome Shout. Then Sam and Adam conclude their speech, shouting over each other and the commotion of campers getting up from the tables: "Let's make this year one to remember! Everyone reports to the beach at twelve-thirty—that's in about thirty-five minutes. Don't be late!"

I look for Mari to suggest we walk back to the bunk together to get our bathing suits and towels, but she's already gone.

Jessica stands up with her tray, and Chelsea immediately drops her last bite of hot dog to join her. "Hey, Amber," Jessica says, "are you coming with us or not?"

"Um, actually, I'm not quite finished, so I'll catch up with you later at the beach," I say. The truth is, I already need a break.

"Okay. Whatever. See ya," Jessica responds coolly. Chelsea offers a little wave and follows her like a little duckling following its mother.

Waiting for them to turn the corner, I get up to clear my tray. As I'm scraping the remnants of potato salad into the trash, Duke appears at the neighboring receptacle. His introduction catches me off guard. "Hey, you're new. I'm Duke," he says.

"Hey, I'm Amber."

"Cool. I like your socks," he says, then quickly adds, "See ya."

"See ya," I respond, adding my empty tray to the growing stack to the right.

Heading out of the mess hall alone, I turn toward the trail leading to the bunks, thinking about Miranda again. I've come to grips with the fact that our friendship was shallow. I thought I could tell her anything, but I never admitted how often I worried I wasn't good enough to be her best friend. Keeping up with the most talented, most popular girl in school was exhausting, and I had to make sure I never took a wrong step. I could never tell her how much energy it took to prove I could hold my own next to her. What was I supposed to say to her? *Hey, Miranda, you know, underneath all these bright colors, crazy socks, and silly slogans, I'm just an average girl with average talent who will never measure up to the go-getters and top achievers like you.*

I can only imagine how dumb my average art will look next to the pieces of the most talented kids from all over the country at the Congressional Art Competition. Remembering the letter stuffed under my mattress at home makes my head pound.

As I step into the shaded woods, I feel the temperature drop a few degrees. The sudden chill pulls me from my pity party. I feel a vibration in my back pocket and mindlessly reach for my phone. Remembering it's not there, I laugh. *Phantom vibrations.* Maybe going a week without a phone will make me realize it's an unnecessary distraction, and I won't ask Mom for a new one.

Relax. I said maybe.

Chapter 14

MARI

The midday sun is sweltering, which is the only reason I'm sort of looking forward to the "beach." I snuck out of the mess hall about the time they were chanting that stupid welcome shout to get a head start back to the bunk, where I knew I could change into my bathing suit without Amber seeing my cuts and scars and asking a bunch of questions.

Stopping briefly at the path leading to the boys' bunks, I'm tempted to sneak off again to the secret pond I discovered earlier, but I decide against it in case they take roll call and realize I'm missing. I don't want to draw any attention to myself.

Up ahead, I see Amber at the end of the trail, looking like she's trying to find something in her back pocket. I watch as she giggles and think again how odd she is. She continues to walk toward me, and when she's close enough not to shout, she waves and says, "Oh, hey! I was just looking for you at the mess hall after lunch."

"Yeah, it was so hot I couldn't wait to get into my bathing suit and cool off at the beach." I stop myself from mentioning the freshwater pond. Maybe no one else knows about my hideaway, and I'll have it all to myself for the week.

"Same. Okay, I guess I'll see you at the beach in a bit." Amber smiles as she continues to make her way to the bunk.

My plan to beat the rush to the beach is foiled when I see the same boys who seem to follow me everywhere in this place, wrestling a canoe into the water. I remember some of their names—Josh and Eric, the camp clowns, and the third one, Pete, who introduced himself at registration. But I don't know the fourth boy's name—Eye Contact Boy—who also broke my fall earlier in the food line. Recalling the incident sends another flush of embarrassment to my cheeks, but I'm pretty sure no one noticed or really cared, and the feeling dissipates quickly.

"Yo, Duke! Bro, grab that paddle over there," one boy shouts. It's Eye Contact Boy who makes his way to a metal rack with paddles and life preservers neatly organized before any campers have had a chance to disturb the orderly display. He tiptoes his way to the rack as if the sand is hot lava; I can't bring myself to look away from him.

I watch as he chooses a paddle. The name Duke suits him, with his shoulder-length, wavy blonde hair and his height. He must be at least six feet tall. Even from several feet apart, I remember his intense, blue eyes from when he looked at me this morning. He had to be the best-looking guy at camp. Out of my league, for sure.

Making his way back, Adam calls to him, "Mr. Duke, you and your buddies forgetting something?"

Looking at Adam and then his friends, Duke returns to the rack to grab life preservers for everyone.

"Thank you, Mr. Duke. Mr. Howser, Mr. Taylor, Mr. Colvin! Get those life jackets on before you shove off, please," Adam playfully scolds, calling the boys by their surnames like a parent would call their kid by their first *and* middle name when they're in trouble.

Amber appears next to me wearing a multi-colored fluorescent one-piece bathing suit, loose-fitting gym shorts, and sunscreen streaked across her face. "You remember your sunscreen?" she asks, holding out a bright orange tube of Banana Boat SPF-50. I'm not sure if I packed any at all, so I accept the lotion and squeeze a generous amount into my hand. As I smear the sunscreen in all the usual places, I ask, "Is Duke his first name or his last?"

"According to Jessica, it's his last name. She said no one knows his first name. Surprisingly, even *she* doesn't know. She seems to know *everything*," Amber says, trying to hide an eye roll. I have no idea which camper Jessica is, but I make a quick scan of the beach to see if I can take a wild guess. Before I can ask Amber to point her out, she says, "I'm going for a swim. Are you coming in?"

I toss the sunscreen onto her towel and look down at my feet, cursing my Chucks for the second time today. It takes me a few minutes to free my feet from the high tops before stepping out of my shorts. Folding them neatly, I place them on my beach towel, carefully laid out in the sand. The sun is relentless, and for a second, I think I might ditch the T-shirt, but I remember its purpose is to keep people from seeing the marks on my arms. I notice Amber is still wearing her shorts, so I guess leaving a T-shirt on won't attract any attention.

Joining her at the shore, I step into the icy water without any hesitation. It's not as cold as the hidden pond in the woods, and I venture further into the water until it's up to my waist.

"You're brave!" she says, standing in the water, only ankle-deep. "It always takes me a while to get used to the water before I go all in." I can appreciate taking your time before making a decision and being unsure.

I smile at her and shrug, then submerge myself completely under the water. Holding my breath, I dive deeper and swim as far as I can until my lungs start to burn from lack of oxygen. I fight the urge to return to the surface, but the familiar panic alarms sound, startling me enough to reconsider my decision.

Exploding at the surface of the water, I gasp for air and wipe the water from my eyes, immediately grateful my eyeliner is waterproof. Facing away from the shore, I see an island of trees ahead that seems miles away. Turning around, I see how far I am from the beach, now crowded with campers, and hear someone shouting my name. I see a commotion, arms flailing, and water splashing everywhere. It's Amber, frantically swimming toward me.

"Mari! Mari, are you okay?" She stops to catch her breath when she sees I have finally surfaced.

"Yeah, I'm fine," I say, beginning to swim in her direction.

"I thought you got trapped by seaweed or something. You were under for so long, my gawd, you scared me half to death."

"Sorry, I didn't mean to scare you," I say, feeling genuinely bad. Amber has been nice to me, and I didn't mean to give her a scare.

"You want to grab a canoe with me?" she asks, still paddling her arms to keep her head above water.

"Sure, I guess." It's the least I can do, considering how upset she was about my vanishing act.

As we swim back to shore together, several campers already paddling canoes pass us on their way out to the middle of the lake. "Are we allowed to paddle out to that island?" I ask, the words chopped up between arm strokes and sloshing water.

Amber stops swimming and stands, the water now up to our shoulders. "No, we're not supposed to dock or go exploring," she answers, brushing wet hair off her face and wiping the water from her nose.

"Why is that? Doesn't Camp Evergreen own the island?" I ask, wondering why there are so many stupid rules about everything.

"The counselors don't say much, but my mom told me that older campers like to tell the younger campers, especially newcomers, that the island is where campers who don't follow the rules are dropped off without any food or water or supplies to survive until their parents come to pick them up. Apparently, there have been several campers that never returned from the island—likely mauled by a wild animal or eaten by the cannibal, George."

"A cannibal named George?" I laugh at the absurd story.

"He lives on the island," Amber says deadpan.

"Maybe the counselors just don't make a big deal out of it because they're smart enough to know that the more you forbid kids from doing something, the more likely they are to want to do it."

"I don't know," she says with a shrug as we wade through the water, now waist deep. "I do my best to stay out of trouble, no matter how curious I am."

"Not all curiosity leads to trouble, you know," I say, looking back at the island. "Sometimes curiosity can lead to discovering there's more than one answer to a question. And maybe some of the answers are in the places we haven't been allowed to explore." I submerge myself under the water, and when I resurface, Amber looks at me with a thoughtful expression. "Besides," I continue, "threatening kids with being dumped off in the wilderness to fend for themselves if they break a rule doesn't sound like Camp Evergreen spirit to me," I say as we reach the shallow water close to the shore.

"You're right. It's just a stupid story. I'm sure no one actually believes it," she says unconvincingly as we tiptoe across the sand to the canoe rack. She grabs two life preservers and, pointing at the paddles, says, "The big wooden ones are for the canoes. Pick two." Then she tosses one of the life preservers to me. "Safety first!"

We haul the canoe into the shallow water, and Amber begins to instruct me on how to get into it. I've never been in a canoe before and have absolutely no idea what to do. How is it that Dad never thought of getting a canoe or even a rowboat for our newly built pond at the apple farm? If he had, I wouldn't be seconds away from looking like a complete idiot in front of everyone—again.

"You want to sit in the back or the front?" Amber asks, standing knee-deep in the water, holding the canoe to keep it from floating away.

"Um, whichever, I guess." I'm not sure what the difference is, honestly.

"Ever done this before?"

She has picked up on my uneasiness. "Am I that obvious?" I respond, a little embarrassed but relieved not to admit it outright.

"It's okay. I'll take the back so I can do the steering. If you sit in the front, you'll mostly just help keep the canoe moving," she says, somehow managing not to make me feel like a complete idiot.

She wades through the water before hoisting herself up into the canoe. It rocks violently but doesn't tip over. She makes it look easy, but that doesn't help my lack of confidence at all.

Keeping her body bent, she scootches to the back seat, a narrow piece of wood, and grabs the paddle from the floor of the canoe. "Okay, your turn," she says encouragingly.

I have no idea how I'm going to get into this thing without tipping it over or falling overboard myself. I'm convinced this won't end well, but—whatever. I take a deep breath and reach over the edge of the canoe to grab the opposite side, the way Amber did.

The canoe rocks toward me, nearly ninety degrees, but Amber repositions herself on the seat to put more weight on the opposite end, preventing the worst from happening. "You've almost got it," she says, cheering me on.

I push off the ground and heave myself up onto the canoe, landing in a heap in the middle. I can't believe I made it in without the darn thing tipping over. There seems to be no need to worry that I have made a fool of myself—until…

I hear a round of applause from the beach. Sitting upright carefully and grasping for the seat at the front of the canoe, I follow the sound and see two girls on the beach watching us. One of them is laughing and hooting: "You did it! Good for you!" The thing is, she isn't saying it in a nice way—not like Amber would, anyway. I can't really describe her tone, but it makes me feel stupid and embarrassed for the fiftieth time today.

"Don't mind her. She can be a little much, but she's harmless," Amber says about my *spirited* cheerleader.

"Who is she?" I ask, thinking that *harmless* is not the word I would use to describe her.

"Jessica." Her earlier comment about the girl who knows everything and the eye roll that couldn't be helped now make sense. "The girl with her is her bunkmate, Chelsea. I met them this morning before lunch. Chelsea is sweet. Very, *very* quiet. She follows Jessica around like—" She stops herself. "Anyway, it's not really any of my business," she adds.

Turning to face the front of the canoe, paddle in hand, Amber instructs me to put the paddle in the water on the left side. "Push the paddle all the way back, then lift it up out of the water." She demonstrates, then continues, "Dip it back into the water in the front, as deep as you can, and push it back again." I do as she says, and the canoe lurches forward to the left. "Okay, now put the paddle into the water on the other side," she instructs again. After a few strokes, the canoe rights itself and pushes straight ahead. "Good. Now, just keep switching sides every three or four strokes."

After only a minute of alternating paddle strokes, the canoe finds a good rhythm and glides through the water easily. I watch as the paddle breaks the water's perfectly still surface, creating its own swirling river within the water, ripples multiplying in its wake. The sight of it, combined with the sound of the water dripping from my paddle as I lift it out of the water, distracts me from the intrusive thoughts that always torture my mind.

For a moment, I feel lighter. I concentrate on counting each paddle stroke, alternating when Amber says to. The quiet is comforting rather than lonely or oppressive.

"How did you get to be a pro at canoeing?" I ask.

Amber shrugs and downplays the compliment. "I learned the basics in the Adirondacks with a friend of mine. We went to her family's lake house every summer." Abruptly changing the subject, she says, "It's beautiful out here, isn't it?"

"It really is," I respond quietly, unsure if she can hear me.

"Hey, guys!" Jessica, my cheerleader from the beach, shouts at us from her canoe a few yards away. "I wasn't sure you'd make it this far. Nice work!"

"Hey, Jessica," Amber responds politely. "Yeah, we made it."

"Want to race to the island? Or would that be too much for you—sorry. Did I get your name yet?" Jessica asks, directing the question at me.

There's something about this girl that makes me want to smack her. "Mari," I say instead of what I actually want to say, which is, *none of your darn business, now bugger off.*

"Mari, like, rhymes with sorry?" she asks sympathetically.

"Sure, like, rhymes with sorry," I respond tightly, using every available muscle in my body to keep from being catty. I imagine lifting the paddle from the water and *accidentally* whacking this girl on the back of the head.

"Mari. Okay, that's actually more lovely than I thought. It's nice to meet you. This," she says, pointing to her canoe partner in the front, "is Chelsea."

I offer a simple hello as our canoe begins to move away from theirs. Amber then says to Jessica, "Maybe we can race another time. Bye!"

We paddle a good distance away from them before Amber announces it's time to take a break from paddling. "Let's just drift for a few. I forgot that paddling a canoe is a workout."

"Fine with me," I say, resting the paddle in my lap. "You know, Jessica reminds me of my older sister. They both act like they're better than the rest of us." The second I say it out loud I regret it. Laura doesn't do it on purpose and I love her. Besides, constantly feeling inferior isn't something I really want to talk about.

"I don't have an older sister, but I know what it's like to live in someone's shadow, constantly trying to keep up. People like Jessica are so… extra," Amber says, her voice catching as she fumbles with the canoe paddle. "It's like they take up all the space—and there's barely any left for the rest of us average people who have to try twice as hard just to be good enough, never mind the best."

My first impression of Amber is anything but *average*. "Yeah, well, I bet Jessica couldn't teach someone how to paddle a canoe as patiently as you just did."

"What good is a thirteen-year-old that can teach someone how to paddle a canoe?" she asks, rolling her eyes.

"I know I couldn't be patient enough to teach anyone anything. And I can be pretty mean sometimes."

"You don't seem mean to me."

"Yeah, well, that's because you couldn't read my mind when that Jessica girl challenged us to a race," I say.

"Oh really? And what exactly went through your mind?"

I hesitate to admit the truth, unsure if she will join the *No One Likes Mari Club* if I do. My intuition has failed me before, but what have I got to lose? "It may have had something to do with my paddle *accidentally* making contact with the back of her head."

Amber instantly laughs. "Oh, that *is* mean!" She shakes her head and grabs the paddle from her lap, signaling it's time to get back to work.

Following her lead, I turn around to face the front of the canoe and begin alternating paddle strokes. My energy renewed; I realize maybe I'm actually making a friend, but a prickle in my gut reminds me, "Careful, Mari. You know what happens when you let people get too close." I ignore it and focus on the swirling water beneath my paddle, hoping with each stroke that the thought will get swept away with the ripples cascading away from the canoe.

# Chapter 15

AMBER

The sun has finally retreated beneath the trees surrounding the camp, and the drastic change in temperature makes me shiver. Digging through my duffle bag, I pull the contents out before locating my neon pink hoodie with the lime green word "NOPE" across the chest. It clashes with my yellow socks, but it's getting dark—no one cares.

Lying on her cot across from me, Mari places a strip of paper that looks like it was torn from a magazine into the book she's reading and asks, "What kind of music do you listen to?"

It seems like a random question until I notice her looking at the discman poking out of the mound of socks and shirts that my hoodie had previously been buried under. "Oh, you know, just whatever is on the radio, I guess," I answer before pulling the hoodie over my head. "My favorite band is Paramore."

"Never heard of them," Mari says, shaking her head and scrunching her nose. Then she points. "Is that Paramore?"

"No, it's my mom's," I say, freeing the discman from the pile of clothes. The flimsy headphones are still attached, and a pair of my underwear dangles from the cord like laundry hanging from a clothesline. I flush with embarrassment and quickly snatch them off, but Mari doesn't notice. *Hallelujah!* "You want to listen? It's got a bunch of old songs on it, nothing I really know," I say, offering her the headphones.

"Sure," she responds eagerly. "My dad listens to the oldies station on the radio, so maybe I'll know something."

Positioning the headphones on her ears, she pushes a button and listens. As I sit in silence, Mari lights up with recognition. "Oh, I know this one. It's not *old*," she says, rolling her eyes.

She begins to sing along, and I catch most of the words. *"Like a candle in the wind, never knowing da da dee da, when the rain sets in,"* she hums when she's unsure of the words. *"And I wish I could have known you, da da dee da, candle burned out long before da de da…"*

She removes the headphones and says, "That song only came out like last year when Princess Diana died in that car crash."

Princess Diana? I'm completely stupefied until I remember my Instagram feed, overrun with royal wedding pictures. "Oh, right. Princess Diana—Prince Harry's mom. Meghan Markle's wedding dress was iconic—"

"Knock-knock! It's time for Community Campfire!" Jessica interrupts.

"Already?" I ask, standing up. Opening the flap to the bunk, I see it's noticeably darker now, and the smell of burning oak and birch permeates the air.

Returning to sit on my cot so I can tie my sneakers, I notice Mari looking—I don't know, exactly—like she's trying to solve an algebra problem. "Are you coming?" I ask. My voice seems to snap her out of the weird trance.

Quickly looking around, she spots her high tops and, reaching for them, says, "Yeah, I guess. Where?"

"Community Campfire. It's a huge bonfire every night with the whole camp," I say, as she squeezes her right foot into her first shoe. It's painful to watch as she takes nearly a full minute to get her foot in.

Deciding to wait for her outside the bunk while she wrestles with the other shoe, I stretch my arms high above my head and crane my neck to peer at the night sky. The treetops, their leaves clustered together, create an impenetrable canopy for the bunks, but a few tiny openings allow me a glimpse of the first stars emerging from the night sky, a deep navy blue. I'm still trying to figure out what that song was—the one Mari just sang. If my phone wasn't broken, I could ask Google about it.

Finally, Mari emerges from the bunk with both shoes securely on her feet. "Hallelujah!" I shout at her with a smile.

"I was beginning to worry you'd make us miss Community Campfire!"

"Yeah, sorry. These Chucks are a pain."

We walk in silence away from the bunk, but as we reach the final turn to leave the forest, Mari stops briefly and looks down the path toward the boys' bunks. She asks curiously, "Have you been down that way before?"

"No, that's boys only. They're not allowed down our path either." I keep walking but she doesn't move to follow me. "What's wrong?"

"Nothing," she says after a second. "I'm coming."

As we leave the chill of the woods, the brilliant light of the campfire appears. The flames, touching the night sky, burn so hot that we feel their heat from across the wide field—the length of two football fields. A few stray campers are still making their way toward the fire set to the left of the beach. We can see fireflies twinkling at the top of the hill, where the blackberry bushes are.

As we arrive at the circle of logs, Jessica waves us over. "Amber! Mari! Over here!"

"This should be fun," Mari whispers to me before we make our way to the log where Jessica and Chelsea have saved us a spot.

"Goo-oood evening, Camp Evergreen Campers!" Sara hollers happily. "Welcome to our first Community Campfire of the week. Tonight's fire was built by none other than our very own Sam and Adam! Can we get a round of applause to thank them for their fantastic fire-building skills?" The campers applaud wildly, and of course Josh and Eric add their typical *whoop-whoop!*

"Thank you, thank you, everyone." Adam and Sam stand up, both taking a humble bow to acknowledge their adoring fans.

Joanna playfully pushes Adam and Sam from the spotlight and continues. "Wonderful, thank you, everyone! We are thrilled to have all of you here at Camp Evergreen, where we encourage you to let loose, be yourself, make some new friends, and maybe—*hopefully*, learn a new skill or two!"

"That's right, guys and gals," Sara addresses the campers. "Camp Evergreen is all about leaving the outside world behind, enjoying the great outdoors, and the fresh air, but of course, always keeping in mind safety first!" she says, looking directly at the camp clowns, Josh and Eric.

Sara and Joanna run down the safety rules, answer a few quick questions from newcomers, and then turn things over to Adam and Sam.

"All right, thank you, Sara and Joanna, for that detailed rundown of the Camp Evergreen safety rules," Adam says. "And remember, if in doubt—"

"Ask for help!" the campers shout in unison, finishing his sentence.

"That's right! You're all good listeners. I don't care what your parents say about you."

Laughter lingers as Sam addresses the campers. "Okay, folks, it's the moment you've all been waiting for… the camp spirit award—The Starburst Staff!" A few people clap excitedly but are hushed by their neighbors, not wanting to miss anything Sam says. Newcomers, unsure what happens next and curious to find out what the Starburst Staff is all about, sit up a little straighter.

Sam continues: "Camp Evergreen was founded in 1982 by Martin Hill and his son, Nathan. This great camp was built on the principles of friendship, kindness, helping others, and gratitude after they traveled to the Dominican Republic as volunteers for the United Nations Disaster Relief Organization. They assisted with the cleanup and rebuilding efforts after Hurricane David ravaged the island in 1979. Upon their return, they wanted a place—a retreat—where they could revisit their experiences of friendship, kindness, and acts of service, like they had in the Dominican Republic.

"While in the Dominican Republic, Martin and Nathan discovered a beautiful bush—one they had never heard of or seen before—the Starburst Bush. It is the national tree of the Dominican Republic, representing growth and resilience. When this exotic bush flowers, its blossoms burst open like a firecracker or, as some would say, a shooting star.

"In awe of its beauty, Martin and Nathan were inspired to create the Starburst Staff the first year they opened the beautiful grounds of Camp Evergreen to teenagers from diverse backgrounds. Bestowed upon individuals who embody the founder's core values—friendship, kindness, helping others, personal growth, and gratitude—the Starburst Staff serves as a reminder of the importance of these values and is the highest honor that all campers should strive for."

Sam then motions to Adam. "Adam, would you please give me a hand?" he asks, reaching into a large wooden box with the Camp Evergreen crest, the Starburst Bush, carved on the side.

The camp is silent with the exception of the crackling fire, its embers burning hot and bright, as Sam produces the Starburst Staff from its resting place. Audible *oohs* and *aahs* escape the first-timers' mouths, none of them embarrassed at their reaction to the sight of the most beautiful replica of the exotic plant from the founder's story.

Shiny strips of fabric, the colors of emerald, pine, and grass-green brightened by the light of the fire's flames, cascade from the top of a meticulously hand-carved staff, like Maleficent's from Sleeping Beauty. Nested inside the green foliage, deep pink blossoms surrounded by lighter pinks and vivid whites flourish and sparkle on a sturdy stem.

"This year, the Starburst Staff will be given to not one but two campers who, on this first day of camp, were wonderful examples of friendship, kindness, and helping others. And so, tonight, our first recipients of the Starburst Staff are… Pete and Duke!"

A collective sigh of campers hoping they'd be selected is overtaken by enthusiastic applause, whistling, and admiring cheers as Pete and Duke make their way to accept the Starburst Staff.

"Congratulations, Pete and Duke! And thank you for your display of camp spirit on this, the first day of Camp Evergreen!" Sam congratulates them both, shakes their hands, and offers them the staff. Duke and Pete, returning to their seats, are greeted by campers who want to take a closer look.

"All right, now who's ready for marshmallows and camp songs?" Adam says, clapping his hands together.

Mari looks over at me, exasperated. "I guess I shouldn't be surprised."

The first camp song is easy, perfect for newcomers like us. We sing the same verse over and over—loud at first, then quieter, until we're practically whispering:

"John Jacob Jingleheimer Schmidt. His name was my name, too. Whenever we go out, the people always shout, 'There goes John Jacob Jingleheimer Schmidt!' Fa-la-la-la-la-la!"

When we can't possibly sing it any softer, the counselors give the cue, and we belt it out at full volume one last time.

Soon, the fire dies down, along with the singing and excitement. The four camp counselors, now standing in a row in front of the dwindling fire, announce the final song of the night: The Camp Evergreen Anthem, which is ceremoniously sung at the close of Community Campfire each night.

Camp Evergreen is my favorite place,
Friends and laughter fill the space.
At the door, be yourself, leave your woes,
Feel the grass beneath your toes.
'Round the campfire we sing our songs,
You'll soon see that you belong.
Hey-ho! Camp Evergreen! Hey-ho! Hey!
Come see for yourself, I'm not a liar,
Row your boat and build your fire.
Enjoy the great outdoors with a friend,
A helping hand, you should lend.
With gratitude for all that you have,
Remember the Starburst Staff.
Hey-ho! Camp Evergreen! Hey-ho! Hey!

Chapter 16

MARI

"Hey-ho! Camp Evergreen! Hey-ho! Hey!" Campers sing in unison to close out Community Campfire. Then, all at once, everyone stands and retreats to their bunks for the night.

"Remember, quiet hours begin at eleven!" Adam shouts.

Amber, by my side, says, "It's not surprising Duke and Pete got the Starburst Staff."

"Why do you say that?"

"Well, for one thing—" she begins but cuts herself off as Pete and Duke pass us on the left, Duke carrying the Starburst Staff.

"Hey, guys," Pete says.

"Congratulations on the Starburst Staff," Amber offers as they move ahead of us.

"Thanks," Duke replies over his shoulder as they increase the gap between us.

When they're out of earshot, I ask, "How do you know Pete?"

"We go to school together. Honestly, we hardly know each other even though he also lives up the street from me," she says with a shrug. "You said you have a sister, right? Do you have other siblings?"

"No, just one sister. She's going to college this fall at BYU."

"BYU? Isn't that in Utah?" she asks, surprised. "That's so far away! Camp is two hours from where I live, and it's the furthest I've ever been from home."

"Yeah. She and my mom flew out there last fall to visit the campus."

"Do you think you'll go that far away for college?"

"What makes you so sure I'm going to college?" I scoff.

"Oh. Isn't it just the thing to do after high school?"

"I guess, but I don't know. I haven't really thought that far ahead. Been a lot going on for me—lots of things on my mind, that's all," I respond. Thinking so far ahead into the future is an impossible task.

"Right. I get it," Amber says, but really, I don't think she does.

Reaching our bunk, I suddenly feel so tired I can't wait to get into my cot. I hope the pool float will remain inflated, allowing me to get comfortable. I worry I won't be able to sleep. I imagine forest critters letting themselves into our tent in search of forbidden snacks. I'm slightly comforted knowing that Amber certainly wouldn't break that rule since earlier, she mentioned her mom's uninvited guest raccoons when she went to camp. I know I have nothing that would entice the creatures, but still… I know all too well that uninvited guests tend to make their way into my thoughts in the form of memories and dreams—especially at night.

"Wow, I'm exhausted," Amber says, reading my mind.

"Ditto," I mutter.

"Ditto?"

"Yeah. Ditto. You know, like, me too." I can't believe I have to explain this to her.

"I know what it means," she says, "it's just that my mom used to say that all the time until I told her these days we say same."

"Hm. If you say so."

After a trip to the outhouse to brush our teeth and wash our faces, Amber removes her sweatshirt and explains, "As much as I love the smell of smoke from a campfire, I don't really prefer it when I'm trying to sleep. I'm going to hang it outside." But she doesn't make any movement to head outside. After a few seconds, I realize she's waiting for me to take the hint that I should do the same.

I shed my sweatshirt, pulling it up over my head. My T-shirt underneath clings to the sweatshirt and exposes my belly and the dark scars that haven't faded yet. Grasping the hem of my shirt, I yank it down to cover myself and see the look of worry and panic on her face. My face turns hot, and I quickly turn away, too exhausted to explain myself. Bracing myself for her overblown reaction and questions, she takes me off guard when she only mentions the shimmering diamond nestled inside my belly button.

"My mom let me get a nose ring last year for my thirteenth birthday," she says as she turns to leave the bunk with her sweatshirt.

I follow her outside and wonder how I hadn't noticed the nose ring before. When we return to the bunk, I look closer at her face in the light of the lantern and see the tiniest hoop in her right nostril.

"That's cool," is all I say before squeezing into my sleeping bag, hoping it will swallow me whole.

Holding my breath, I wait for the interrogation from Amber. Instead, I hear the zipper of her sleeping bag before she turns the lantern down. The light grows dimmer before fading completely away. My uninvited guests know that's their cue— "You'll never be enough; you don't belong; you don't know who you are; just keep your mouth shut."

But then I hear Amber faintly humming, almost to herself, a song I know well that James Taylor sings; *You've Got a Friend.* I want to tell her my mom sings it when Laura plays it on the piano, but I'm choked up and can't speak. Besides, I'm not sure if she knows I can hear her. Instead, tears dampen my pillow as she continues to hum. I can't keep my eyes open and slip into sleep.

There's a sofa on her left and a recliner behind her, both covered in multi-colored crocheted blankets. With the coffee table in front of her, the furniture boxes her in.

The piano nestled in the corner is lit up by a small streak of sunlight that breaks through the tiny opening where two thick curtains meet, drawn closed so she can't see out, and no one can see in.

There's a board game on the coffee table. She tries to lean forward but is yanked backward by an invisible force. Her right collarbone burns. She reaches up, her fingers following a fabric strap crossing the length of her torso.

It's a seatbelt that holds her back.

Reaching to find the belt's buckle, she presses the latch to release herself, but it's stuck.

Gathering all of her strength, she wrenches the buckle free and is thrown forcefully toward the coffee table.

It's a Monopoly board game that crashes silently to the ground. The usual rainbow colors at the top of each property square are dull and gray. Their names are all wrong: "Brimstone Avenue. Sinner Place. Why Should You Collect $200 After What You Did?"

The dice roll themselves, and she watches as the silver Scottish terrier game piece moves itself to the square:

"GO TO JAIL."

Chapter 17

AMBER

Facing away from Mari's cot, I open my eyes and yawn. "Hey, are you up?" When there's no response, I roll over and see her empty cot. Sitting up and stretching my arms above my head, I let out another yawn that morphs into a strange groan. My back aches despite my pool float's efforts to be something it isn't—a mattress.

Unzipping my sleeping bag, I pull my knees to my chest to break free from the cocoon. Swinging my legs over the cot's edge, I shove both feet into my sneakers, squashing the heel backs (Mom doesn't like it when I do this). Missing my Nike slides, unacceptable footwear for Camp Evergreen, I quickly tie my laces and pull on a fresh T-shirt—Shrek and Donkey frolicking through a field of wildflowers, with SQUAD GOALS printed across the top.

Exiting the bunk, the smell of pancakes and maple syrup smacks me square in the face, my stomach acknowledging it with a growl. Looking toward the outhouse, I wonder if Mari is there or if she got a head start to the mess hall for breakfast.

As I leave the bunk, I think about Mari and the marks on her stomach. Concern edges its way back into my mind. I'm pretty sure they are scars and cuts she's inflicted on herself; the crisscross pattern was too perfect to be brought on by some sort of accident. I could tell right away that she was upset that I had seen them and didn't want to press her for details. It's none of my business, but I can't help but feel a pang of sadness for her.

Life isn't easy, I get it, but the thought of hurting myself has never crossed my mind. Miranda was a jerk and embarrassed me in front of everyone at school *and* the entire social media world, and that hurt enough. The thought of hurting myself—*physically*—makes my head buzz.

I can't imagine what terrible things Mari has been through that would make her hurt herself. A familiar heaviness settles in my chest, like water that keeps me submerged, unable to breathe. It's the same weight I carry at school, where I work so hard to keep up appearances, smiling when I don't feel like it, doing everything right so I won't disappoint Mom (or Miranda, before that all went to crap). It's the ache that burns when I think about telling Mom what's really going on, like how nothing with Miranda was ever real, that she was never my true friend. But then I remember: I have to protect Mom. I can't let her see that I'm not always okay. I don't want her to worry. I don't think she'd understand anyway.

"Hey, Amber!" Jessica's voice interrupts my thoughts. "Where's your bunkmate?"

"Hey, guys," I say as Jessica and Chelsea catch up to me. "I'm not sure. She had already left the bunk by the time I got up."

"She's an early riser, huh? Well, we're going rock climbing after breakfast. You guys should come with us," Jessica says.

"Okay. I'll mention it." Just like Miranda, Jessica isn't one to argue with.

The three of us settle into our seats at the mess hall, each with a stack of pancakes. Most campers are groggy, still wiping the crusties from their sleepy eyes. A few are "bright-eyed and bushy-tailed," how Mom describes cheerful morning people. "The ones that are bright-eyed and bushy-tailed drive me nuts," she often says, her hair not quite done, searching for keys, running late as usual.

I scan the room looking for Mari when Charlie (*speaking of bright-eyed morning people*) steps in front of me with an enormous grin on his face. "Hi, I'm Charlie," he says. "Pancakes are my favorite, so I'm really happy today we are having pancakes and not boring oatmeal or Cheerios. Pancakes. I could eat them all day," he says all in one breath. "What's your name?"

"It's Amber. Nice to meet you, Charlie. Do you ever put whipped cream and strawberries on your pancakes? That's my favorite," I say, taking my first bite of sweet, warm pancakes. Ms. Wolcott, still the camp cook after all these years, has really outdone herself today.

"No, I don't like strawberries. I only like apples and sometimes grapes, but only the green ones. And not bananas. Bananas are mushy. Apples are crunchy. But sometimes apples aren't crunchy, and that makes me mad. Dad always makes sure he gets crunchy ones for me."

"That's really nice of him. My mom always makes sure to get the snacks I love, too."

"Come on, Charlie. Let's sit and eat your pancakes before they get cold," Molly says as she passes behind us.

"Bye, Amber. Bye, Jessica. Bye, uh, I can't remember — oh, I know. Bye, Chelsea." He wishes us all a good day and turns to take his seat, digging into his stack of pancakes, which is double the height of ours, by the way. *Clearly, Ms. Wolcott has favorites.*

After licking our fingers and plates clean, we dispose of our trash and grab a few individually wrapped *Wet-Wipes* to clean our sticky hands.

"I forgot to apply sunscreen, so I've got to head back to the bunks," I casually say to Jessica and Chelsea, quickly turning in the opposite direction. I don't feel like forcing myself to chit-chat with Jessica, and I'm relieved when she offers a dismissive, "Okay, that's fine. We'll see you in a bit."

"Right. The rock-climbing wall. I'll bring Mari."

The walk back to the bunk is slower than usual, with my belly full of pancakes and syrup. As I turn the corner, Mari is up ahead just arriving at our bunk.

I finally make it to the bunk, and since I don't want to startle her or invade her privacy, I call out, "I'm coming in. Hope you're decent," I add for good measure.

Stepping inside, I see Mari sitting on the edge of her cot, looking like she's working on that algebra problem again. "There you are! Jessica and Chelsea want us to meet up at the rock-climbing wall in a bit. You up for it?"

"Rock climbing? As in helmet and harness rock climbing?" she asks, her eyes practically bugging out of her head.

With a laugh, I confirm she has it right. "Yes, as in helmet and harness. Have you ever climbed before?" I ask.

"Never," she says, shaking her head.

"Me neither. We'll figure it out together, I guess."

"Okay. Sure, why not?" Mari agrees with a *what have I got to lose* attitude.

"I just came to get my sunscreen, so I'm ready when you are." I reach for the Banana Boat SPF-50 that had been kicked under the cot and notice Mari's feet. "Hallelujah—you've got your Chucks on!" Then, throwing my hands in the air to praise the gods, I add, "I won't have to wait an *hour* for you to be ready!"

"Funny," she says with a smile.

After applying a generous amount of sunscreen and offering a dab to Mari, we make our way to the rock-climbing wall. It's cleverly hidden in a wooded area further up the hill from the mess hall, camouflaged by the blackberry bushes. "Jessica showed me the blackberries on the first day of camp," I say as we reach the top of the hill.

"It's okay to eat them?" Mari asks, reaching for a drooping branch so full that it's a miracle it hasn't snapped.

"Definitely! They're amazing, too," I say, plucking the plumpest berry I can find. Still stuffed from my pancake breakfast, one berry is all I can manage, but Mari can't seem to get enough. The sight of her eating fresh blackberries by the handful is a bit comical, and I can't help but let out a little chuckle. "Someone skipped breakfast this morning," I tease.

Mari stops herself from popping the next two berries in her mouth, but not without great effort. "Can you blame me? Like you said, they *are* amazing!" The remaining berries in her hand meet their fate as they go airborne, then directly into her mouth. Grinning as she chews, she exclaims dramatically, "Mmm-mmm-good!"

"Come on, leave some berries for the rest of the campers, would ya?" I say, reaching for her arm to guide her away from the bushes. As my hand wraps around her left upper arm, her laughing abruptly turns into a wince, and she immediately pulls away from me.

"I'm coming," she says, diverting my attention from her recoil.

I find myself feeling worried again. It's still none of my business, but I'm conflicted about how to approach the situation. If I mind my own business, will she think I don't care? If I ask any questions, will she think I'm being nosey? The battle rages in my head as Mari walks quietly alongside me.

Breaking the silence, Mari says, "I meant to ask if you have any siblings."

"Nope. My dad left before I turned two. It's just me and Mom."

"Sorry about your dad."

"It's okay. I don't know why I even mentioned it. It bothered me when I was little, when I figured out not having a dad was something to even be upset about, but not so much anymore. My mom and I are pretty close."

"That's good. My mom and sister are close. She's four years older than me, and I've always felt like my mom doesn't really need me since she already has a daughter to bond with."

"What do you mean, *doesn't need you*?"

"I don't know—it's just a feeling, I guess. They do things together, like watch crime shows, which I don't really like, and sing songs together at the piano. They love shopping and trying on new clothes, and they sometimes drag me along, but I'm miserable when I go. Nothing fits or looks right on me, and anything that does—they love, and I hate."

"I know what that's like. Clothes are hard when you're short, right?" I carefully nudge her with my elbow. Shoulder to shoulder, we're just about the same height.

"Yeah. I don't even bother with shorts anymore. My parents are really strict about how short a pair of shorts is allowed to be, so unless I want to wear boys' soccer shorts that fall at or below the knee all the time…" She rolls her eyes.

"I wondered," I say, looking at her long black jeans. "Why are they so strict? About the shorts, I mean?"

"If only it were just the shorts." Mari keeps her eyes down, and for a second, I think she's going to ignore my question completely, but then she says, "It's our religion. There are strict rules." Mari crosses her arms in front of herself and kicks at a tree root emerging from the dirt. "It drives me crazy. Everything is written in stone—in black and white—no debating allowed."

An image of the Ten Commandments etched onto stone tablets flashes in my mind. I highly doubt God wrote, "Girls must not wear shorts that don't reach below the knee," but I know it's not the time to make a joke about it.

As we follow another bend in the trail, the rock-climbing wall appears, seemingly out of nowhere. Mari stops, her eyes darting to the top. "*That's* the rock-climbing wall?" she shrieks.

"The one and only!"

Mari gawks at the wall, reaching at least three feet higher than the tallest trees, and says, "You have *got* to be kidding me."

Adam is helping Chelsea with her harness as Jessica, already suited up for her climb, waves when she sees us. "Guys! You made it! Come on! Chelsea and I are going up together. Gonna see who can reach the top first," she shouts as we approach. She leans her head in between us and whispers,

"I'm going to go a little slower than I can *actually* go so I don't make Chelsea feel bad. I might even let her win."

I want to say *how noble of you*, but instead, I smile and nod. I hold back a small laugh as I remember Mari saying she wanted to whack Jessica with a canoe paddle.

Jessica leaves us to pump herself up for her climb. Chelsea timidly assumes her position to the left as Adam double-checks the harnesses and the heavy-duty carabiners.

"All right, you two. On the count of three. One! Two! Three!"

Jessica mounts the first hold with her left foot and grabs another with her right hand. Chelsea follows her lead, hesitantly taking her first step, but can't quite reach the next hold. Dismounting the wall, she tries another hold closer to the bottom and finally makes progress. After they both clear the first three feet, Chelsea's right foot slips, but she recovers quickly and remains neck and neck with Jessica.

"You're doing great, Chelsea! Nice save!" Adam shouts encouragement as Jessica turns to look over her shoulder.

"Hey! What about me?" Jessica asks Adam with a pout.

"You're amazing as usual, Jessica! Eyes forward!" Adam placates her as he turns from the wall and rolls his eyes.

Mari's eyes are glued to the top of the wall. I think she might be breaking out into a sweat, and I swear I can feel the vibrations from her racing heart rumbling through the ground. "You'll do fine, Mari." I give her a reassuring pat on the back, but it doesn't seem to help.

"You really think the view at the top is worth it?" she asks doubtfully.

In response, I repeat one of Mom's favorite quotes: "Nothing worth having comes easy."

Mari whips her head around, taking me by surprise, and looks at me intently. Inhaling sharply to say something, she reconsiders and lets the air out between pursed lips. Turning away, she seems to be thinking about something, but I'm not sure what.

"Nothing worth having comes easy," she finally says, but to herself, not to me.

Chapter 18

MARI

It's only the second morning waking in the wilderness, and I'm *so* over it. Amber remains asleep; even the birds haven't started their morning songs. I lie here fidgeting and picking at my fingernails, wishing I could escape to the freshwater pond. But it's barely light out, so instead, I reach for my suitcase and slowly unzip the front pocket where my sharps are hidden. It's sad they've become my comfort object instead of a fuzzy teddy bear or a soft blanket.

Time blurs as I fall into a trance. My thoughts fade into the background, and the familiar sting numbs all the other pain. I watch as a faint line blooms red, but I pull myself back before it can go any further. I cover the open wound with a bandage and tuck my sharps away in my suitcase.

As morning birds finally begin their singing and Amber stirs, I ask, "So, what's on the agenda today?"

She yawns and says, "There's archery, fire building, hiking, or arts and crafts." Sitting up, she adds, "Unless you want another go at rock climbing."

Yesterday, I did the best I could but chickened out two-thirds of the way up the wall. I made the mistake of looking over my shoulder and saw how far I had climbed. It was enough to make me dizzy, and I panicked. Adam and everyone else on the ground tried to be encouraging, but ultimately, it was decided that if I didn't feel I could regain my focus or my nerve, the safest choice was for Adam to help me down using the belay device attached to my harness.

"I think I'll pass," I say. "Arts and crafts sound harmless enough."

Amber lights up and says, "I could use a less physically demanding activity for today. Between canoeing on Monday and rock climbing yesterday—"

"And sleeping on these cots!" I interject.

"Hallelujah! Definitely a good day for something a little more chill," she says, pulling out a pea-green shirt with the menacing face of The Grinch sketched on the front. I raise an eyebrow when she tosses a pair of red shorts on top. "Are you hungry?" she asks.

Before I can say a word, my stomach responds with a growl. It's so loud it spooks a flock of birds in the trees outside our bunk. The unexpected flapping frenzy makes us both jump and then burst out laughing.

After a breakfast of scrambled eggs and sausage links, I follow Amber to the camp office, where the arts and crafts are set up. I really hope it's not something cheesy like rainbow-colored plastic beads we string onto pipe cleaners or basket weaving.

The door to the office has been left open, and two long tables lined with brown craft paper are arranged in an L shape. On the tables are easels, each with a blank canvas waiting to be brought to life with paint. Another table has an impressive variety of two hundred or more paintbrushes, neatly displayed in a giant Maxwell House coffee tin. Against the wall in the back corner is a small table filled with dozens of paints in every color imaginable.

Sara looks up from setting out cups of water and cheerfully greets us. "Mari! Amber! Welcome! Gosh, the two of you look like you could be sisters!" she chirps, placing a hand on her heart.

Amber and I exchange looks, silently agreeing that we don't see a resemblance.

"Well, anyway, it's wonderful to have you here. Not sure if any other campers are gonna join us, but you don't have to wait around. Help yourself to whatever you need," she says, as Amber makes her way to the table of paint in the back before Sara finishes her instructions.

I watch Amber as she carefully selects three brushes, inspecting several of them closely.

"I have no idea what to paint," I admit, as she chooses the canvas with the most natural sunlight shining in from the window.

"Start with picking colors," she recommends.

"How do I pick colors if I don't know what I'm going to paint? If I pick out red, I can't paint a blue jay." I know it sounds dumb, but I start to panic. "What if I want to paint a blue jay?"

"If you want to paint a blue jay, grab the blue, silly goose. If you change your mind, you can get up and find a different color," she says with an appropriate amount of exasperation.

I realize I might be overreacting. But here's the thing: I can't think of a time I have ever been given a blank canvas to do whatever I want with. In art class at school, a canvas always comes with a set of strict requirements. There are certain elements we have to show we understand from reading a textbook. There's no creativity involved, only restrictions. Funny how this train of thought leads me directly to the source of my panic: I have a choice. I can do whatever I want. I can *express* myself however I want. I thought my biggest problem in life was not having any choices. Now, having *too many* choices sends me into a tizzy.

I don't want Amber thinking I'm a nut job, so I finally decide that primary colors are a good place to start. Then, I remember that white and black can transform any color, and I grab those, too.

Arms full of paint, I head to the canvas next to hers and sneak a peek at her brushes—I don't want to have another fit trying to choose those. I dig through the pile until I find ones that look just like the ones she's using and watch as she swipes the biggest brush back and forth horizontally on her canvas. Bright blue paint splashes across the top, then gradually lightens as she returns to her paint palette to add a touch of white. She makes it look easy.

Squeezing the paint from the bottles, I place a puddle of each color around the paper plate Sara provided as a palette, making sure to put the red next to the blue. I begin to mix them, watching as they swirl together and create a deep purple. I fill the fattest brush with the purple paint and carefully swipe it back and forth across the canvas.

I have no idea where this is going, but the burst of purple paint exploding in front of me is soothing. It's not exhilarating like music used to be, but I almost feel… something.

I continue to add purple, covering every inch of the top half. Then, copying Amber's technique, I add white to the deep purple, which becomes a shade of violet, then lavender. By the time I reach the bottom, it's a soft lilac.

"I figured you'd pick purple," Amber says with a smile. "Looks good, so far."

"It's nothing yet. Just color," I say, a little embarrassed, not knowing how long she has been watching and wondering if I was making any weird faces or sticking out my tongue as I worked.

"You've got to start somewhere."

"What are you going to paint?" I ask.

"Haven't really decided yet. Not completely, anyway. I have a few ideas," she says, returning to her canvas. "What about you?"

"Whatever it is, it's obviously going to be abstract." I can't think of anything I'm capable of painting. Rinsing the remnants of lilac from my brush, I consider that flowers won't be too hard.

Using the medium-sized brush, I start at the bottom and paint a haphazard row of vertical, curved lines to create the stems. I switch out the medium brush for the tiniest one I can find. I saturate it with black and return to the canvas. At the top of each stem, I paint a small x, then another one, overlapping it in the opposite direction to create little stars. The finishing touch is a circle wrapping around each of the pointed stars. It's not perfect, but after several minutes of working, I sit back to admire my work.

"Dandelions!" Amber says, sitting back in her chair, peeking at my canvas. "Iconic!"

Iconic. Not ironic. "Uhm, thanks? Does that mean you like it?"

"Like it? I love it. And I love that you did them as silhouettes," she says, complimenting my creativity before turning her canvas *away* from my view.

Pretending to stretch, I lean back, sneaking a peek at her progress. Several shades of blue are perfectly blended, reminding me of a summer night sky after the sun has set and the stars begin to twinkle. On the right, there's a large tree trunk with a single thick branch extending across the sky. Two parallel lines coming from the branch are clearly ropes of a swing, like the one Dad hung at the farmhouse. A perfectly round, full moon shines light on every detail of her painting, so intricate that it appears more like a photograph than a painting. Before seeing her impressive work, I was somewhat content with my dandelions. Now, I feel a little embarrassed staring at my childish artwork.

"Wow, it looks so real!" I say, forgetting I'm supposed to be *sneaking* a peek.

Startled, her cheeks turn pink with embarrassment, and she quietly says, "Thanks, but it's not really *that* great. You should see some of the work kids do in my art class. Their stuff puts this to shame."

"Are you kidding me? It's incredible, Amber!" I say, having to pick my jaw up off the floor.

"I dunno," she says, shrugging and applying more paint to the tip of her brush.

"Seriously, Amber. You could have your own art gallery!"

"An art gallery? I don't know about that."

"I'll be the first in line when you open it!" I say, looking back at my crooked dandelions, which resemble a first-grade finger painting compared to her incredible life-like painting.

Ignoring me, she continues to work, and I notice something change on her face as she concentrates on each brushstroke. It's as if she's silently speaking to the brush, the paint, the canvas, willing them to do as she wishes. The brush, a vessel for the paint, obeys her commands as the exquisite details of a girl on the swing emerge. She makes it look effortless. I can't believe she doesn't see how talented she is.

Turning back to my canvas, I add my initials, MAC, to the bottom left corner. In a moment of inspiration, I fill the medium brush with black and get back to work. Starting on the left side and working my way to the right, I add a long, slender, curved line. I use the medium brush to create the illusion of hundreds of tiny lines emanating from the first curved line. A feather finally takes shape, suspended in the air, floating above the dandelions.

My painted feather of a bird reminds me of the Emily Dickinson poem hanging on the wall above the piano at home. Laura and I both have it committed to memory:

"Hope" is the thing with feathers-
That perches in the soul-
And sings the tune without the words-
And never stops- at all-
And sweetest- in the Gale- is heard-
And sore must be the storm-
That could abash the little Bird
That kept so many warm-
I've heard it in the chillest land-
And on the strangest Sea-
Yet- never- in Extremity,
It asked a crumb- of me.

Scrawled in delicate cursive below the poem, the caption reads, "The bird symbolizes hope. Hope is always within us—no matter how dark our world may seem. Hope has the ability to bring us out of our greatest trials, yet it asks for nothing in return."

Hope. The thing with feathers that seems to be flying away from me.

Chapter 19

AMBER

The temperature rises as the sun hovers directly over the camp, turning the office into a sauna as we finish our paintings.

"I think that's it," I say, even though I'm still touching my brush to the canvas in places I feel need a little more shading.

"It really is beautiful," Mari says.

Deflecting her comment, I ask, "Is it just me, or did it get *really* hot all of a sudden?"

"It's definitely hot."

"I'm ready to cool off at the beach. You?"

We set our canvases by the window to dry in the sun and pause to admire each other's work. Mari's feather floats effortlessly in the center of a purple sky and makes me wonder what that must feel like—being so carefree, gliding wherever the wind takes you, trusting you'll land somewhere safe.

Her compliment about owning my own art gallery swirls around in my head. I think about the Congressional Art Competition letter stashed beneath my mattress at home. I don't mention it to her, of course, because I've decided I'm not going to accept the invitation. The last thing I need is for her to pester me the rest of the week about entering my work.

We make our way to the bunks, and after changing and applying our sunscreen, we leave the bunk as Mari says, "I've got something to show you." We walk together through the woods, but as we come to the turn leading to the campgrounds, she continues straight

"That's the boy's side. We aren't supposed to go that way!" I warn.

"We're not going to the boys' bunks, I promise. Just follow me," she says, continuing forward. After she walks further down the path, she turns left and disappears.

"Wait up!" I call after her. I start to run, then remember I *don't* run and slow to a brisk walk. Mari is waiting for me, pushing aside branches of a thorny bush just off the path. "Are you *sure* we're allowed to go this way?"

"Relax! It's just up here a little," she says, laughing at my panic about breaking the rules.

Catching my breath (*I told you I don't run!*) I nervously follow her, hoping that whatever she wants to show me isn't dangerous or forbidden territory.

"I'm surprised you've never been this way before. You seem to know camp so well."

"I *do* know camp pretty well—the parts that are on the map and *aren't* prohibited!" I say in a harsh whisper. "Where are you taking me?"

"Look." Mari stops abruptly.

I stop short of crashing into her and look up. Before us are massive boulders and patches of lush, green grass surrounding a freshwater lily pond with a small waterfall trickling down a large boulder on the other side.

"Holy crap!" I blurt. "This is beautiful."

"I know. I found it the first day we were here."

Thinking back to Mari's disappearance after we had finished blowing up the pool floats for our cots, I ask, "Is this where you were hiding before lunch on the first day?"

"I wasn't *hiding*," she says defensively. She hesitates before admitting, "Well, maybe I was. I wasn't exactly down with being here. It was my parents' idea—signing me up for camp."

"I wondered if you were miserable or just shy when I met you at the camp office." I realize too late that maybe I shouldn't have said that out loud. Mari laughs, and I join her with relief. At least I left out the part about being a Debbie-Downer.

"Sorry. I hope I didn't come across as rude," she mumbles regretfully.

"No, definitely not rude," I tell her honestly.

"I didn't mean to be a party pooper. So far, camp has actually been… okay, I guess. It's just that I'm already not sure about a lot of things, and then my parents just sort of sprung this camp stuff on me, and I didn't really have a choice about coming. They didn't *ask* if I wanted to go; they *told* me I was going."

Visibly upset, Mari kicks a small stone into the pond before settling down in the grass with a row of small boulders. "Do you ever feel like your whole life is scripted for someone else? Like you're not in control of anything you do?"

Joining her on the grass, I have no idea what she means. But then I think of Miranda and how I always followed her lead. "I let a friend talk me into playing soccer once. I didn't want to, but..."

"Yeah, that's not quite the same," she says, a hint of irritation in her voice. She plucks blades of grass from the earth, then tears each blade in half. "It's just, sometimes it feels like I never make any decisions for myself, and I'm always being forced to do things and *be* someone I'm not," she explains, sounding defeated.

We sit together quietly, Mari picking grass while I pick my brain for what to say next. It's hard for me to come up with any advice without understanding what she's going through. But it doesn't really feel like the right time to offer advice anyway.

Mari starts again. "It's kinda hard to explain, you know? I mean, I'm really lucky to have a good family. My older sister is a good role model, my parents are good people, and I know they love me and all, but I don't feel like I can measure up to their expectations. I try to keep up but can never get it right."

"I get *that*," I say with a confident nod.

"I'm forced to go to church *every* Sunday and have to do all the church youth group activities, mostly like service projects and stuff, but there's also this early morning bible study they make me go to every day before school, and I hate it."

"*Before* school? That's gotta be really early," I say, knowing that the first block at my middle school starts at eight a.m.

"I have to get up at five a.m."

"Five o'clock?" I cringe. "Dang, that's early! I have a hard time getting up at six forty-five."

"Seriously. After that, my mom drops me off at school more than an hour before the first bell. There's never anyone around, and I sit there bored by myself."

"My mom and I aren't morning people, and we're always running late," I say, knowing it's kind of random and isn't any consolation. "This church that you go to with your family, is it like Jehovah's Witnesses or something?"

"I don't know about that. The church I go to has missionaries that go door to door like they do, but I don't know anything about what they teach or believe."

"Oh," I say, pausing for a second to think. "Wait, I think I've seen those people. They're the guys that wear white dress shirts and ties and have the black name tag on their shirt pocket, right?"

"Yup, those are the ones."

"Those are Mormons," I say proudly, finally right about something.

"Yup. Also known as The Church of Jesus Christ of Latter-Day Saints," Mari says with lackluster enthusiasm. "They should call it The Church of We Have All the Answers Don't Bother Looking Anywhere Else."

"I've never understood how people can think there's only one right way to do something or one right thing to believe," I say indignantly. "You're allowed to change your mind—especially when you keep an open mind and learn something you didn't know before. That's what my mom has always told me, anyway."

"Exactly. My whole life, I've been a Mormon, but when you're little, you're just a kid who goes to church with your family. I was baptized when I turned eight, and I guess that's when I officially became Mormon."

"I thought people baptized babies. Eight seems old."

"If you ask me, eight is still too young. The church calls it "the age of accountability" and tells you that being baptized is a *choice*. I don't know any eight-year-olds who would say to their parents, 'Sorry, I know who I am and what I believe, and I don't think getting baptized into this church is the way I want to go with my life.' Do you?"

She has a point. I certainly didn't know much when I was eight.

"Everyone in the church is committed and so sure of everything," Mari says, making it clear she isn't including herself. "They spend all their energy convincing each other that what the church teaches is," she air-quotes, "the true gospel," and makes a face of disgust. "If you don't believe that, well, you just won't make it into the Celestial Kingdom."

"Celestial Kingdom? You mean, like heaven?" I ask curiously.

"Exactly," Mari confirms.

"I've never heard of heaven being called the Celestial Kingdom. It *does* sound more romantic than plain old heaven," I admit.

"*Romantic*," she repeats sarcastically. She pulls her knees close to her body and rests her chin on them. She swats at a fly that lands on her arm—the same arm I touched yesterday, which caused her to wince.

The wind picks up and rustles the leaves overhead as a pair of robins swoop down from a nearby branch, crossing over the pond. A bumble bee bounces from one blossom to the next in the flowering bushes to the left. Out here in the woods, watching the critters and listening to the bugs go about their simple lives makes me wonder how people manage to complicate everything.

"Sometimes," Mari begins, "I'm afraid I'll never figure things out for myself."

"We're only thirteen. There's no rush, is there?"

"No matter what age I am, figuring things out for myself could hurt my family."

"Hurt them how? Why wouldn't your family want you to be confident about who you are and do what you feel is best for *you*?"

"It's the church. My parents, my sister, and even my best friend, Rachel—like everyone else at church, they believe that the only way to be truly happy is to be baptized, follow the rules, and do everything that will allow you to be with your family forever, even after death, in heaven."

"Celestial Kingdom, you mean." I'm careful not to make it sound like I'm making fun, hoping it might make her smile.

"Right," Mari says with a smile, thankfully. But then her smile fades. "I wish I believed the way they do, but…" She stops and looks over at the waterfall. "If someday I decide that trying to live up to the rules and expectations of the church isn't for me—if I decide that I don't believe what they teach and leave the church, it will crush my parents."

I understand not wanting to disappoint your friends and family. The thought of being abandoned just for following your heart and being true to yourself puts a lump in my throat and an ache in my chest. I can't imagine being unable to decide things for myself—to be forced to believe something that doesn't feel right.

It makes me think of all the choices Mom gives me: "What do you want for dinner? Where should we go for a weekend trip? Do you want to take lunch to school or buy cafeteria lunch? Pick out whatever clothes you want. Choose whatever makes you feel good. I can't tell you who you are; only *you* can know that for sure. *You* decide. Be yourself, Amber."

Then I think about how I'm usually annoyed by always having to make so many choices and feel a pang of guilt. I'm not about to mention this to Mari since, obviously, there's nothing she wouldn't do to be given choices.

Mari, sounding like she's holding back tears, says, "My parents only want what's best for me and my sister, but nothing feels right. I just feel lost. Empty. Afraid—afraid that even *if* I figure it all out—if I walk away from the *church*, my family will walk away from *me*."

Her words echo in my ears. "I get your fears about that," I confide quietly.

"I'm sorry. I always feel stupid and ungrateful when I complain about my family life and the whole church thing. I know plenty of kids have it far worse than me."

"You don't have to apologize. We all have our problems," I say, trying to be comforting. "You're struggling now, Mari, but you'll figure it out. Maybe not right away, but someday."

"Someday," she says doubtfully.

"I know you will. My mom says living and experiencing things is how we eventually figure things out. Just got to be patient and not worry so much about what other people think."

"Easier said than done."

"Believe me, I get that. It doesn't happen overnight. Give it time."

"I don't think," Mari begins, but is interrupted by the lunch bell ringing. Neither of us wants to leave the pond, but our hunger motivates us to get to our feet and make our way to the mess hall.

I really wish I could say or do something more to help her. The ache in my chest burrows its way deeper inside of me, binding itself around my ribcage. I wrap my arms around myself, trying to keep the ache from taking over completely as we leave the freshwater pond behind.

"Mari, I hope—" I start but have no idea what I want to say. Mom's daily farewell, "Remember who you are," comes to mind. I try again: "You'll figure things out. My mom always says, 'Remember who you are,' and honestly, sometimes it's annoying, but I guess—" I stop, realizing something for the first time. "I guess she knows that who we are is always inside of us. We just forget who we are because of all the noise around us. We have to shut everything else out so we can *remember*."

"Remember who you are," she repeats the words quietly to herself.

"Life is overwhelming," I say. "Everybody has an opinion about who they think we are. Keeping up appearances can be impossible sometimes. There's so much we have to unlearn— *to forget* in order to *remember* who we are."

"There are definitely a lot of things I need to unlearn *and* forget," Mari says.

I respond, "Same."

At lunch, Jessica talks our ears off about all the talent camps and clinics she's been to over the years: horseback riding, ballet, theatre, pottery, and even American Sign Language. "This year, I'm going to a photography internship." She's not very humble and goes on and on about everything she's good at. The thing is, I'd rather be good at nothing than be good at something and act like I'm God's gift to the world.

After reciting her resume, Jessica says, "Joanna is announcing the theme for tomorrow's talent show during lunch today. You guys are going to do something, right? It's important to showcase your talents."

…we are pleased to inform you that you have been selected to enter your artwork…

I push the thought from my mind as Jessica carries on. "People need to know how awesome you are. And you can't let the haters get you down. They're just jealous they're not as good as you are at something, and that's their problem, not yours."

I can tell Mari is biting her tongue as hard as I am. She finishes her lunch quickly and whispers, "I'll meet you at the beach in a bit. Just need a break."

I completely understand. "Okay. Don't forget we're going to kayak today!"

"I won't forget," she promises, standing with her tray.

Jessica gives Mari a small, dismissive wave and continues her monologue about being confident and believing in yourself, no matter what. I'm not really listening as I continue to eat, unable to keep my mind off the Congressional Art Competition.

Jessica doesn't understand it's not always easy to put yourself out there for people to judge (*or comment on Instagram, for example*). The fact is, no matter how good you are at something, there's always someone better at it than you. It's sad that we make everything a competition, but it's hard not to. Especially when social media constantly makes comparisons and makes it look so easy to excel in everything—academics, athletics, *and* art. I'm smart enough to know that social media only shows the highlights, not the struggles and real lives of the people behind the stories, but it can be hard to remember that.

We're only supposed to put our "best selves" on display. Doing anything *but* that is a *huge* risk that not many are brave enough to take. Even putting your *best* self on display is a risk. There will always be the jerks lurking in the shadows whose mission it is to tear people down. I still feel the hurt, fresh and raw, every time I think of my painting of Grandma, vandalized in the school lobby.

"The moment you've all been waiting for!" Joanna shouts, getting everyone's attention. "This year's camp talent show theme is… 'Shine!'"

Jessica claps her hands and says excitedly, "I love that song!"

"It's a song?" I say, completely clueless.

"Of course it is. By Collective Soul."

"Collective Soul," I parrot, feeling ignorant.

"They're one of my brother's favorite bands, and *Shine* was one of their biggest hits," she says as she begins to sing the words she knows. "Show me where to look, da-da-do, da, I find, da-da-da, fly me in the sky, do-do-da, teach me how to share, where to go, da-da, love will be there."

Joanna's voice interrupts Jessica. "So, practice up, people! You can do anything you want—a magic act, a dance, sing a song—we've got 'Ole Faithful there in the back if anyone wants to tickle the ivories," she says.

"I'm assuming 'Ole Faithful is a piano?" I ask Jessica. If I'm wrong, I don't have much to lose after not knowing who the heck Collective Soul or Punky Brewster is.

"Yes, it's a little out of tune, but they keep it around. It's in the custodial closet with the mops and brooms," she replies, gesturing to the back of the mess hall. "They rolled it out for one of the campers to play for last year's talent show."

Joanna said it's not mandatory to participate in the show. It is, however, mandatory to attend as a spectator to cheer on and support those who decide to show off their talent. I've got plenty of experience in *that* department.

"Amber, you'll do something, won't you?" Jessica asks. The gold emblem of the University of Visual Arts floats above her head. "I'm sure there are lots of things you're good at, and you're just holding out on us."

"I'm not holding out. I don't have any real talent, trust me," I say, feeling guilty for telling the little white lie. But talent shows aren't exactly meant for artists to showcase their paintings. What am I going to do? Get up on stage with an easel and paint in front of everyone, like that old guy with poofy hair on PBS? "The last thing you want is for me to get up in front of everyone to sing or dance," I say, spooning the last bite of pasta salad into my mouth. "I might be able to shake a tambourine or some maracas if you want to throw together a girl band act," I say, completely kidding.

"That's a great idea!" Jessica leaps out of her seat with excitement.

"I was kidding, Jessica." Her face immediately falls, annoyed that the carpet has been yanked from under her, along with her vision of being the star of the talent show.

"Well, I think it would be fun," she pouts. "We could do an easy song like *MMMBop* by Hanson."

"Who the heck is Hanson?" The question slips out of my mouth.

"Are you serious, Amber? You know Hanson." Jessica sings the chorus, "MMMBop. Oh, oh, MMMBop..." then stops abruptly. "You know it! Who doesn't?"

I don't want to sound like I live under a rock, so I give a lame, "Oh right, sure." *My list of things to ask Google keeps growing.*

"Besides," she continues, "I know most of the words, and I'll sing lead. Chelsea, you can play air guitar, and Amber—I don't think any of the Hanson brothers played the maracas, but you can play the air drums. Oh! And Mari! We can figure something out for her, too."

Jessica is determined to get her way, and I know there's no point resisting. "Okay, you win," I relent and picture myself waving a white flag.

"I remember Joanna saying there's a boombox and a bunch of CDs in the camp office. Maybe it's on one of those, and we can just lip-sync! I'll go check with her," she says as she walks—no, *skips* away, anxious to turn her vision into reality.

Chelsea immediately gets up to follow her, as she always does, leaving me alone with my empty food tray and a knot in my stomach. The thought of us singing along to a boombox in front of everyone and not *actually* showcasing any *real* talent makes me feel sick. I don't want to have anything to do with Jessica's silly act. With a sigh, I try to shake it off and remember this is camp. It's not that serious.

I get up to return my empty lunch tray and glance at the clock. I have thirty-five minutes before meeting Mari at the beach to kayak. It's not enough time to go back to the bunk for a nap, but maybe I could find a shady spot of grass to stretch out and close my eyes.

Stepping into the heat of the sun, the panoramic view of the beach is beautiful. I take a deep breath of fresh camp air, trying to decide where I will most likely find a comfortable place to rest. Looking to my left, I see Jessica and Chelsea walking with Joanna to the camp office. I send a message out to the Universe: *Please don't let her find a CD with MMMBop on it* and laugh as I imagine her finding something fifty times worse, like *Don't Charge Me for the Crime* by The Jonas Brothers.

Making my way down the path from the mess hall, the beach in front of me sits abandoned. No one goes to the beach right after lunch because everyone knows you're supposed to wait at least thirty minutes after a meal before swimming. I'm honestly not sure if it's true. I'll ask Google.

At the bottom of the hill, I change course to the right, where the tetherball sand pit is. Just beyond that is an inviting patch of shaded grass perfect for a quick snooze. I'm about halfway there when I see Pete approaching me, proudly carrying the Starburst Staff.

He stops a few feet away from me and looks up at the bright green and pink Starburst sparkling in the sun. Without a proper hello, he says, "Something tells me they're going to pick someone else at Community Campfire tonight."

"Maybe." It's all I can think of saying. *Awkward, I know.*

"You wanna play some tetherball?" he asks as I take a step toward the shady grass that's calling my name.

I feel bad saying no and figure since I'm so good at doing things just because someone else thinks I should, I might as well be consistent. "Sure."

After staking the Starburst Staff into the ground at the edge of the sand pit, Pete takes the first punch at the tetherball, sending it sailing through the air. The rope it's attached to begins to wrap itself around the pole, slowly at first and then faster and faster.

The objective is to hit the ball in the opposite direction of your opponent to prevent it from wrapping around the pole entirely. I'm not very good at it, and I tend to get a little dizzy as I watch the ball circling the pole. It's also not as easy as it sounds, depending on how hard your opponent hits the ball.

I give it my best shot but miss the ball entirely on the first attempt. It's always embarrassing when this happens, but it's also probably what makes the game so fun. You can't help but laugh when someone misses. Feelings don't really get hurt because *everyone* misses at least two or three times, so we're essentially laughing *with* each other, not *at* each other.

After we alternate hitting the ball several times, Pete finally takes a miss and lands on his knees in the sand. "Are you okay?" I ask, but he's already getting to his feet and brushing himself off.

"Yeah, yeah. I'm good," he says, laughing and shaking the sand from his hands. "I could use a break, though."

Together, we move to the shaded area I had longed for earlier to take refuge from the sun's persistent heat. We both collapse heavily on the cool grass.

"Hey, that was fun," Pete says, holding up his hand for a high five. The Pete sitting next to me seems completely different from the one on my street back home. In all the years that we've been neighbors, I don't think I've heard more than twenty words from him.

"Hey, can I ask you something?" I ask, sitting up and leaning on one elbow.

Mirroring my position, Pete looks at me and says, "Sure. What's up?"

"It's about my bunkmate, Mari. I think she…" I hesitate because I don't think it's really my place to tell anyone about her personal business. But I'm worried about her, and I need to talk to someone about it. "I don't know. She…"

"What about her? Everything okay?" His genuine concern takes me off guard. I don't know him all that well, but there's something about this version of him that I've never seen before, and it makes me feel like I can actually talk to him.

"I don't know," I say carefully. "I think she's depressed. I think she's going through some heavy stuff, but I don't know how to help her." I wait for him to respond, unsure if he'll say something helpful.

He nods in acknowledgment and pushes himself up onto his elbow. "I get that you want to help," he says, "but the thing is, sometimes when people are going through stuff, the heavy stuff, like you said, there's nothing you can say that they haven't heard already."

"That's true. There's a lot of clichéd advice out there: 'Fake it 'til you make it' and 'everything happens for a reason.' That one's my least favorite."

"I hear ya," Pete grunts. "And some people hear the same thing over and over again, but it doesn't make any difference until the person is ready to, like, really hear it."

"And what if they're never ready? What if it ends up being too late?" I ask, a hint of panic in my shaking voice.

His concerned face frightens me a little, but he doesn't hesitate to say, "It's never too late. Sometimes people just need to know that someone will be there for them and listen." He shrugs before adding, "I know it's probably more complicated than that, but it's a good place to start."

I offer a single nod and a quick smile. I don't have the courage to ask, *what if the people who are supposed to be there for you are the ones who leave?*

Chapter 20

MARI

After having to suffer through a mostly one-sided conversation with Jessica at lunch about all the things she's good at, I need a minute to myself.

I sneak out of the mess hall and make my way down to the beach. To the right, behind the kayaks, a small path leading into another wooded area catches my eye. Wondering if I could find another hidden gem like the freshwater lily pond, I look over my shoulder to make sure no one is watching before making my escape.

It certainly isn't a secret trail. The roots, exposed by the constant traffic of campers over the years, resemble giant rattlesnakes. I'm anxious to see where the trail will lead as I make my way up and over a steep incline, and archery targets come into view. Several arrows are stuck in one of them, and out of nowhere, an arrow whizzes through the air, nailing the center bullseye.

Then I see Duke reloading his bow. He's focused and doesn't know I'm here. I don't want to scare him—not with a loaded bow in his hands—so I remain still and quietly watch.

Thwack! Another arrow snaps from his bow, just barely missing the bullseye. Duke sets the bow down on a nearby log and makes his way to the target to retrieve the arrows, neatly bunched together in the center.

After plucking them from the target, he turns and spots me before I can hide. "Come out, come out, wherever you are!" he teases as I step out from behind the tree, embarrassed that I've been caught stalking him.

"Hey," he says, arranging the arrows in his hands. "Don't tell anyone you saw me here alone. We're not supposed to do this without a buddy, but I needed to get away from Josh. That guy can be a bit much sometimes."

Heading back to the archer's line and without looking my way, he asks, "Have you ever done archery before?" He doesn't wait for my response before loading another arrow onto the bow. Getting into position, he draws back the string, aims, and releases. Within seconds, the arrow is lodged in the center of the target. "Bullseye!" he shouts.

Deciding I had better stop acting like a peeping Tom, I move away from the tree. "I've never done archery before," I say, making my way down the slope, careful not to lose my footing. I've fallen once already in front of Duke. I don't need to do it again.

"Grab a bow," he says, pointing to a rack constructed from old logs and branches.

I wonder how hard it can be and shrug passively as I select the first bow at the end of the rack.

"Actually," he stops me, "that looks a little big. See the color at the top? The blue ones are the biggest. I'd recommend the smallest one, the yellow, for you."

A large crate is filled with hundreds of arrows at the end. There doesn't seem to be any system to distinguish any differences between them, so I blindly reach for five or six arrows and join him.

"Good. So, you just take the tip of the arrow with the feathers and see this little notch?" Duke points. "That's where you put it on the bowstring. It's called nocking. Like this." I watch carefully so I won't have to ask him to repeat himself. I don't want to look stupid. "Then you just put the other end of the arrow here, like this. Now, pull back the bowstring and tighten it as much as possible. Take your aim, and when you're ready, release," he says, as his arrow barrels toward the target as if a strong magnet forces them together.

Mirroring his stance, I follow his instructions. I pull the bowstring back and feel it get tight. My left arm holding the bow shakes from the tension, and I worry I'm about to make a fool of myself.

Duke carefully moves behind me and places his hand under my left forearm to help steady the bow. With his help, I release the arrow. It proceeds to bounce off the tree trunk to the right, missing the target by several feet.

"Hey, not bad for your first time!" he congratulates me.

"It didn't even come close to the target!" I say, embarrassed.

"But your arrow had good speed and went a good distance. Most people's arrow lands about five feet from them in the dirt on their first try," he says encouragingly as he hands me another arrow. "Try again."

I repeat the same process, placing the arrow's notch on the bowstring, raising my left arm to aim, and drawing back the bowstring. This time, the arrow hurls itself straight ahead and into the top right corner of the target.

"There you go! See? And it stuck!" Duke says.

"Barely," I say with a little less embarrassment this time.

"You'll get the hang of it. Every time you miss, you'll start to figure out what adjustment you need to make for the next shot to go where you want it to."

Taking a third arrow from him, I think about the adjustment I need to make. Waiting for my bow to settle down after drawing back the bowstring, I aim, and—*thwack*—the arrow hits the outer black circle.

"Nice shot! You're a natural!"

It's the first time I've heard that. "Where are you hiding your Starburst Staff?" I ask, remembering that the day before, he and Pete dug a hole in the sand to keep it standing upright while they went kayaking.

"Pete's got it. Pretty sure it's going to be awarded to another camper tonight. We were both surprised no one was picked last night."

"Has anyone ever had possession of it for the entire week before?" I ask curiously.

"Not that I can remember."

"It's a beautiful work of art. The Staff, I mean," I say stupidly. Of course, I mean the Staff. What else would he think I'm referring to? The heat of humiliation ignites again, rising up into my cheeks, but a cool breeze and Duke's response keep it from burning too hot.

"I heard Joanna tell another camper it was made by the founder's wife before she passed away."

"That's sad," I say, looking down at my feet as I draw a half-circle in the dirt with the toe of my Chucks.

"Yeah, I know."

There's a brief, awkward pause before Duke reaches for the arrow in my hand and takes it for his own bow. He prepares the arrow on the bow and assumes the archer's position. Within seconds, he is already aiming the arrow and fires—*thwack*—he hits another bullseye effortlessly.

"How do you do that every single time?"

"A lot of practice," he says with a shrug. "It's not so hard once you figure out what you're aiming for. After you know where to place the tip of the arrow so that it hits where you want it to, the rest is just building up your strength to hold your ground and have confidence."

"I think you know how to make it look easier than it actually is."

Duke smiles and gets into position to take another shot at the target. "The girl with the funny socks, she's your bunkmate, right?"

"Amber? Yeah, why?"

"Pete said she's a character. Not in a bad way," he adds quickly.

"She's *got* character, that's for sure," I say, thinking about her Christmas-in-July outfit. "She said Pete is her neighbor, and they go to the same school."

"Oh, I didn't know that. Pete didn't mention it." After sinking another arrow into the bullseye, he asks, "What do you think about Camp Evergreen so far? Not so bad, right?"

"It's okay. Not nearly as bad as I thought it would be."

"My first year, I wasn't looking forward to it either," Duke says. "My parents didn't even tell me about it until the day before. My dad said, *Find your swim trunks, pal—you're going to camp.* I had it coming since I sat around all day in my room as soon as school was out for the summer. Guess he was tired of watching me rot," he says as he settles onto the log behind us.

I join him, careful not to sit too close. "That's basically how it went down for me, too. My parents left the camp brochure on the kitchen table, and when I saw it, I was desperate for it to be for my sister. I don't have that kind of luck, so of course it was for me."

"Your parents sound like mine. They like to say, *you're doing this, like it or not*. It's so annoying."

"Sounds about right," I say, thinking about all the times I don't have a choice.

"I mean, how are we going to learn anything if they don't let us decide some things for ourselves? Big whoop if we're wrong about it. As long as we aren't going to do anything super dangerous or stupid, they should just let us figure it out," he says, picking up a small twig and breaking it in half aggressively. Goosebumps prickle on my arms.

Duke bumps the bow propped against the log next to him, catching it before it crashes to the ground. Repositioning the bow, he leans back to right himself on the log and bumps my arm, making the cut I etched there early this morning burn. Crossing my right hand over my chest self-consciously, I apply pressure to my arm.

"There are probably worse things than parents forcing their kids to go to summer camp, though, right?" I say with a knowing laugh.

"True. I guess we lucked out that Camp Evergreen is pretty great. But you know, the other stuff..." He trails off.

"Yeah, I get it," though I'm not sure what the other stuff is for him.

Before I can ask about it, he looks at his wristwatch and says, "It's almost time for us to be at the beach. We should probably head back."

My immediate thought is, *You mean together?* As I get up from the log to follow him, my mind will not shut up. He's going to be mortified when everyone sees him with the miserable new girl with purple hair. I'm sure Josh and Eric will have something to say about it. Following him, my legs try to keep up with my self-doubting, racing thoughts. Why am I always so hard on myself?

Noticing I'm having a hard time keeping up, Duke stops and waits patiently for me. I pick up the pace and notice his eyes again—a shade that probably doesn't exist on any color wheel.

Standing at the top of the steep slope, he reaches out his hand. I accept it, and he pulls me forward, holding my hand only a few seconds longer than is probably necessary. My sweaty palms are grateful to be freed from his when he finally lets go.

I'm sweating like a pig, but at least my breathing isn't out of control. I guess my lungs are strong from marching around a football field and playing the French horn.

The goosebumps on my arms become firecrackers as we walk together, shoulder to shoulder, in silence. It isn't uncomfortable. Instead, the silence is strangely natural. My silly crush on Aaron pales in comparison to this. I scold myself for automatically feeling there might be some kind of romantic connection with Duke. I only just met him! Seriously, I need to stop turning everything into a soap opera.

"I've got to head back to the bunks to change for the beach. Are you headed straight to the beach, or…" Duke hesitates, running a hand through his thick hair and fumbling for words.

"Amber and I put our bathing suits on before lunch, so I'm heading to the beach now. She'll probably be there any minute. She wants to show me how to kayak today."

"Cool. Okay," he says, looking ahead. "I'll see you at the beach in a bit."

"Cool," I say as we step out of the shade and into the blaring sun. Duke heads toward the bunks, and I shake my head to bring myself back down to earth.

The beach, only a few steps away to my right, is definitely calling my name. I'm dripping with sweat and can't wait to step into the icy lake water. My Chucks delay that pleasure by a full three and a half minutes. Blast these darn high tops.

After setting my socks and sneakers next to a small rock, I see Amber and Pete sitting in the shaded grass by tetherball. Such a strange game. She explained it to me, but I didn't understand the objective or the appeal.

The usual intrusive thoughts that constantly swirl around in my mind grow louder. I rub my temples, trying to silence them as I tiptoe across the hot, coarse sand toward the foamy water's edge. A small ripple forces the water over my feet. It makes my breath catch, but I focus on relaxing as I walk a few feet deeper in.

Each step gets easier as I slowly ease myself into the water, rising to my calves, then my knees, and finally, my stomach. I stop and look around to see if anyone has arrived for canoeing and kayaking, but there are only a few stray campers wandering between the woods and the mess hall. We aren't supposed to swim without a buddy, but Pete and Amber are still sitting nearby in the grass. I'm not technically alone, but I stay in the shallow water anyway.

I've been holding my arms above the water this whole time, but now that my body has acclimated to the icy temperature, I'm feeling brave and let them drop. Beneath the surface, I push the water back and forth, trying—and failing—to push the hopelessness away with it.

# Chapter 21

AMBER

As Mari and I dock our kayaks, Jessica and Chelsea confirm that a boombox and CDs are in the office. "Meet us in five minutes," Jessica says. "You too, Mari. Hanson only had three members, but we can figure out something for you to do."

"Good thing I put my kayak paddle away already," Mari whispers.

"Stop it!" I laugh as we follow them. Remaining a good distance behind them, I catch her up on the Hanson act that Jessica was dreaming up at lunch.

"Sounds like you walked right into it," Mari says, laughing.

"I was being completely sarcastic. Believe me, I wish I hadn't said anything. Getting up in front of the whole camp to play air drums is not my idea of a good time," I say as we enter the camp office.

Joanna is in the back, searching through a closet. "I'm sure the boombox is hiding in here somewhere," she says, setting a few boxes on a table. Finally, she finds a shoe box labeled CDs. "Here we go!"

Jessica eagerly takes it from her, hoping to find her golden ticket to fame. After a minute of searching, she says impatiently, "I haven't seen Hanson yet. Are you sure this is the only box?"

"I'm sure," Joanna says, apologizing for the lack of variety, "but there are some good alternatives there. Keep looking!" She finally finds the boombox and begins to return boxes to their spots in the closet.

Mari stops her. "Can we look through that one?" she asks.

The box is labeled "vinyl," and if it weren't for Victrolas being all the rage right now, I would have to add, "What is vinyl?" to my growing list of questions to ask Google.

"Why would we look through a dusty old box of vinyl?" Jessica asks, annoyed. "If we find something in that box, it's going to be some oldies band our grandparents used to listen to," she adds, rolling her eyes.

"Maybe there's something that will inspire us," I say, coming to Mari's defense.

Still feeling deflated after not finding a single CD with Hanson on it, Jessica doesn't have the energy to argue. "Whatever," she says as she moves closer to look over Mari's shoulder.

Mari starts to flip through each vinyl, scanning the album titles. Her face remains neutral and gives us no hint as to whether or not there is anything worth getting excited about. After at least the ninth or tenth vinyl, she finally shows a sign of interest. "Here's a good one!" she says, her eyes lighting up. We all look closer when she flips it over to read the back. In the center, there's a man on a surfboard and a giant wave. At the crest of the wave is the artist and title:

THE NO.1 SURFING GROUP IN THE COUNTRY

THE BEACH BOYS—SURFIN' USA

"Nice find!" Jessica says, surprising all of us since it's a far cry from Hanson. "Everyone knows *Surfin' USA*. And The Beach Boys is made up of four guys, right? There are four of us! It's perfect."

"But we don't have a record player, just the boombox," I remind her.

Our shoulders sink a little. The plan is to lip-sync, not actually *sing*, so Mari sets the album on the table and continues the search.

"Are we sure none of the CDs were The Beach Boys?" Jessica asks as she goes back to double-check them.

I look back at Mari and see her quietly pulling out another album. It's at least half the size of The Beach Boys album. "What's that one?" I ask.

"It's a 45 RPM; The Beatles." She answers without taking her eyes off it.

"A what?"

"It's basically just a smaller vinyl. It can only hold a few songs," she says. I wonder how she knows that, but I'm relieved I don't have to remember another question to ask Google.

"I know a lot of music by The Beatles," Jessica says. "What songs are on that one?"

"*Paperback Writer* and *Rain*," Mari reads from the sticker on the record she's taken from the sleeve.

"Oh. I don't know either of those. I know *Yesterday*, *Let It Be*, and *Here Comes the Sun*. I know a lot more, actually, but I'd have to hear them to remember," she says, in her usual *there-is-nothing-I-don't-know* tone.

"Any luck with The Beach Boys over there?" I ask Jessica to change the subject.

"No, still nothing. But there's one by The Cranberries that we missed earlier." I'm relieved to know who they are, thanks to *Y94-FM*. Jessica is probably keeping score on how many times I've said, *"Huh? What's that? Who?"*

"Their song, *Dreams*, is my favorite," Chelsea says. I make a mental note to count the words she just said; it might be the most I've heard her speak all week.

"Let's listen," Jessica says kindly. She pops open the top of the boombox—its size striking me as completely ridiculous. It reminds me of *The Fresh Prince of Bel-Air*.

Mom and I recently watched the show's reruns after she noticed it was streaming on Netflix: "We have to watch it!" she said before singing the *entire* theme song like she was Snoop Dogg, breakdancing around the room. She cracks me up.

When the music ends, Jessica asks, "Well? What should we do?" She's *freaking out*.

"We'll figure something out." I console her as best I can. She's taking this whole thing *very* seriously.

Jessica shrugs and says, "I guess. I need a break." She stands and leaves the camp office, Chelsea right on her heels. I start to follow but notice Mari is still looking at the box of vinyl and pulling out another one. Turning it over in her hand, she appears lost in thought.

"Finding more treasures?" I ask, returning from the door to look over her shoulder.

"There's a lot of great stuff in here, actually," she says, handing me an album with the title *John Williams Conducts the Tokyo Symphony: The Star Wars Trilogy.*

"I've heard of John Williams. He wrote the music for *Jurassic Park*, right?" I can't remember why I know that little piece of trivia. Mom probably told me once upon a time.

"That's right. He's a genius *and* my favorite. My sister got me a CD of his movie scores for Christmas last year. I listen to it pretty much every day," she says. For the first time, I think I hear a bit of enthusiasm in her voice.

"Do you play?" I ask as I set the John Williams vinyl on the table.

"An instrument? A little. Not much."

It's clearly something she doesn't want to talk about. I understand because I don't usually like to talk about my painting. But I'm still curious. "Which instrument?"

She hesitates. "French horn in concert band, mellophone for the marching band, and…" she trails off, busying herself with the vinyl again.

"And…?"

"That's it." She turns away and continues organizing the vinyl, even though they are already neatly filed. She stops and points at our paintings by the window from this morning. "Maybe you could show off your canvas painting at the talent show."

I laugh. "Maybe." *Maybe not.*

# MARI

Later, the smell of smoke fills the air, signifying Community Campfire is about to commence. Since I didn't remove my Chucks after dinner, I'm ready to go right away.

After tossing me a bottle of *OFF!*, Amber throws her hands up and says, "Hallelujah!" when she sees I still have my Chucks on.

"Are you going to say that every time?"

"Probably," she teases.

A minute later, we exit the woods. The campfire's flames illuminate the entire camp, and we see a couple of stragglers still making their way to the giant logs surrounding the fire pit. After a few general announcements about tomorrow's activities, including another pitch for the talent show, Sara and Joanna ask Duke and Pete to come forward with the Starburst Staff. Everyone makes some kind of noise—applause, whooping, oohs, aahs—and whispers about who will be chosen next to be the keeper of the Starburst Staff.

"We would like to take a moment to recognize Duke and Pete, once more, who have been the keepers of the Starburst Staff for the last two days," Joanna says as campers applaud and hoot again.

As everyone settles down, Sara says, "Thank you for your wonderful example of camp spirit. Now, we do not *take away* the Staff, but rather, we *give* it to another who demonstrates the spirit of camp and invite them to *join* Pete and Duke as Starburst Staff recipients and honorees."

Everyone is quiet. The only sound is the crackling fire and an owl's who-who in the distance. I look around at the faces of all the kids, their expressions intensified by the glow of the fire. They're eager to find out who's about to be recognized, but I've learned over the years that it's better not to get your hopes up. Expect the worst; if things go right, it's a pleasant surprise. Otherwise, you risk getting crushed by the debris of everything falling apart.

Sara's voice cuts through my pessimistic thoughts and the suspenseful silence with excitement. "This evening, we welcome Chelsea to our circle of Starburst Staff recipients!" Sara leads everyone in applause as Chelsea, completely shocked, looks first at Jessica and then back to Sara. It takes an encouraging shove from Jessica to get her to stand to join Duke and Pete in front of the fire.

"Chelsea is being recognized for being a team player and having the courage to step out of her comfort zone to try new things," Joanna says as Pete places the Starburst Staff in front of her. She reaches for it reluctantly, but as everyone begins clapping and cheering again, she stands taller, firmly taking hold of the Staff with a smile.

"I didn't see that one coming," Jessica whispers to us from the vacant spot Chelsea abandoned to accept the Starburst Staff.

"I think it's great," Amber says, applauding with the rest of the campers.

"I just hope it's not a pity award," Jessica says, concerned.

I shoot Amber a look, but Chelsea returns to her seat before I can speak my mind.

Community Campfire proceeds as usual with camp songs and marshmallows before we're dismissed for the night. After leaving Jessica and Chelsea at their bunk, I can't hold it in anymore. "Why is Jessica so rude? I can't believe what she said about Chelsea and the Starburst Staff possibly being a pity award."

"She's a lot to handle, I know," Amber says. "But I don't think she meant to sound cruel when she said that."

"Look, I'm not perfect in any way, but at least I know that not everything that comes into my mind needs to be said out loud. She has no filter. Maybe her parents neglected to make her watch Bambi," I say, still frustrated.

"The Disney movie? You mean what Thumper says about if you can't say something nice?"

"Yes, I mean Thumper. It's the most basic thing you learn as a kid, isn't it?"

"True. I definitely remember learning that early on. I've never understood people who seem to go out of their way to say or do something that they know might hurt someone," Amber says, kicking a small branch on the ground. "I go out of my way to make sure people *don't* get hurt. Sometimes, I think I care more about everyone else's feelings than my own. I keep a lot of stuff from my mom—stuff about school and friends, I mean—because if she knew how hard things have been for me, I know it would upset her. I hate seeing her worry—especially about me."

"I understand that," I say, thinking about not having the courage to open up to Rachel or my parents about what I'm going through.

"Maybe that's kind of how Jessica feels about Chelsea. Worrying about her getting hurt, I mean," Amber says. "I think what she said just sort of came out wrong. I know a lot of times what I say out loud doesn't always sound the way it did in my head."

"Ditto," I say. Amber shoots me a look. "Sorry—*same.*" We both laugh. "You really think Jessica means well?"

"Can't say for sure, but maybe. I know she seems kind of stuck-up, but I think she *tries* to be nice and encouraging."

I stop and try, just for a minute, to see Jessica in a more positive light. Maybe Amber's not completely wrong. I think about Jessica's cheering on the beach and wonder if she really did mean well. "You're a good egg, Amber."

"Uh, thanks?" she laughs oddly. "I think you're pretty great too, Mari," she says convincingly, even after I was so judgmental about Jessica.

For the first time in a long time, I don't feel the sting of rejection or hate myself for saying something I probably shouldn't have. Amber seems to get me and… I just hope I don't screw things up.

"So, where did you disappear to this time?" Amber asks with mock accusation.

"Disappear?"

"After lunch earlier. When you left me in the lurch during Jessica's monologue about believing in yourself and throwing yourself into the spotlight."

"Oh. She didn't let up, huh?"

Amber laughs. "No. But I survived. So?"

"Nowhere special. Just archery," I say nonchalantly.

"I thought I saw you coming from that way—with *Duke,*" she says, sounding like Rachel, but I know she's teasing playfully, and I don't mind.

"Yes, with Duke," I respond, mimicking her teasing tone. After a brief pause, I ask, "Did you know he's really good at archery?"

"It wasn't something Jessica mentioned when she was swooning."

"Swooning, huh?"

"Oh yeah, she *definitely* has a thing for him," Amber says.

"He's nice. He showed me how to use the bow and arrow, and I actually *hit* the target once," I say, rolling my eyes.

"Archery is hard. I've never understood how to get that stupid arrow to go where you want it to go. You can't just *tell* it. Even asking nicely doesn't make that arrow listen," she says.

Duke's words drift through my mind: *It's not so hard when you know what you're aiming for.*

As we reach our bunk, we shed our smoke-saturated sweatshirts and hang them from a tree branch. I tilt my head back, gazing at the sky through the rustling leaves. The Starburst Staff flashes through my mind—the vibrant pinks, the soft greens, the careful stitching. Did the founder's wife know how beautiful it would become when she first gathered those scraps of fabric? Or did she just start with an idea, trusting it would come together piece by piece?

Then something clicks. The first step isn't hitting the target; it's knowing what you're aiming for—even if it's just a rough idea. It's about steadying yourself, building your confidence, and accepting that you might fail. But trusting yourself to adjust, to learn from every misstep, and to keep moving forward—that's when things fall into place. That's when the arrow sticks.

Amber's right. I won't figure everything out overnight. But the same way the Starburst Staff began as scattered pieces of fabric and became something whole, something meaningful, I can piece things together too. And for the first time, I might know where to start.

Chapter 23

AMBER

Mari is reading her book long past quiet hours. The light from her flashlight casts shadows of little flies and mosquitoes on the ceiling of our bunk. I lay there thinking about Jessica, wondering if I really believe what I said about her looking out for Chelsea and protecting her. I thought Jessica was like Miranda, but I realize that's not true. Miranda hadn't protected me. Instead, she threw me to the wolves.

Mari switches off her flashlight, and I listen as she moves around to find the sweet spot in the pool float to get comfortable. They've held up surprisingly well, and I'm glad Mom gave me two. Still, I can't settle in and fall asleep. Mom swears that if you start listing unrelated things—the more random, the better—you'll drift off to sleep within minutes. Sometimes, it works, but it's not foolproof. Usually, I end up imagining a slice of pizza teaching a yoga class for garden gnomes.

Maybe listening to music will help. I reach over the side of my cot and pull my duffle bag out from underneath. I rummage around in search of the bulky discman—*seriously, how can I be having trouble finding this massive thing?* I find an envelope instead.

Reaching for the dial on the lantern, I turn it the tiniest bit, just enough to see what this mysterious envelope could be. My name, Amber Luna, is written on the front in Mom's cursive. I pull a piece of folded paper from the envelope and read the words:

The moon can't shine on its own. It reflects the light of the sun. When things are at their darkest, it's the moon's borrowed light that helps us find our way. I've had some dark times in my life, and during those times, I was lucky to have people whose light helped me keep going. I borrowed their light, like the moon borrows from the sun, and found my way. Amber has taught me so much. She has helped me through so many hard times without even knowing it.

Her words wrap around me and settle comfortably into my heart as I fold the paper and put it back inside the envelope. The discman practically bites me when I reach into my bag to put the envelope back. Burrowing myself into my sleeping bag, I zip it closed, put on the flimsy headphones, and push play.

Maybe it's okay to let the light we borrow from someone else help us grow into our own. Maybe I was borrowing Miranda's light for a time, but along the way, I forgot that I had my own. My light, however dim, might be someone else's light, too. *Maybe?*

I settle back into my pillow as the music from Mom's discman reminds me of a show we saw at Hollywood Studios a few years ago. That makes me think about roller coasters and Mickey Mouse. *Not helping.* I guess there's no harm in giving Mom's advice another shot... *pencil, ponytail, socks, mushroom, glass, puppy...*

"Jessica is going to throw a fit if we're late to rehearsal," Mari warns as I scramble out of my cot, throw on my tie-dye Crayola Experience T-shirt and a pair of orange shorts before slipping on my sneakers.

"I know, but she'll live," I say, grabbing my toothbrush and paste. "I just need three minutes." Mari gives an exasperated pout—*and did she just stomp her foot at me?* "That's less time than it takes you to get your Chucks on!"

"Touché," she says with a grin. "I'll wait." Mari easily agrees since she isn't exactly looking forward to our talent show rehearsal.

After hastily brushing my teeth, Mari and I speed-walk to the mess hall for breakfast. We're twenty minutes late, but there's still plenty of hot scrambled eggs and bacon left. Thinking about performing in the talent show later makes me feel a bit queasy, so I choose a box of Cinnamon Toast Crunch and grab a half-pint carton of 1% milk.

Jessica and Chelsea are sitting at our usual table with the Starburst Staff leaning against the wall just a few feet away.

"Where have you guys been?" Jessica asks frantically as Mari and I set our food trays on the table. "We only have three hours before lunch to figure out what we're *actually* doing tonight, and then we still have to rehearse!"

Mari gives me a look that says, *I told you so.* I acknowledge her look with a shrug and respond to Jessica, "Sorry. Overslept a little."

"A *little*? Breakfast is nearly over. You've got less than ten minutes to suck down that cereal before it's time to clean up." Jessica is really freaking out about this talent show business.

"Sorry. We'll eat fast," I say, slowly pouring the milk onto my cereal. There's plenty of time. Worst case, nothing comes together, and Jessica will just have to go solo. I'm sure she can think of something to entertain everyone for two minutes.

Jessica rolls her eyes and stands to clear her tray. Mari waits for her to be out of earshot before asking, "Do we have to stick with the boy band idea?"

"Other than the fact that Jessica has her heart set on it, I don't see why not," I say. "You have an idea to pitch?"

"I was thinking maybe a skit."

"What about a skit?" Jessica asks, returning to the table so quickly that she makes me jump.

Unfazed, Mari says, "For the talent show. It could be fun to do a skit. When I was in kindergarten, I used to make up skits with my friend, and we'd perform for his parents after they got home from work."

"That's a good idea. What could we do?" I ask before Jessica has a chance to shoot down the idea.

"I don't know," Mari says, scooping the last of her scrambled eggs onto her plastic fork. "Something funny."

"Gonna need something more specific than that," Jessica says, glancing at the clock, a worried expression returning to her face.

"What about a game show skit?" Chelsea asks.

"A game show! Good one," Mari says quickly.

"How about The Price Is Right?" Chelsea continues to surprise us by chiming in. "The items to bid on can be camp supplies, and Jessica, you can be Bob Barker!"

Bob Barker? I thought the host of The Price Is Right was Drew Carey. My questions to "Ask Google" were beginning to get out of hand, so I started writing them down. So far, the list is:

Punky Brewster?

Elton John song about candles?

Collective Soul/Shine?

Hanson/MMMBop?

When I get back to the bunks later, I'll add:

When did Bob Barker stop hosting The Price Is Right?

Before I can correct Chelsea about the host of The Price Is Right, Jessica lights up at the thought of being the host, the star of the show, and shouts, "Yes! Let's do it!"

I know that means it's time for me to drink up the last of my cinnamon milk and prepare myself to deal with Jessica taking charge for the next three hours.

"Where should we go to come up with the act?" Chelsea asks, her word count well over thirty. I may have to stop counting. *Hallelujah!*

"Between the camp office and the first aid station, there's a nice shady spot that's private," Jessica says, "and I'll ask Joanna about borrowing some items from the first aid station for our prize props."

"I'll go with you," Chelsea says.

Jessica then gives us orders like a Marine: "Amber. Mari. You go check with Ms. Wolcott to see if she's got anything in the kitchen we could borrow."

I put my hand to my forehead and give her a friendly salute. Mari and I turn and head to the kitchen. "Are you ready for this?" I ask.

"Not at all," Mari laughs, "but we'll survive."

"Let's go before *Drill Sergeant Jessica* makes us do push-ups for being late again,"

"Sir, yes, sir!" We laugh, somehow both of us knowing that together, we've got this.

Chapter 24

MARI

Even with Amber by my side, I have zero confidence that I'm going to make it through a whole afternoon with Jessica. She is definitely a natural at taking charge, and right out of the gate, she quickly assumes the role of Commander in Chief.

"Chelsea, you stand here," Jessica says, grabbing her by the shoulders and physically putting her in place. Then, grabbing each of us in the same way, she says, "Amber and Mari, you'll stand on either side of her." She could do this with verbal instruction, but we all agree with a solemn look that it would be best to let Jessica do her thing and be as compliant as possible. "Joanna said there is a small folding table in the custodial closet we can use for all the prizes—and nice work on this mess kit, guys!" Jessica congratulates us as she organizes the items in a neat row on the grass. She has a box of gauze pads, a tube of something called bacitracin, a tube of SPF-50, and a can of *OFF!* bug spray. "Joanna also agreed to be the announcer at the beginning of our skit. You guys remember how the show starts, right?" Unsure if we are supposed to answer her question, we stand at attention, not daring to move a muscle without her instructing us to do so.

Without waiting for our responses, Jessica continues with her directions. "Joanna will say, *'Welcome to the most exciting hour of prizes! The fabulous sixty-minute The Price Is Right! Amber, come on down! Chelsea, come on down! Mari, come on down! You are the first three contestants on The Price Is Right!'* When she calls your names, you'll make your way to these spots."

"I have a question," Amber bravely interrupts.

Jessica, somewhat annoyed, quickly responds, "Yes, fine. What is it, Amber?"

"Where are we when Joanna calls our names?"

"You're just going to be sitting in the audience with the rest of the campers. Remember, just like on the show, you're part of the audience." Jessica says impatiently. "Now, once you're all in your place, Joanna will say, *'And now, here is the star of The Price Is Right… Jessica!'* And everyone will cheer as I make my entrance." Jessica waves at the invisible crowd and then at us, standing there like dopes. "You guys, you have to clap too! You've watched the show, right? The contestants are supposed to be really excited about being chosen as contestants, *and* they love Bob Barker, so they're even *more* excited to see him—well, in this case, *me!*"

It takes a lot of energy not to roll my eyes, but I use what little I have to join Amber and Chelsea in a round of enthusiastic applause. Chelsea even gives a *'whoop-whoop'* like Josh and Eric. We look at each other, all of us thinking, *who is this girl, and what has she done with Chelsea?*

"Good! Good! That's really good, you guys. You're all very good at cheering!" Jessica says like a kindergarten teacher praising our coloring skills. "Once I've made my entrance and everyone has finished their *enthusiastic* applause, I will welcome everyone to the show."

We don't have many lines to memorize since Jessica is mostly portraying Bob Barker as the game show's host. We essentially just have to follow her lead and answer her questions. She's quite entertaining, and the three-hour rehearsal passes quickly.

Finally, the mealtime bell rings, and Jessica says, "Guys, that was great. After lunch, we'll check out the custodial closet for a table and make sure we can get it set up quickly when it's our turn to perform." In her best director voice, she shouts, "That's a wrap!"

Amber and Jessica collect the "prizes" from the ground, leaving me with Chelsea, who picks up the Starburst Staff leaning against the side of the first aid station.

"I'm starving," I say.

"Ditto," Chelsea says.

"It's really cool that you were picked for the Starburst Staff."

"I guess," she says, looking up at the Starburst. "I'm not sure why they think I deserve it. Everyone at camp is trying new things and being," she air quotes, "a team player."

"Maybe. But being a team player and trying new things is easy for a lot of people. I think they recognized you because they know it's not as easy for you, but you're doing it anyway." I'm not sure if it comes out right, but she smiles.

"Maybe you're right. I've always been shy, and making friends doesn't come easily to me. It's probably why my parents signed me up for camp: to get me to come out of my shell."

I wonder for a minute why *my* parents signed me up before Chelsea continues. "Thank God Jessica was my bunkmate last year and took me under her wing. I know she comes across as a know-it-all, but she means well. She's pretty hard on herself. She understands it's not easy to try something new, knowing you might fail. I was terrified of joining everyone in the activities last year because, I don't know, I had never had a friend who encouraged or believed in me, so I didn't believe in myself."

Listening to Chelsea describe Jessica makes me think maybe Amber was right. Maybe Jessica's *I hope it's not a pity award* comment was actually genuine concern.

"I would have spent my days reading in the bunk," Chelsea laughs, "if it weren't for her."

"That's cool. I guess I could say the same about Amber. If it weren't for her, I would probably be in my bunk reading all day too," I admit, thinking the truth is that I'd be hiding away at the freshwater pond.

"You like to read!" Chelsea says. "Have you read Philip Pullman's *The Golden Compass*?"

"Of course! It's one of my favorites! Did you bring anything to camp to read?"

"I did. I'm reading *Ella Enchanted* by Gail Carson Levine. Nothing heavy since I can hardly keep my eyes open by the end of the night."

"I love that one. It's a fun read."

"What about you? What did you bring?" Chelsea asks with sincere curiosity.

I hesitate to admit I brought a Jane Austen classic. Most girls our age aren't interested in the classical genre, but I absolutely love it. "Actually, I brought *Emma.* By Jane Austen. I'm sure you know it."

"Of course, I know it. That's some heavy reading, though. I sometimes have a hard time with the old English language. I did start *Northanger Abbey* but gave up after the first three chapters," Chelsea admits with a laugh.

"Believe me, I get it. It definitely takes some getting used to. I once had a teacher—an *English* teacher, of all things— basically mock me for reading a Jane Austen book."

"An *English* teacher? What did they say to you?"

"She asked why I had *that* book on my desk and questioned if I understood it as if she didn't believe I could."

"What did you tell her?"

"I didn't know what to say other than, 'It's a good book.'"

"Maybe she felt threatened by you and how smart you are."

"I seriously doubt she thought I was *smart*. That's probably why she wasn't impressed. I shoved the book into my backpack and made sure not to pull it out in English class ever again."

"That's sad. You shouldn't have to hide something like that."

"I know. But sometimes it's just better to go along with what's expected of you and not make waves."

Chelsea looks at me as if she's about to disagree, but we're interrupted by Josh and Eric greeting us at the door to the mess hall.

"What's up, ladies?" Josh asks, his hand suspended above his head, offering a high five.

Eric asks, "You gals doing anything for the talent show tonight?"

Chelsea, holding the Starburst Staff firmly in her hand, is the one to respond. "We sure are. It's going to be the best act in the show."

Both of them gawk at her, their mouths hanging open like apes. This new Chelsea is going to take all of us some getting used to.

"Chelsea is right. We've got a solid act planned. You'll see," I say as we confidently move past them to take our place in the food line. I look back at them over my shoulder as Josh points at Chelsea and mouths, "Did she just speak?" I stifle a laugh and shrug with a smile.

I admit I didn't understand why everyone made such a big deal about the Starburst Staff at first, but it seems to be having a magical effect on Chelsea. Maybe the power of the Starburst Staff isn't really about the award itself. It could be the validation and acknowledgment it represents, coming from the people around you. Being recognized for the good things you're doing and the effort you're putting into being the best possible version of yourself certainly is a powerful thing.

I like this new Chelsea. She's smart and interesting, and I'm proud of her for coming out of her shell. Looks like her parents were right about camp helping her do that. I'm still wondering about my parents' motives for sending me to this camp.

Is it possible they see I've got walls up all around me? Maybe they really *do* want me to figure myself out—not just *who* I am but also what *I believe*. Maybe they thought that making friends with kids who aren't from the church would help me figure that out.

I dismiss the thought immediately. There's no way they would send me out into the woods to seek answers to questions they already know the answers to. It would make more sense for them to expect me to see how lucky I am to have all the answers, unlike the other kids. They probably think I'll feel sorry for them and hope I'll *convert* them.

The idea that I'm supposed to feel like I'm better than everyone else just because I'm a member of the church irritates me to no end. I remember finding a book by C.S. Lewis in the library that said when our religion makes us feel superior to others, we are likely under the influence of the Devil, not God.

I doubt either of them is wasting their time on me. It's the monster that haunts my memories and dreams, not the Devil or God, who has a hold on me.

The sunlight breaks through the small opening in the curtains, drawn closed. The light beats down on the monster sitting at the piano in the dark, musty living room.

He nestles closely to the small girl next to him, placing an arm around her shoulder as her tiny fingers pluck at the keys.

The melody of "I am a Child of God," the first hymn every Mormon child learns in primary class, cuts through the sounds of a busy neighborhood outside—children laughing, a basketball hitting the pavement, the ice cream truck's jingle, a mother calling out, "Be home before dark!"

Abruptly, every sound goes silent.

The monster, his breath warm on her ear, whispers, "I warned you not to tell anyone. Now look what you've done."

Chapter 25

AMBER

Jessica is doing a fantastic job channeling her most authentic game show host persona for our silly skit.

Our audience approves with constant laughter and wild applause as she congratulates the winner of today's show. "Let's see what you will be taking home, Chelsea," she says, whipping off the beach towel with theatrical flair as if hosting game shows were her true calling. "A brand new pair of swimming goggles and this expired bottle of SPF-50 sunscreen! Congratulations, Chelsea! Thanks for playing our budget version of *The Price Is Almost Right*! Tune in next time for more random household prizes and sunscreen giveaways. And remember—help control the pet population; seriously, people, get those pets fixed!"

We take our bows as everyone claps, and Jessica, still on cloud nine from the adrenaline of her performance, starts hugging each of us. "Amber, oh my gosh! That was fantastic! Right, Mari? And Chelsea, you were—Chelsea?" She turns, and immediately, her eyes grow wide. "Chelsea!" she says excitedly, then covers her gaping mouth with her hand.

Chelsea, who remains on the talent show stage with the microphone, smiles back at the three of us, standing still as statues, forgetting to take our seats. "Hello. I'm Chelsea, and I'll be singing 'Tomorrow' from Annie the Musical."

"Did you know anything about this?" Jessica asks, looking at me and then at Mari.

"Nope!" I say.

"Not a clue!" Mari adds, then gestures for us to hush and sit.

"This is absolutely the most exciting thing ever!" Jessica squeaks. "I can't believe she's up there on stage to sing—all by herself!" She then sits on the edge of her seat, watching like a mother in the front row of her baby girl's first dance recital.

Mari watches Joanna tinker with the boombox to the right of the stage. It becomes clear there is a problem when Sara starts jabbing at the buttons, too.

After several minutes, Joanna quickly approaches Chelsea and whispers in her ear. Her shoulders drop as she hands the microphone to Joanna. "It appears the boombox isn't cooperating due to faulty batteries and the absence of a power cord. But Chelsea says she can still sing without it."

Joanna hands the microphone back to Chelsea as Mari suddenly stands and moves quickly toward Chelsea. I can't hear what she's saying, but Chelsea lights up and says loud enough for everyone to hear, "Yes, yes! That would be so awesome, thank you!" Then she turns her attention to the audience and says, "Okay, guys. Mari has agreed to play the piano for me! We just need a minute to get 'Ole Faithful from the back."

"Mari plays piano?" Jessica turns to me abruptly. "How did you not know? How did *I* not know?"

"She never said," I respond, somewhat amused. Then I remember the "and" Mari left hanging in the air after telling me she played the French horn. But why was playing the piano something she didn't want to admit?

A minute later, Sara and Mari appear, pushing 'Ole Faithful toward the front of the room. Everyone cheers as they park the piano next to Chelsea, and Mari takes her place on the bench. As she plays a short introduction, Chelsea looks over at her, obviously impressed by her playing and relieved she isn't going to screw her up. She begins to sing, "The sun will come out tomorrow," her voice soft and delicate, like a small child. But as the song progresses, her voice becomes louder, stronger, and more powerful, until she's no longer a child but a mature young woman, singing from her heart and soul. She belts the final words, "You're always a day away!" as Mari punctuates the end with a dramatic final chord.

Everyone claps, and goosebumps prick my arms as I watch Mari sneak away from the piano, likely making sure the spotlight remains on Chelsea.

"Thank you, Chelsea and Mari. That was absolutely stunning!" Joanna says. "Okay, our next act is Charlie! Charlie, come on up!"

Charlie hesitates, but Molly encourages him, saying, "Go on, we practiced all day. You're going to be awesome!"

Finally standing, Charlie makes his way to Joanna to take the microphone. "Hello, is this thing on?" he says, tapping the microphone as everyone giggles.

From the back, Eric and Josh holler their "whoop, whoop!" and add a supportive, "You got this, man!"

This is what encourages Charlie to jump right in. "Did you hear about the circus fire?" he asks Molly, standing a few feet away to his left.

"What about the circus fire?" she replies.

"It was in tents," Charlie answers nervously, unsure anyone will get the joke. But we all do, and the laughter helps him continue more confidently for his next joke.

"Why did the orange lose the race, Molly?"

"I don't know, Charlie. Why did the orange lose the race?"

"It ran out of juice," he says, slapping his knee.

Molly gives him a reassuring thumbs-up and whispers, "Keep going! You're doing great, buddy."

Charlie has everyone rolling for at least another ten minutes, then closes out the act with his best joke. "I went to buy some camouflage pants, but I couldn't find any! Thank you, everybody. Thank you very much," he says in response to everyone's laughter and applause. He takes several bows before turning the microphone over to Joanna.

"We want to thank *everyone* for participating this evening," Joanna says. "All of you are so talented, and we know it takes a lot of courage to get up in front of your peers to perform. So, thank you, and congratulations to everyone tonight!"

Adam, Sam, and Sara appear on stage next to Joanna. Adam takes the microphone and says, "You are all such a great group of people! We hope everyone has been enjoying camp this week, and I know you're all probably just as sad as we are that tomorrow is our last full day at Camp Evergreen."

Everyone agrees, acknowledging their disappointment about camp ending so soon with cries of, "Oh, man, for real?" I look around the room searching for Mari, but she's nowhere to be found.

"I know, I know," Adam responds to everyone's cries. "It's always tough when camp ends, but remember, the spirit of Camp Evergreen—friendship, kindness, helping others, learning something new, and having gratitude in your heart—can remain with you throughout the year. You can demonstrate these values every day at home and at school."

Sam adds, "Adam is right, folks. We hope that you take the experiences you've had here at Camp Evergreen—"

Leaning over Chelsea's shoulder, I quietly whisper, "Hey, did you see where Mari went?"

"Isn't she at the back?" Chelsea says as she turns to look over her shoulder. "Over there in the—oh. I guess not."

Returning my attention to the counselors making their speech, Sara addresses everyone: "Sometimes it's hard to notice all the things in your life that you have to be grateful for. We know that life can be hard, and sometimes you might feel hopeless. But we're here to tell you—there's *always* hope. There's always a way out of any problem you're facing. Your families, parents, friends, teachers, and coaches—all of these people are here for you."

I try to listen but can't shake the feeling that something isn't right. I keep telling myself that Mari is a big girl and is probably just sitting in the back. She's short, like me, and can easily get lost behind tall kids. I'm overreacting.

The sound of Sam plucking the strings of his guitar pulls me out of the panic I'm fighting. Adam's voice, a soothing baritone, begins to sing as I breathe and concentrate on listening.

This little light of mine, I'm gonna let it shine.

Usually, I hear this as an upbeat, cheerful anthem, but he sings it like one of Mom's favorite Celine Dion love ballads.

Then Sara, her voice, a soft soprano strikingly different from Adam's, sings the next line and makes the hair on the back of my neck stand at attention.

This little light of mine, I'm gonna let it shine.

Letting your light shine is risky. It takes a lot of courage to let people in, to see you for who you *really* are. Holding back, containing my light—it's always been a move to protect myself. I've always had to guard my light, even if it is dim.

This little light of mine, I'm gonna let it shine.

Everyone else's light seems so much brighter than mine, but maybe that's because each time I doubted myself, feared I wasn't enough, and compared myself to others, my light dimmed a little more. And what about the vultures—the jerks that make it hard to believe there's any good left in the world? The image of Grandma picking apples from the tree, my painting—vandalized with the mustache and googly eyes— flashes through my mind. They certainly didn't help my light.

Let it shine, let it shine, to show my love.

Maybe believing in myself a little more and putting myself out there *is* a risk, but it's time to stop hiding and see what happens. Maybe the good people will outnumber the vultures circling overhead. Chelsea and Mari found the courage to sing and play piano in front of everyone tonight; maybe I could be brave, too.

…It is an honor and pleasure to inform you that you have been selected to submit your artwork to this year's Congressional Art Competition…

The sound of clapping pulls me back to the moment— except, no one is clapping. Sam's final guitar chord hangs in the air, and I realize it's rain, pounding against the mess hall roof, that has fooled me. It intensifies as the campers *actually* begin to clap and cheer.

In lieu of s'mores, Ms. Wolcott quickly rolls out a cart with ice cream and sundae fixings. She looks concerned that campers will be disappointed about Community Campfire being rained out, but it will take more than a little rain to dampen everyone's spirits after such a fun talent show.

I join Jessica and Chelsea at the toppings station, still feeling uneasy about Mari's disappearance. "I don't see Mari anywhere," I say to Chelsea as Jessica hands her a bottle of chocolate syrup.

"I'm sure she'll show up," Jessica says. "It's been a wild night! Who knew Mari *and* Chelsea were so talented? I *knew* you guys were holding out!"

We finish our ice cream sundaes as the rain finally tapers off enough for people to scamper off to their bunks for the night. "Great job tonight, ladies!" Jessica says as she pulls the strings of her hood tightly around her chin and darts out of the mess hall. "Last one to the bunks is a rotten egg!" she hollers as she takes off running.

Chelsea shrieks as she runs after her, carrying the Starburst Staff in her hand, which doesn't slow her down. Shaking my head, knowing full well I'll be the rotten egg, I step out of the mess hall and walk. The rain is just a light sprinkle, almost a mist. *Hallelujah!*

Looking up at the sky, I let the rain wash over my face, its coldness refreshing after the warmth of the mess hall. By the time I reach our bunk, I'm damp enough to catch a little chill, but my bunk, dark and empty, is what gives me the shivers. I'm expecting to find Mari with her flashlight and a book curled up in her sleeping bag, but there's no sign of her anywhere.

I don't walk, I *run* to Jessica and Chelsea's bunk to ask them for help to find Mari. "I haven't seen her since she played piano for you, Chelsea, and she's not in our bunk," I cry breathlessly.

"Calm down, Amber. Did you check the outhouse? Maybe she's just brushing her teeth or something," Chelsea suggests.

"You're right. I hadn't thought to look there," I say, calming down only a smidge.

"Chelsea and I will go check the outhouse," Jessica says calmly. "Why don't you go back to the mess hall and see if she turns up there?"

"That's a good idea," I say, slightly reassured.

"Ms. Wolcott is probably still there cleaning up," Chelsea says. "Maybe Joanna and Sara are there, too, and can help us look for her."

I give a solemn nod and make my way down the path to head out of the woods. Then it hits me. Of course! She's probably at the hidden freshwater pond. That's exactly where she'd go if she wanted to hide.

My heart begins to beat faster as I pick up my pace to a light jog. Turning left down the path to the pond, I'm sure I'll see her there and feel some relief. It's nearing quiet hours, and the rain clouds cover the moon and stars, leaving the woods in deep darkness. I hope she has a working flashlight because mine keeps flickering and shutting off randomly. The batteries must be getting low because I've had to smack it twice to make it work properly.

"Mari? You here?" I shout as I come to the pond, casting my flashlight around its perimeter. But there's no response and no sign of her.

Panic rises within me again. The image of the marks on her body flash through my mind. I have a feeling she's dealing with something heavier than just a religion crisis. I know Jessica and Chelsea said she'd turn up, but something in my gut tells me she's in trouble.

I leave the pond and make my way to the campgrounds. Without the Community Campfire's blaze to light up the grounds, the darkness fills me with dread. I can barely see the mess hall from across the field, but it's completely dark and abandoned anyway.

The rain starts to come down heavier, but at least there isn't any thunder or lightning. I'm completely drenched within seconds, and I try desperately to think where Mari might go. I can see the camp office in the distance, but it's just as dark as the mess hall. If she *is* there, she's sitting in the dark. The possibility sounds reasonable enough to justify making the trek across the field. But first, I flash my light up and down the beach, then out over the dark water. I call out her name twice and hope against all odds she will magically appear and ask what all the shouting is about.

I notice something slightly off on my second pass of the beach with the flashlight. I slowly scan the rack of canoes and stop when I see a vacant spot between two kayaks.

I hear Mari's voice in my head from the first day of camp, asking, "Are we allowed to go to the island?" I told her no, but then she said, "The more you forbid kids from doing something, the more likely they are to want to find out more."

The island. She's gone to the island.

Fear grips me as I imagine Mari lost in the deep, dark waters of the lake. Running to the row of kayaks, I grab the nearest life preserver and a paddle. Quickly shoving the kayak away from the rack, the adrenaline coursing through my body gives me the strength to heave it into the water. I quickly mount the back deck and slide my feet into the cockpit. I push off with more strength than I knew I had.

I paddle feverishly toward the island. Forbidden or not—if Mari is there, I need to find her. The rain clouds part just enough for a sliver of moonlight to shine on the lake. Straight ahead, I can barely make out the outline of the island and dig the paddle deeper into the water, hoping to gain as much speed as possible.

My arms feel like Jell-O, and I'm completely winded, but I don't stop paddling until I've reached the island. Ramming my kayak into the dirt, I crawl out of the cockpit and call out, "Mari! Are you here?" I shake my flashlight again, begging the Universe to keep it lit as I look around for some kind of trail that Mari might have followed. Several feet from my own kayak, I see Mari's left abandoned in the dirt. At least I know she's here and hasn't drowned in the lake. "Mari!" I call out again as I walk urgently toward her kayak.

Up ahead to the right, there's an opening to the woods where she may have gone. I follow the overgrown path that's a little difficult to navigate, tripping over an exposed tree root within the first few feet. Crashing to the ground, my flashlight flies from my hand, landing further up the trail, and the light goes out. *Dang it.*

I fumble in the darkness on my hands and knees and find the flashlight without too much trouble. *Hallelujah.* After a hefty whack on my wrist, the flashlight cooperates and lights the way. Getting to my feet, I shine the light up the path. It seems to go on for miles. Beyond the flashlight's range, there's nothing but darkness—a black hole like the one we learned about at the planetarium in sixth grade.

My determination to find Mari overrides my fears and moves me forward down the path, looking for places she may have found shelter from the storm. After several minutes of walking with my heart in my throat, I call out to Mari again.

There's a commotion to my left, and I think I hear something that sounds like an animal whining. Campers being mauled by wild animals and the tale of Cannibal George race through my mind. "Mari, please! If you're here, answer me!" I shout.

I don't know how I manage to keep moving, but I do. Determined to find her, I venture further up the path until finally, off to the right, I see a dim light. Mari's flashlight, I hope. "Mari! Are you okay? I'm coming. I'm almost there."

I begin shoving prickly branches aside; some of them snap as I force my way through to get to her. Mari sits with her back against a giant log, hugging her knees. Her head is bowed, resting on her arms, with the flashlight beside her; its beam lighting the bushes surrounding the small clearing.

She sits very still, like a deer that fears a hunter has discovered her. I'm not sure if she heard any of my calls earlier. I don't want to startle her, so I use my flashlight to shine a ray of light in her direction, hoping the light will let her know she's not alone anymore.

Now, standing a few feet from her, I speak quietly. "Mari? You okay?"

Chapter 26

MARI

Sitting on the brown braided rug of his living room, I hear the neighborhood kids playing outside. A dog is barking, and an ambulance siren sounds. I wonder if it's on its way to save me from this monster, but the sirens fade, and no one comes.

As the monster moves closer to me, I hear a fire crackling. Then, I hear my name: "Mari! Are you okay? I'm coming. I'm almost there."

The sunlight shining through the small opening of the curtains moves around the room like a spotlight, looking for its main character on stage. A little girl's voice speaks to me: "Mari, you okay?" she asks, touching my shoulder gently.

"I won't tell anyone. I promise. I'm sorry," I say, burying my face in my hands.

"Mari, it's okay. You don't have anything to be sorry for." A river of warmth runs down my arm as I hear the little girl's breath catch. "Mari, you're bleeding!" she says, wrapping soft fabric tightly around my arm just above my elbow.

The braided rug beneath me morphs into mud. The furniture fades, and the walls and dark curtains of the living room completely dissolve as she squeezes my arm. The sharp point of the arrow I snatched from archery drops from my hand.

"Amber?" I say and wait to hear her voice to make sure she's really here and that I'm *safe*—not in the dark living room as a little girl where the unthinkable happened.

"Yes, Mari. I'm here. It's okay."

She sits quietly next to me, keeping pressure on my arm. She doesn't attack me with questions or give me any sort of lecture about breaking the rules by coming to the island. She's just—here, and it's the only thing I need right now.

After a moment, Amber hums the melody of *You've Got a Friend*— the same tune she has hummed softly in her cot every night this week before going to sleep. I rest my head on her shoulder as fresh tears begin to fall down my face.

"Thank you, Amber," I say when she stops humming.

"Do you want to talk about it?" she asks cautiously.

I know she cares, and it's not that I don't want to talk it's just—I don't have the energy or courage to let her in. It's too painful. There's *so* much—I don't even know where to begin.

"It's okay if you don't want to," she says.

Sitting up straight and wiping at my tears, I turn and see her face, lit up by the moon that has returned and shines through the trees. "You've been a good friend, Amber. I wish I could talk about it, but it's just too much."

"I get that, and I'm sorry you were hurt. I don't know what happened, but I know the pain of being hurt by someone you thought you could trust. It's not your fault. You didn't do anything to deserve what happened to you. There wasn't anything you did that made any of it happen."

"It doesn't matter if I believe that or not. There's still no escaping it."

Amber looks away for a second but then turns back to me. "Is that why you cut yourself? Because you're trying to escape?"

I take a minute to calm my nerves. "I guess that's part of it," I say quietly. "At first, I didn't *know* why I was doing it, but it made me feel like I had control over something." Saying these things out loud for the first time makes my mouth dry and my palms sweat. The two opposite sensations remind me of the constant battle that rages within me—wanting it all to *end* but wishing I could actually *live* my life. If only I could take control of it. "I'm not brave enough—*strong* enough to face it alone."

"It was really brave of you to get up in front of everyone tonight to play for Chelsea. And you may not feel strong enough right now, but you'll get stronger over time. The more you try, the more you'll believe in yourself. Nothing worth having comes easy, remember?"

"Remember who you are," I add, the words feeling a little less hollow than they did before.

"Yes, Mari. Remember who you are—the person you really are, the one who's been buried and forgotten. She's still there. You can still find her."

"But what if she's not? What if she's too broken, and I can't put the pieces back together?"

"There's only one way to find out. You're not alone, Mari. And I think finding yourself is worth any risk."

Still unsure, I look at Amber and see how confident she is that what she's saying is true. "I've never been able to trust anyone, especially myself, but I trust *you*."

She smiles and asks gently, "Are you ready to head back to camp?"

I give a small nod, and Amber gets to her feet. Offering me her hand, I take hold of it. As I stand, we notice we're both covered in mud.

"We look like we were mauled by a wild animal," Amber says mischievously, "but at least there's no sign of Cannibal George."

We push through the thorny bushes to find the trail leading to the shore, where our kayaks await. The rain has stopped, and the clouds have parted just enough for the moon to light our path. The walk back feels shorter this time. Earlier, I had run for what seemed like miles before collapsing in the clearing, exhausted and lost. I guess the way back is easier, especially when you're not alone.

Chapter 27

AMBER

The moonlight reflecting on the lake is like a lighthouse guiding us back to the beach. The sky above us is clear and gives no indication of rain, as if the storm never happened. We paddle together, too exhausted to speak. The comforting sound of the water lapping off our kayaks and the stars reappearing in the night sky help ease the fear and adrenaline that almost made my heart explode earlier.

Reaching the shallow water, Mari and I climb out of our kayaks and push them onto the beach. I'm afraid we're going to be met by camp counselors searching for us, prepared to give us a stern lecture about leaving camp without permission, and especially how dangerous it was for us to paddle to the island where we are strictly forbidden to go. Instead, the camp is dark and quiet as we carefully replace our paddles and kayaks on the rack where they belong.

As I hang my life preserver next to the paddles, a small light catches the corner of my eye. "Jessica? What are you doing here?" I hiss. Now, I'm definitely worried the consequences of breaking the rules are looming.

Jessica steps out of the bushes with Chelsea, each of them with a small flashlight. "Thank God you guys are okay!" she says, wrapping her arms around my neck and then Mari's. Taking a step back, she puts her hands on Mari's shoulders and says urgently, "Pete and Duke! They went after you!"

"They did what?" Mari asks.

"They didn't want you guys to get in trouble," Chelsea says as we make our way back to the beach to look out over the dark water, "so they went looking for you."

Before we can do anything crazy like jump back in a canoe to go searching, Duke and Pete appear at the shore. As their shadows approach and their faces become visible in the moonlight, we let out a collective sigh of relief. But as they reach the sand, we all start hammering them.

"What were you guys thinking?"

"You shouldn't have done that! It wasn't safe!"

"You could have gotten into a lot of trouble!"

"Whoa, whoa!" Duke puts up both of his hands and tells us all to settle down. "Listen, we didn't do anything that the two of *you* didn't do," he says, wagging a playful shame-on-you finger at Mari and then at me. "We docked at the island and found you, but we didn't want to fight through the pricker bushes to get to you," Duke says. "You were having a pretty deep talk, and we didn't want to interrupt."

Pete says, "We got back in the canoe and stayed hidden behind a rock to wait for you to return to your kayaks. We wanted to wait until you shoved off and were far enough ahead so we wouldn't spook you."

"We weren't going to let on that we followed you," Duke says to Jessica and Chelsea. He might as well have said, "Nice going, guys."

"Oops," Chelsea says as Jessica shrugs an apology.

"The important thing is that everyone is safe, right?" Jessica says reassuringly.

The six of us make our way back to the bunks in silence, not wanting to draw any attention to ourselves. It's long past quiet hours, and we are supposed to be in our bunks, not soaked to the bones and wandering the camp.

When the path splits into two, Pete says quietly, "This is where we part ways. Good night, ladies."

"Stay out of trouble, would ya?" Duke says warmly, looking only at Mari.

"Promise we will," Mari says, looking back at him long enough for me to wonder if there's something going on between the two of them. It's kinda sweet.

"Thanks, guys," I say to both of them.

After leaving Jessica and Chelsea at their bunk, Mari and I continue up the trail until bunk sixteen finally comes into view.

Neither of us is sure we can make it, but we manage. We change out of our damp, muddy clothes quickly and crawl into our warm sleeping bags.

"Good night, Mari."

"Good night, Amber."

Despite my exhaustion, I'm unable to sleep again and lie there listening to the sound of raindrops making their way through the branches and leaves, *plop, plop, blip*. Thinking about Mari and whatever awful things she's going through, I remember something Mom said to me once: "Bad things happen to good people. It's unfair, but never experiencing the bad means we can never appreciate the good."

But no one should have to go through something so terrible that it causes them to hurt themselves and feel worthless and alone. I'm comforted knowing that, just like Pete said, I could be there for Mari tonight and listen to her when she needed someone.

Everyone really is going through their own heavy things, but Mom also said, "Everything we go through makes us who we are, and there's always going to be someone who needs you just as you are."

Chapter 28

MARI

Waking this morning, I'm surprised at how refreshed I feel. Memories didn't haunt my dreams last night like they usually do—I don't think I dreamed at all. I remember saying goodnight to Amber, and then, almost instantly, morning light nudged me awake.

Amber is still sleeping, and I can tell from the gray light in the tent that the sun won't rise for at least another thirty minutes. I think about heading to the freshwater pond, but if I leave the bunk, Amber might wake up and panic when she sees my empty cot. I've caused her enough worry already.

Instead, I carefully reach over the edge of the cot and quietly unzip the front pocket of my suitcase. My fingers graze one of my sharps, but instead of giving in, I pull out my journal.

I open it to the last entry I had written before being forced to come to Camp Evergreen. I was so angry when I wrote that entry, and it shows in my handwriting. My usual flowing cursive is replaced with sharp and jagged edges. I was sure it would be the longest week of my life and didn't think I'd survive. That was only four days ago, and in that short amount of time, my perspective has drastically changed.

I turn the page and start a new entry.

Camp Evergreen ended up being a lot of fun. I was dreading it and was pretty miserable from the moment I arrived, but that changed pretty quickly after meeting Amber. She's my bunkmate, and this was her first year at camp, too. She already knew a lot about camp because her mom used to come when she was our age. Thank goodness, too, because her mom knew that the cots were hard as rock and sent two inflatable pool floats for Amber and her bunkmate (me!) to sleep on. Amber's mom is a hero! It's pretty crazy the things I've done this week. First there was canoeing, then rock climbing, painting on canvas, archery, and kayaking. But the hardest thing I did this week wasn't any of those things. No, it was playing piano for Chelsea's singing act at the talent show in front of EVERYONE. It's been forever since I've played. I don't even know what came over me. I guess it was Chelsea that inspired me. She was so quiet and shy when I first met her. I think the first time I heard her speak was on the third day of camp. She won the camp spirit award that night, it's called the Starburst Staff, but anyway, she won that award, and it changed her somehow. The next day, she was more confident and talkative and surprised everyone by getting up the courage to sing at the talent show. Anyway, I don't know if it makes sense, but I just thought—if Chelsea could come out of her shell, maybe I could too.

The crinkling of Amber's pool float makes me stop writing. "Good morning, sunshine," I say.

"Morning," Amber replies through a massive yawn. She pulls her arms out from the sleeping bag and stretches them high above her head. "You sleep okay?"

"Believe it or not, I did. I barely remember getting into my sleeping bag," I say, closing my journal.

"How is it the last day already?" she asks, slowly sitting up to lean her weight on one elbow.

"It's funny. When I first got here, I thought it was going to be the longest week of my life, and now I can't believe it's over."

"Ha!" Amber laughs. "I'm glad you came around," she says, shifting from her elbow to sit up. "My mom said she wasn't thrilled about coming to camp her first year either."

"And just like me, she ended up having a good time, didn't she?"

"Of course she did," she says, freeing her legs from her sleeping bag. "She has a lot of great memories of camp, and it's all she could talk about for the last few weeks."

"Would she have forced you to come to camp?" I ask, then quickly clarify, "If you didn't *want* to go?"

"Mom doesn't *force* me to do anything, really," she says in a way that makes me think she hates to admit it. She quickly looks away. "I know you said you hardly ever get to make decisions for yourself, but with Mom—" she stops to put on her sneakers. I'm envious of how effortlessly they slide onto her feet. "She has always told me that she wants me to decide things for myself because she trusts I'll make the right choice."

"And if you don't?" I ask.

"Well, when it comes to the not-so-serious stuff, she knows I'll figure it out for myself. She says that's part of how we figure out who we are and what's important to us. But the more serious stuff? It's not like she'd let me decide to do anything extreme or dangerous just because I *want to*. I'm not a wild child on the loose without parental supervision!"

"That's good," I say with a sarcastic sigh of relief.

Amber pulls her scrunchy from her messy hair. Stiff with bug spray and knots, her ponytail holds its position at the top of her head. She grabs hold of it and runs her fingers along her scalp before tying it back again. "Mom says that as long as you're not going to hurt anyone, think through the pros and cons, and listen to what your heart is telling you, then there's really no such thing as a wrong choice. Everything is a learning experience, and she says she'll be there to support me and help me figure out the better choice if what I decide doesn't go the way I thought it would."

"I wish my parents had that attitude," I say, rolling my eyes.

Amber nods. "One day, you'll be able to choose, Mari. Maybe you don't feel you can now, but we won't be thirteen forever."

"Hallelujah!"

"Hey, that's my line!" Amber laughs, then stands and stretches again. "I'm starving."

My stomach agrees. I respond, "Same."

We are the first campers to arrive for breakfast at the mess hall. The menu is a hodgepodge of everything we have already eaten this week, and we have our pick of scrambled eggs, sausage, bacon, pancakes, and cold cereal with milk. We can't decide on just one thing, so we take a little of everything until our plates are almost too heavy to carry.

Jessica and Chelsea join us when we're more than halfway finished with our breakfast, and we talk about our plans for our final day at Camp Evergreen. "We've done just about everything, haven't we?" Chelsea asks, dipping a bite of fluffy pancake in a bath of maple syrup.

"Just about," Amber responds, after looking as though she has made a list in her head and checked off each box.

"There is one thing that someone *started*," Jessica says, looking at me, "but never *finished*."

My stomach flips.

"That's right!" Chelsea says. "Mari, you never made it to the top of the rock-climbing wall! You didn't get to see the view from the top!"

"I don't know, guys. I really don't think I can do it," I protest.

"We'll go up with you!" Jessica says.

"Yeah, we can do it together," adds Chelsea.

After several minutes of persuasive pleas from Jessica and Chelsea, I look to Amber to help me out of this one. She smiles back and reminds me, "Nothing worth having comes easy."

So, here I am, halfway up the monstrous rock-climbing wall, Amber on my right and Chelsea on my left. Adam, Pete, and Duke are manning the belays directly below us, and Jessica, our fearless cheerleader, shouts encouraging mantras: "You can do it! You're almost there!"

The end is closer than the beginning. Maybe a dozen holds stand between me and the view from the top of the wall. My palms are sweating, and my legs are shaking. I admit to Amber, "I don't think I can do it."

"Mari, you've already come twice as far as you did your first time. Don't look!" she shouts as I begin to turn my head to look down. She laughs as I jerk my head back. "Keep your eyes forward and focus on the top."

I take a deep breath, carefully release my sweaty palm from one hold, and reach for the next. I slip, only a little, but don't lose my footing. I repeat the steps slowly, slipping only once or twice more. With each move, I find a rhythm and feel myself getting stronger. Once or twice, I hesitate and think, *I can't do this*, but Amber and Chelsea cheer me on.

"You've got this," Chelsea says. We're right here."

I keep my eyes forward like Amber keeps telling me, and I secure the next hold. The anchor at the top of the wall, glistening in the sunlight, is within my reach. I can make it. I can do this. One more hold, and I'll be there.

Amber and Chelsea patiently wait for me to make my next move. They're just below me and want *me* to get to the top first. A surge of adrenaline gives me enough nerve to let go and reach for the last hold, where I finally clamp my harness onto the anchor at the top of the wall.

"Mari, open your eyes and look!" Chelsea says.

The hard part is over. I'm at the top but still afraid to open my eyes. I can hear my heartbeat and the familiar voice from my nightmares echoing in my mind: "You think you're special just because you made it to the top? Everyone else did long before you. You're the one who couldn't do it, remember?"

I close my eyes tighter and take another deep breath. Silently, I tell the voice in my head—*that was before. It's behind me. I aimed for the top, and I made it. I did it.*

The voice laughs at me; "It means nothing. You can't even open your eyes."

I will open my eyes when I'm ready.

"You'll never do it. You don't have what it takes."

Amber's voice interrupts: "The view is iconic, Mari! Totally worth it."

Then Chelsea suggests, "How about on the count of three?"

I nod once and suck in a quick breath. "On three," I agree.

"One."

You just need to know what you're aiming for and have confidence.

"Two."

Remember who you are.

"Three."

Nothing worth having comes easy.

Releasing the breath I had been holding and opening my eyes, I'm not disappointed by the view. It's incredible. I can see everything, just like they said. I don't look down but keep my eyes focused on the panorama of the camp stretching before me like a comforting patchwork quilt. I can't make out the ugly weeds protruding from the sand at the beach. The mess hall doesn't look ready to collapse like it does from the ground. The scent of pine and remnants of this week's Community Campfires drift through the air, tickling my nose. The taste of a toasty, sweet marshmallow smacks my tongue, and distant laughter from campers echoes happily in my ears. This time, the laughter doesn't sting or remind me of my isolation. Instead, it feels lighter, as if this climb proves I belong, too.

Everything looks, feels, and sounds so different from this new perspective up here with my friends. I couldn't have done it without them believing in me. They helped me believe in *myself.*

I *am* stronger and braver than I thought. I know there are more walls for me to climb, but for the first time, I *know* I can do it. Something tells me, without a doubt, it will be worth it.

Chapter 29

AMBER

It's really exciting being here with Mari as she reaches the top of the wall. I know she was scared, and for a minute, I thought she'd need Adam to rescue her again before she got up the courage to keep going.

Now that she's finally opened her eyes, it's as if she's seeing camp—the world—for the first time. *Everything looks different after you do something you didn't think you could.*

We quickly descend from the top and unfasten our harnesses on the ground. Jessica, skipping and hopping her way to us, says, "That was so exciting!" She gives Mari a brief hug.

"It was definitely worth it!" Mari says. "Hand me your harness, Amber. I'll put it away."

"I'm really proud of those two," Jessica says after Mari and Chelsea leave to return their equipment. "I know they both struggled at the beginning. Last year, I still hadn't successfully convinced Chelsea to let loose and be herself before camp ended."

"Chelsea is lucky to have you," I say, standing and tightening my ponytail that had come loose during my climb.

Jessica smiles and replies, "Believe me, it's the other way around. *I'm* the one that's lucky to have *her*." She looks around to make sure no one is close enough to hear before saying, "My parents got divorced last year, just a few months before camp. I was pretty angry about the whole thing. They put so much pressure on me and my brother to be perfect, and we both did everything right. I couldn't understand why it wasn't enough, even after working so hard to live up to their standards." She stops briefly, fighting the emotion that has snuck up on her. "Chelsea was the one who helped me understand that my parents' divorce wasn't because of anything I did wrong or because I wasn't good enough. She helped me lighten up and not worry so much about being perfect at everything."

I think back to the first day of camp when Jessica scoffed at Mari's purple hair and depressed attitude. I immediately wrote her off as another Miranda, with her snarky tone—*some girls got it, some just don't*—but I can't think of a time this week she ever tried to tear any of us down just to build herself up.

Jessica clears her throat and says, "I'm sorry if I came off a little strong when we first met." A vision of her standing at a podium in front of an American flag, waving to adoring fans on the campaign trail, *almost* makes me laugh. "I know I probably try too hard. It's just…" She looks up to the top of the rock-climbing wall, then down to her hands, clenched in tight fists. "I'm always scared people are going to judge me right away. If I don't distract them, they'll notice everything that's wrong with me."

I nod, thinking about how easy it is to judge someone based on the surface. "You don't have to be perfect, Jessica. Nobody is."

"I know I go on and on about everyone being good at *something* and encouraging them to put themselves out there," she says quietly, "but I get that it's hard."

"Hallelujah!"

Jessica laughs and unclenches her fists. She brushes the hair away from her eyes. "We're all in this together, right?"

I can't resist breaking out into song. "We're all in this together…" I sing, channeling my best Gabriella Montez. I expect Jessica to join in after the first line. Instead, she smiles and claps along in rhythm as I continue through the chorus.

"That was great!" she says, applauding my performance. "Did you make that up yourself?"

"Are you serious?" I gloat a little and say, "It's High School Musical, silly goose! Zac Efron, Vanessa Hudgens?" She still looks at me with zero recollection. "Really?" For once, there's something Jessica doesn't know. (*Chelsea's and Mari's hidden talents don't count. No one saw that coming!*)

"So, you're saying you didn't make that up?" she asks seriously.

My gloating quickly turns to guilt for being so smug. I apologize and say, "I guess it's not as popular as I thought. It's just a movie I used to watch with my friend."

"High School Musical," Jessica repeats.

"It's probably on Netflix now."

"Netflix?"

"Yeah, you know—"

"Great climb!" Duke interrupts, waving as he and Pete leave the woods with Adam.

Chelsea and Mari join us a second later. "I'm really proud of you, Mari," Jessica says as the four of us stand together, looking up at the top of the wall.

"Thanks. I couldn't have done it without you—without *all* of you," Mari says.

Jessica then pulls us into a group hug. "This is so great, you guys!" she cries.

"Okay, okay. That's enough," I say, freeing myself from the group hug. "I'm ready for a swim after all that exercise. Who's with me?"

Everyone quickly agrees and turns to leave the woods. Chelsea is chatting with Mari about a book she's reading, and Jessica joins their conversation. "I read that one. Did you ever read…"

I remain behind them, several paces away. The realization that camp is ending and we will be returning to our regular lives hits me like a punch to the gut. I don't want to go back to real life—texting, scrolling, notifications, the constant scrutiny, always feeling like everything I do is being judged and could end up on the internet for the whole world to see—where it's hard to know if your friends are *truly* your *friends*.

"Are you always this slow?" Mari asks, stopping abruptly and looking over her shoulder at me. Chelsea and Jessica stop, too. The three of them stand there waiting patiently for me to catch up.

"Pick up the pace, Camper!" Chelsea says, reaching out her hand. "No one gets left behind at Camp Evergreen."

As I grab hold, Jessica clasps my other hand. Chelsea extends hers to Mari, and together, the four of us charge forward, singing *John Jacob Jingleheimer Schmidt* at the top of our lungs.

Dinner in the mess hall is a mix of subdued campers who have run out of steam and others who have somehow found their second wind. The four of us belong to that first group of exhausted campers and mostly focus on eating our dinner of hamburgers and fries.

Just as we finish our plates, the camp counselors hustle us outside for a Camp Evergreen group photo in front of the mess hall. "Say Cheeeeeese!" Adam says as the timer on the camera, one of those old Polaroid-style ones I have only seen in the movies, runs up and snaps the photo.

We only have a few hours before Community Campfire, the final gathering for the week, and Mari and I agree we have to visit the freshwater pond one last time.

The sun sinks low on the horizon, casting the pond in gray and dark shadows, but not in the threatening way it looked last night when I came looking for Mari. It's inviting and soothing, mostly because we know how beautiful this place is when the light shines on it.

We venture to the other side of the pond and settle onto a large boulder just a few feet from the trickling waterfall. The boulder is low enough for us to dangle our feet over the edge to dip our toes in the water, and Mari suggests we take our shoes off.

"Girl, we do *not* have time for you to take those high tops off your feet." I laugh and count on both hands the times I've had to wait for her to put on (and take off) her Chucks throughout the week. "We'll miss Community Campfire by the time you get them back on!"

"I know, it's the only thing about these sneakers I can't stand," she confesses.

"So, what was your favorite part about camp?" I ask, kicking my feet back and forth as they dangle over the water.

Thinking it over carefully, Mari answers, "Conquering the rock-climbing wall. That was the best."

"Hallelujah!"

Mari laughs. "Well? What about you?"

"Everything was fun, just like my mom said it would be. It's definitely hard to pick just one thing," I say, taking my time to think about everything we did together. "The talent show was fun, and Charlie's comedy act was iconic. He's a sweet kid," I add, continuing to think.

"I guess I missed that act," Mari says, and I remember she disappeared before Charlie took the stage.

For a few minutes, we sit quietly, surrounded by the sounds of the waterfall, frogs, and buzzing insects. A light breeze rustles in the treetops, carrying the scent of fresh moss. I'm really going to miss this place.

"Okay, okay," I say. "I think I have an answer. My favorite part was when you admitted to me that you wanted your canoe paddle to *accidentally* hit the back of Jessica's head!"

We burst into hysterical laughter. "Oh, stop! That was *not* your favorite part, Amber!"

"How do you know?" I ask, barely managing to stop laughing.

"And here I thought you were a *good* egg," she teases.

After finally getting a hold of ourselves, I admit to Mari, "Maybe you're right that it wasn't my favorite part of camp this week. I think we've both come around to understanding Jessica a little differently than we did at the beginning. I think she feels a lot of pressure to be perfect. She just wants everyone to get out there and do their best at something—*anything*."

"I guess we all could use a supportive cheerleader like her in our corner," Mari says.

I sing, "We're all in this together, da-da-da, we can make it, da-da-da." I stop and search Mari's face for *any* sign of familiarity. "High School Musical?"

"What in the world?" Mari asks.

"Never mind," I say, a little miffed.

She laughs. "You're an odd one, Amber," and quickly adds, "but I still think you're a good egg."

"Knock-knock!" Jessica makes her usual announcement to enter our bunk—the bunk *without* an actual door to knock on.

"Enter at your own risk," I shout, looking around our disorganized bunk.

Jessica pops her head inside and says, "Ah, yes. I see what you mean," her eyes scanning the floor, clothes strewn about. "Before Community Campfire, I wanted to make sure we all exchanged contact information. Chelsea and I already swapped, but here—" she produces a few sheets of paper torn from a spiral-bound notebook and a bag of colorful glitter gel pens.

Each of us takes a paper and pen—Mari choosing the purple one, of course—and writes down our info. After I've written my cell number and Instagram handle on all three papers, I watch Jessica carefully tear her paper in half and then fold each of them neatly. I do the same before everyone exchanges papers.

I stuff everyone's papers into my pocket as the official signal—the smell of burning oak and birch—tells us Community Campfire has commenced.

"Okay, let's go!" Chelsea says. "We can't be late for Community Campfire tonight!" Her excitement seems a little extra until I remember she's in possession of the Starburst Staff.

I groan when I see Mari's feet *without* high tops on them. "We'll be there in, oh, I don't know, what do you think, Mari, an hour for you to get your Chucks on?"

"Funny. I'm working on it now. We'll catch up," she says as Jessica follows Chelsea out of the bunk.

"The Starburst Staff," Mari says as she crams a foot into her shoe. "What will happen to it?"

"I have no idea. My mom never mentioned it. She usually gets caught up in her memories of her first love she met here at camp."

"Oh *really?*" Mari gushes. "That is so sweet! Wait, don't tell me she married her first love, and you're—"

"Immediately, no!" I shut her down abruptly. "I think they stayed in touch for a little while, but she never mentioned how it ended. All I know is that she met my dad right after high school, and they were married a year later."

"Wow, your mom was really young when she got married."

"She'd agree with you. I've heard her say more than a dozen times that she was too young and hardly knew herself before tying the knot."

"But she has you! So, I guess it wasn't a bad choice after all."

It had never occurred to me that Mom *chose* to have me. For the woman who can never make up her mind, deciding to have a baby—that's huge. *Deciding* to have *me…* well, I'm just glad she did.

Chapter 30

MARI

After four minutes of wrestling with my Chucks, Amber and I finally leave the bunk and head to Community Campfire. The path is easy, and I could probably walk it with my eyes closed, as if I've known this place my whole life, when, in fact, it's only been five days.

The denim color night sky stretches before us as we exit the woods. The full moon, like the one in Amber's painting earlier this week, shines brightly. "You know, Amber, this week has been…" I hesitate, searching for the right words. "It's just... I want you to know that you've been so cool, and I—" struggling to get the words out, I finally manage to say, "Thank you for not judging me and for giving me enough space to come around on my own. I know I was miserable at first."

Amber gives a soft laugh. "Miserable is a strong word."

I smile, but my eyes sting a little. "Maybe. But you didn't make me feel like a lost cause. You have a gift for making people feel accepted and cared about," I say, hoping it doesn't sound too cheesy. "Believe me, I know it's hard being someone who feels everything so deeply. I know it opens you up to a world of hurt, but the world needs more people like you—people who show up and know how to be themselves—who help others feel a little less lost." I pause, not caring if I sound like Mr. Rogers. It's the truth.

Amber pulls at a thread on her sleeve, not meeting my eyes. "Why would the world need more average people like me?"

"Amber, there's nothing *average* about you! You've got this—this light about you. I can't explain it, but when you found me last night, the things you said…" I trail off, feeling my emotions start to overwhelm me. I clear my throat, trying to hold back the tears. "I've never told anyone about what I've been through, but last night, you reminded me that I am brave and need to believe in myself. You were there for me, just as you are, when I needed someone."

Amber looks at me, startled, and says, "My mom says something like that all the time."

"Your mom is pretty smart," I reply.

"I am pretty lucky to have her," she says, wiping away a tear.

"I think she's just as lucky to have you."

"Maybe," she replies softly.

"There's no *maybe* about it, Amber." My tears threaten to spill over, but I don't want to turn this into a sob fest. I shift gears abruptly: "And can we take a minute to appreciate your amazing style?" We both laugh as Amber looks down at her dark purple sweatshirt with the words, "Well-behaved women rarely make history," scrawled in neon pink above a calico cat wearing sunglasses and a party hat.

The old saying, "You can't judge a book by its cover," comes to mind, and for the first time, it doesn't sound so cliché. Despite Amber's outwardly confident appearance, she has insecurities and struggles just like everyone else. I guess we don't always know what others are going through, do we?

The final Camp Evergreen Community Campfire concludes as it always does: "Hey-ho! Camp Evergreen! Hey-ho! Hey!" But tonight, the last phrase hangs in the silence instead of the usual excitement and applause.

No one moves as Adam and Sam bring the box with the carved Starburst crest on the side closer to the fire, its glow flickering across their faces. Sara and Joanna join them on either side of the box.

Chelsea steps forward with the staff, walking purposefully toward them. Before surrendering it, she recites: "May the spirit of Camp Evergreen remain in our hearts, allowing its light to shine through each of us. May our thoughts, our actions, and our words always be kind. Let us remember our own lights and never be afraid to let them shine." Her voice carries over the hushed crowd, and for a moment, I expect a collective "Amen."

Instead, the campers sit motionless, their eyes reflecting the firelight as Joanna and Sara lift the lid. Adam and Sam carefully take the Staff from Chelsea and lower it into the chest, their movements deliberate, reverent. The lid closes with a soft creak, like a breath being released.

"The Starburst Staff, its light and meaning, now rests—its spirit lingers in the campfire's glow, in our hearts, and in the memories we carry home."

Chapter 31

AMBER

The next morning, we wait for our rides outside the camp office. After hugging me and Mari, Chelsea turns to Jessica, embracing her fiercely, and says, "I'm going to miss you so much!"

"I'll miss you too, Chelsea!" Jessica says as they reluctantly let go. Chelsea makes her way to her family's car, turning once to give an exuberant wave goodbye.

Another car pulls into the parking lot, and Jessica lets out an exasperated sigh. "That's my brother," she says, her voice filled with disappointment. "Bring it in, ladies!" The three of us engage in an awkward group hug. "Amber, I'm going to check out that movie—what was it called again?"

"*High School Musical.* Check the Disney Channel," I say, as Mari looks at me just as puzzled as Jessica had been yesterday when I broke out into song.

"It's a movie?" Mari asks.

"Apparently." Jessica shrugs as she picks up her perfectly rolled sleeping bag from the ground. "See you guys next year!"

"Good luck with your photography internship!" I remember to add.

"Thanks! And remember," she says, pointing a finger at each of us. "Make sure you show people how awesome you are!"

Mari and I laugh and promise we'll do our best.

Then Duke and Pete come up behind us, and Pete asks, "See you both next year, right?"

"Wouldn't miss it," I say, giving him a high five.

"Cool. Have a good summer," he says, then heads for a bright yellow Jeep Wrangler. The license plate jumps out at me: "HNY BEE." *Cute.*

Duke steps closer to Mari and whispers something in her ear. She smiles, and they hug.

Aww, a real-life High School Musical romance.

Then there's a rumbling noise as an ancient blue minivan—the same one that brought thunder to camp earlier this week—pulls into the lot.

"That's me," Mari says over the growling engine. "Shocking. I'm always the last to be picked up from everything."

There's not much left to say, so we hug each other and exchange a quick, "Bye!" before Mari makes her way to the rusty minivan with her sleeping bag and vintage luggage that reminds me of the one Bing Crosby has in Mom's favorite Christmas movie, White Christmas.

"Mari!" I call out to her. "Remember who you are!"

Her face lights up, and the biggest smile I have ever seen dances across her face. As she reaches the van, the woman driving steps out. Mari drops her luggage and throws her arms around the woman, catching her by surprise. She hugs Mari back, and as they hold each other, the woman—who, I swear, looks just like Grandma—glances over at me and winks.

Mari gets into the van and waves one last time before sliding the door closed. The noisy van leaves the parking lot as gray clouds gather overhead. A rumble of thunder rattles a flock of birds in a nearby tree as fat raindrops begin to fall. I breathe in the fresh air filled with aromas of pine, campfire, and Ms. Wolcott's pancakes and shout, "Hey-ho! Camp Evergreen! Hey-ho! Hey!"

Thunder responds to my shout, and Mom pulls into the parking lot a second later. I grab my things and run to the car as the rain comes down harder. I toss my gear in the back hatch and quickly jump into the passenger seat.

"Sorry!" Mom says. "You know I hate when you're the last one to be picked up, but the coffee maker was on the fritz this morning, and then I couldn't find—"

"Your car keys?" I finish her sentence.

"Right," Mom says with a smile as she puts the car in drive. "I can't wait to hear all about this week!"

"It was great, just like you said! I did a *ton* of new things and made some new friends," I say, stifling a yawn.

"That's wonderful! I knew you would!"

Wedging my pillow between my head and the window, I recline my seat a few inches as Mom turns onto the main road. "I'm so beat, though. Can we save the details for later? Maybe after we get home and I've had time to shower and feel human again."

"Of course, that's fine."

Mom turns on the radio and quickly lowers the volume as I settle in for my car ride nap. Her usual station, *Y94-FM,* is playing *Hero* by Mariah Carey—the only female pop singer besides Celine Dion I know well from the '90s. I close my eyes and drift off to sleep, but don't dream at all.

Mom slows the car to take the exit off the highway, and the abrupt change of speed rouses me from my nap.

"Morning, sunshine," Mom says as she looks both ways before turning left toward home.

"Wow, we're already home," I say, putting my seat upright.

"Just about."

"I can't wait to shower and sleep in my *own* bed," I say. "Right now, both sound like heaven." *Or, as Mari would say, the Celestial Kingdom.*

"What's so funny?" Mom asks.

"Oh, nothing," I say, realizing I didn't laugh silently.

"You're an odd one, Baby Burrito," Mom laughs as she pulls into our driveway. "Home, sweet home."

"At last!"

"I'll grab your duffle bag and throw your clothes into the washer so you can shower."

"Yeah, sorry you had to smell me the whole ride home." Lifting one arm and shoving my nose into my pit, I whistle. "Whew, that's rough!" I make a face as I reach for my sleeping bag.

As Mom lifts my duffle bag, the flimsy headphones fall from the side pocket. Following the mile-long cord, she pulls the attached discman from the bag and cradles it like a baby kitten. "Where in the world did you find this?"

I shrug and say, "It was in the side pocket of my duffle bag before camp."

"I haven't seen this since college."

"Did you actually carry that thing around? It's so big and clunky. I don't see how it would fit in your pocket."

"Speaking of things that fit in your pocket. I knew you probably needed a new charging cord for your phone, but it was also time for an upgrade. After you shower, there's something for you on my desk. It's all charged up and waiting for you."

"No way!" I instantly remember dropping my phone in the lake and am relieved I won't have to break any terrible news to her. "Thanks, Mom. I'll take really good care of it. Promise."

Mom follows me into the house, and we part ways as planned. Halfway up the stairs, I remember my new phone, but my craving for soap—and the urge to lather, rinse, repeat—makes me decide it can wait.

Once the bug spray, sand, and sunscreen residue spiral down the drain, I dress and throw my wet hair into a sloppy bun. Sliding my feet into my Nike slides (*oh, how I missed them!*) I head downstairs to find Mom sitting on the sofa with a frosty cup of iced tea.

"Feel better?" she asks as I enter the room, looking and feeling like a new person.

"Much better!" I admit. "I smell better, too!"

"Hallelujah!" Mom laughs. "Okay! Lay it on me!" she says, setting her cup on the end table and repositioning herself to face me as I plop down on the cushion at the other end of the sofa. "No campers met their unfortunate fate at the hands of Cannibal George, did they?"

"No, Mom. No campers were harmed or eaten by Cannibal George." I humor her, "Not this year, at least."

"That's good."

"Community Campfire was rained out once, but we were inside the mess hall for the talent show, so it wasn't a complete washout, and Ms. Wolcott had ice cream sundae fixings for everyone instead of s'mores," I say all in one breath. Then, remembering Charlie's stand-up comedy act, I recite his last joke out loud: "I went to buy camouflage pants, but I couldn't find them!"

Puzzled by my random joke, Mom laughs and says, "I didn't know you were a comedian! Did you do a stand-up comedy act for the talent show?"

"No, but Charlie did."

"Oh, Charlie. Right," Mom says oddly.

"Yeah. When he introduced himself to me, he went on and on about the breakfast foods and fruits he does and *does not* like." I laugh at the memory of him describing bananas as mushy and Ms. Wolcott giving him extra pancakes that morning.

"Anyway," I continue, "I did all the activities, and rock climbing was probably the best! It was hard and definitely scary at first, but the view from the top was iconic!"

Mom shakes her head knowingly. "I'll never forget that view. I managed to make the climb on my second attempt, but I was terrified to open my eyes, at first."

"I'm sure you were. It was *really* high!"

"I knew I'd regret it if I didn't open my eyes and take it all in," she says as she reaches for her iced tea and takes a long drink.

I think of Mari and the moment she opened her eyes after overcoming whatever was keeping her from taking in the iconic view.

"Dang it! I just remembered I forgot my painting at camp," I say, completely bummed.

"Oh, no!" Mom says as her phone rings. She apologizes for the interruption and quickly reaches for it. "Hello? Oh, hi! Yes! What can I do for you?" Getting up from the sofa, she mouths, "I won't be long; be right back," and heads to the kitchen to check on dinner in the oven.

Her phone reminds me that I still haven't checked out *my* new phone. Standing quickly, I cross the room to Mom's desk and easily spot it. I tap the screen, but it's off. I hold the power button until the little white apple appears on the black screen as I return to the sofa.

Thankfully, Mom remembered my Apple ID and password, and it doesn't take long for my home screen to load the familiar, colorful icons I haven't seen in a week. I feel an instant dread as the red balloons with double-digit numbers pop up above each one. I have some catching up to do.

I settle into the sofa and open Instagram. A photo of Miranda crossing the finish line at a track meet fills the screen. Strands of her otherwise perfect hair, soaked with sweat, cling to her face, twisted in pain. Both arms are extended high above her head—the moment of victory is captured. But it's not the Miranda I know, the girl who's perfectly polished and always ready to triumphantly take the first-place podium. Instead, I see someone exhausted, barely holding on, defeated. Her caption breaks my heart:

I think about all the times I felt I couldn't measure up to Miranda. The times I felt invisible, stumbling in the shadows she cast. But did she ever feel that way too? Is her confidence just a shield, a way to keep her own doubts hidden?

I picture her sparkly red dress in kindergarten, her smile shining brightly like she owned the world. Then I see my own wacky wardrobe, not just a style choice but something more like armor—an attempt to fend off the vultures. All this time, I thought I was so different from Miranda, but maybe we're more alike than I ever realized.

The thought brings me back to Jessica and everyone's papers with their contact information. *Dang it.* I can't remember where I put them. Probably in my duffle bag with the rest of my—

"Okay, thanks for calling," Mom says, interrupting my thoughts. "Bye now." She returns to the sofa, and pointing at my hands, says, "New phone: Who dis?"

I roll my eyes and laugh. "You know, I didn't miss having my phone as much as I thought I would," I say, surprising myself. "The first day was weird, though. I kept feeling it buzzing in my pocket even though I knew it wasn't there."

"Phantom vibrations?" Mom laughs.

"Honestly! It's a *real* thing!" I say, looking back at my phone with Instagram still on the screen. My eye catches a post with one of those selfies using the "Age Yourself Twenty Years" filter. "Hey, check this out." I pull up the filter and snap a quick selfie to show Mom.

"Oh, my goodness, you look like *me*," she says, then adds in mock horror, "you poor thing!"

We both laugh, "Nah, it's not that bad. You should have seen Joseph's. His was *really* bad." I laugh, remembering his wrinkly face and the white hair growing out of his ears.

Mom settles into her cushion and takes another sip of iced tea. "Dinner is almost ready," she says. "I hope you're hungry."

"Starving!" I admit.

"Same. Wait until you taste this braised filet mignon I made. It took me all week to perfect!" she says, like an excited child in a candy store.

I laugh as my stomach growls. "I'm sure it will put Ms. Wolcott's tuna pasta salad to shame." I then describe one of her side dishes, mimicking Mom's MasterChef contestant voice: "Today I have prepared for you tuna macaroni salad made with wild-caught ahi. Finely diced red onion, celery, and tart Granny Smith apples are combined with a creamy mayonnaise dressing made from farm-fresh eggs, extra-virgin olive oil, and a spritz of fresh-squeezed lemon."

"Impressive," Mom says with a nod of approval.

We laugh as the aroma of garlic and onions fills the house. I can't help but think again, *It smells like the Celestial Kingdom.*

"This apple honey bread pudding is amazing," I say, once we've finished every bite of the braised filet mignon Mom mastered and moved on to dessert.

"Apple honey bread pudding, made with pasture-raised eggs, cored and peeled New York-grown Cortland apples, vanilla scraped from vanilla beans imported from Indonesia, hand-whipped heavy cream, and drizzled with honey harvested from Mrs. Colvin's very own backyard beehives."

"Pete's mom has beehives?"

"Oh, not Pete's mom—his grandma," Mom says and rambles full steam ahead about beehives and learning about them when she was in high school.

I take another spoonful of the apple bread pudding, the flavors exploding in my mouth, making it hard to focus on what she's saying. I catch something about going to school with Pete's dad and Pete moving into the house up the street from us just after Grandma passed away. Then I hear Mom reminding me that she moved into this house in ninth grade, right after her first year at Camp Evergreen.

After another bite of pudding, I try to listen a little closer. "I went to school with Pete Senior," Mom says, then clarifies when she sees the confused expression on my face. "Your friend Pete is named after his dad. You should have seen the look on Pete Sr.'s face when he saw me and your aunt unloading the U-Haul—iconic!" Mom laughs.

I'm slowly processing everything Mom is saying, and I try to connect the dots bouncing off the walls of my brain like unruly preschoolers who won't fall in line. I guess I just didn't know Pete was named after his dad, and then I remember Pete's yellow Jeep Wrangler with the HNY BEE license plate. At least that makes sense now.

After swallowing my last spoonful of pudding, I say, "I actually hung out with Pete at camp. We played tetherball and talked. Honestly, I feel bad for not hanging out with him sooner. He seemed different somehow. But it's not like I know him that well."

"Pete is a good kid," Mom says, rubbing her temples, suddenly looking exhausted.

"You good?" I ask.

"Huh? Oh, yes. I'm fine. Just a headache from all the driving today. I think I'm going to turn in early tonight."

"Okay. I'll take care of dinner cleanup."

"Thanks, Baby Burrito," Mom says as she stands. "Oh, I forgot to grab the mail today. Could you bring it in after you're finished? You can just toss it on my desk," she says before kissing my forehead and shuffling out of the kitchen.

I watch her go, the weight of the day clearly catching up to her, as I stand to take our empty plates to the sink.

I finish the last of the dishes and head out to the mailbox. The neighborhood is quiet and still, just as it was the night before camp. The fading sunlight makes way for the moon, its light glistening on the treetops, casting soft shadows across the lawns.

I look up the street and see Pete's house. His porch light glows like the color of the setting sun, shining enough light for me to see him sitting on the front steps with a bright orange cast on his arm. Before I can walk over and ask what happened, he stands and disappears into the house. I'll have to catch up with him tomorrow.

Shifting the stack of mail in my hands, I turn to head inside as a little girl's giggle from across the street carries through the silent neighborhood. I watch as she runs up her driveway, her dad following behind, guiding a small pink bike with the training wheels still attached.

A nostalgic tug in my chest stops me, pulling me back to when Mom, not Dad, taught me how to ride a bike. She always says she doesn't know what she'd do without me, but I feel the same way about her—the way she has always believed in me and trusted me to do the right thing, even when I wasn't sure I could. Life with Mom—just the two of us—is all I've ever known, and I wouldn't trade it for anything. She always makes sure I know I'm enough for her, and she has always been enough for me. We look out for each other.

Still, as I step through the front door, I wonder, *What had Dad been carrying that made him step away?* I used to worry I wasn't enough for him, but now I wonder—did *he* worry he wasn't enough for *me*? I wish I could tell him we were *both* wrong.

After tossing the mail on Mom's desk, I head to my room, exhaustion settling over me. My bed calls my name, but first, I need to do something. I search under my mattress (*no pool float tonight! Hallelujah!*) for the Congressional Art Competition letter. I hold it firmly in both hands and hum, "This little light of mine, I'm gonna let it shine."

Chapter 32

MARI

Dressed in a silky black gown, she looks out over a crowd of smiling faces. Her mom and dad sit in the front row, her sister between them, anxious for her performance.

Mr. Shepherd waves from a few rows back. Mr. Franklin, dressed in his Santa suit, winks. Her friends are there too, though one empty seat beside them tugs at her heart.

A giant framed mirror lowers before her, revealing her reflection: dark clothes, painted black eyes hidden behind a curtain of purple hair. She steps closer, her fingers brushing the glass just as the girl she once was begins to fade.

Her reflection shifts, revealing the truth. She stares at herself—dark hair, bright eyes, smiling—a version of herself she never expected to see. The scars she once hid are now barely noticeable, like words drawn in the sand, gently washed away by the tide.

Turning to the piano on center stage, she strides confidently toward it. The crowd's applause echoes through the auditorium as a girl appears at her side.

"Amber! I've missed you!"

"I told you it was already within you, Mari. You remembered."

"Yes, Amber. I remembered."

"Look at what you've done—everything you've accomplished. And look at all these people, Mari, that love you—that are proud of you."

"Nothing worth having comes easy."

"Yes, Mari. You made the right choice."

Chapter 33

MOM

Giving up on sleep, I make my way to the kitchen for a cup of tea. I fill the kettle with water and place it on the front burner. Reaching into my robe pocket for my glasses, I come up empty. With a sigh, I pat the other pocket and then run a hand through my hair, only to find them perched on top of my head, exactly where I put them before coming downstairs. Laughing at myself, I remove them and put them on to read the tea boxes.

Too many choices, but chamomile is the obvious winner—it will help me settle down so I can sleep. I pull out my favorite teacup—the one with dandelions sketched around the rim—and drop a tea bag inside. As I lean against the counter, waiting for the kettle to whistle, my thoughts drift.

All the stories Amber shared about her first year at Camp Evergreen earlier today and at dinner have my head spinning. Amber had said, "Ms. Wolcott brought out ice cream sundae fixings…" but three years ago, Chelsea sent me the newspaper clipping when Ms. Wolcott passed away. Amber also mentioned Charlie—who could forget Charlie?

The kettle's whistle breaks my thoughts, and I remove it from the burner before it wakes the whole neighborhood. After pouring the steaming water into my mug, I head to my bookshelf beside my desk and pull out my 1998 scrapbook album.

As a teenager, I always avoided mirrors and dodged photos. I hated myself then and was convinced everyone else did, too. When the envelope with my first Camp Evergreen photo arrived twenty years ago, I didn't bother to open it. It got tossed in a box and was lost in the shuffle of moving from the farmhouse to this house just down the street from Pete.

I open my scrapbook and flip through the pages. I stop when I find the 1998 camp photo and Jessica's letter she sent with it a few years ago:

> *Your sweet Amber looks identical to the Amber we met*
> *at camp all those years ago! I couldn't believe the*
> *resemblance when I saw the Christmas photo you sent.*
> *Do you agree, or am I losing my mind?*

I stare at the photo—my friend Amber—smiling in her Cheshire Cat shirt and striped, pink and purple knee-high socks. *My Amber really does look like her.* In the photo, I'm sitting beside her with my purple hair, black clothes, and those maddening high-top Chucks that required a lot of patience to put on and take off.

Amber knew me as Mari—the nickname Laura gave me when we were little, because she couldn't pronounce Marlena. I abandoned that nickname after high school, leaving that part of myself behind when I found my way and reinvented myself. Back then, happiness, hope, and belonging felt so elusive. I struggled to imagine a future where I might feel different.

In the same pocket that held the Camp Evergreen photo, there's a piece of paper torn from a spiral-bound notebook where Amber had written down her phone number; the ink faded, and the digits smudged beyond recognition. I spilled coffee on it years ago when I pulled it out to inspect it before adding the camp photo from Jessica to the album.

Beneath the blurred numbers, Amber had also scribbled what I once assumed was her AOL instant messenger address, though I could never quite make it out. Back then, we didn't have a dial-up web connection for our home computer, and the library's connection was slower than Eeyore. I remember calling her, but it didn't even ring. Instead, three obnoxious tones preceded the operator, saying, "We're sorry, but the number you have dialed is not in service. Please try dialing again."

For weeks after Jessica wrote to me, I pored over the camp photo from my first year, dissecting every detail. But the possibility that *my* Amber, named after the Amber I became friends with in 1998, was simply too much to process. Jessica and I were losing our minds—getting old and likely entering a senile phase. Unable to make sense of it then, I tucked the photo away so Amber wouldn't find it. How could I explain it to her when even I didn't understand it myself?

Once again, I hear Amber's voice crashing into my thoughts— "I actually hung out with Pete at camp." But Pete Jr. broke his arm the day before camp and hadn't gone this year.

Did she actually become friends with Pete Sr.? The same Pete I met at camp, and later discovered he lived just up the street from the house we moved into after the apple farm?

This is madness. How could *my daughter* be the friend I made twenty years ago, who was there for me when I needed someone the most?

Suddenly, I remember something. I creep up the stairs to the attic and switch on the light. Carefully, I make my way past several boxes, looking for the bushel basket I'd noticed when grabbing the duffle bag for Amber to take to camp. The thought of looking under the sheet covering its contents had been too overwhelming then. Besides, I was running late and didn't have the time—or the nerve—to look.

But now, I remove the old sheet and smile at the sight of my purple painting with the dandelion silhouettes and floating feather. My eyes then fall on Amber's beautiful, life-like painting of the majestic oak tree and the girl on the swing, her face turned toward the sky, lost in the light of the full moon.

Amber hadn't returned to camp the following year, so I brought both of our paintings home. Her painting looks just as real now as it did twenty years ago. It truly is a masterpiece.

I bring the paintings down from the attic and put Amber's on my desk under the light. I check the back for a name, but it's blank. As if there were not enough proof that Amber, my Baby Burrito, had somehow transported through time and found me, I turn the painting over and stick my nose as close to the canvas as possible. I probably look like Sherlock Holmes—without a pipe or magnifying glass.

Finally, hidden within the intricate details of the tree bark, I see my daughter's signature, *"Amber Luna Brown."*

Chapter 34

AMBER

Morning light and the aroma of coffee and apples wake me in my *own* bed! *Hallelujah!* For a second, I panic that I'm late for something, but the sound of Mom playing the piano—John Taylor's classic, *You've Got a Friend*—helps me relax. Mom always plays on Sunday mornings.

I come downstairs and see the sun shining through the window like a spotlight on Mom sitting at the piano. "Good morning, sunshine," she says as she finishes playing.

"Morning," I say, yawning.

"Sleep alright?"

"Considering I wasn't on a pool float in the middle of the woods, never better."

"Hallelujah!" Mom laughs as she sorts through the stack of sheet music on her right. "There's nothing better than that first night's sleep in your own bed after being away."

"Right?" Then, something on the wall above the piano catches my eye. "My painting!" I shriek. It's the same one I forgot at camp. *An actual Christmas-in-July miracle!* "How did you get it?" I ask, unable to tear my eyes away from it.

"A magician never reveals their secrets," Mom responds with a coy look. "It's a masterpiece, Amber."

I smile, remembering Mari's words: *You could open an art gallery one day.* "Thanks, Mom. I think I'll enter it into that art competition in Rochester," I say nonchalantly, as if this has been my plan all along.

"That's a great idea," Mom says, looking back at my painting of the girl on the swing and the full moon shining above her.

I think of my self-portrait hanging in my room—the girl with the crescent moon. I used to believe I was nothing like her, but I see her differently now. She was *reaching*, and *reaching* means she was trying. She wasn't giving up.

I picture both paintings side by side at the art competition— two self-portraits: the girl who once held back and hid her talent, and the girl on the swing, soaking up the light of the full moon. As long as I keep reaching for the light and allow my own to shine, I'll always remember: I am enough. I am whole. I am capable of anything.

Mom picks another song to play as I head to the kitchen. On the fridge, a photo of the unmistakable Camp Evergreen mess hall jumps out at me. I see myself in the photo, dressed in my Cheshire Cat T-shirt and Mari's arm around my shoulder.

How did Mom get my camp photo already? We left camp yesterday!

They must have emailed the digital file to all the parents. It's no surprise that Mom would dash out early this morning to have it printed at the drugstore. I shrug it off as Mom begins to play a melody. It sounds familiar, but I can't remember why.

I grab a plate from the cabinet and a spoon from the drawer. After dishing out a generous helping of pudding, I turn to put the container away in the fridge when something leaning against the wall by the front door stops me. The shape resembles a frame—*a canvas?* —and is partially covered with an old bed sheet. Only the bottom corner peeks out, revealing a familiar shade of purple.

Mom's singing pulls me out of a strange daze: "Like a candle in the wind, never knowing who to cling to…" and it hits me! It's the old song Mari knew so well! I was supposed to ask Google about it when I got home.

I take the first delicious bite of my apple honey bread pudding and remember my long list of questions to ask Google *and* the papers with everyone's contact information… ugh, my *pocket!* Of course, I remember where it is *now*. Mom took my duffle bag yesterday and said she'd wash everything. *Dang it.*

Reluctantly leaving my apple pudding behind, I scurry to the laundry room to check the dryer. Pulling out the clothes, I find my list for Google *and* everyone's numbers—crumpled and torn, the writing completely washed and dried away from *all* the papers.

Dang it again.

Well, at least they all have *my* information. I'm sure they'll follow me on Instagram when they settle in at home after camp.

I return to my pudding and take another satisfying bite, hoping it will dull my disappointment. I take three more bites and stop myself from licking the plate clean before setting it in the sink. I turn to leave the kitchen, but my eyes drift back to the mysterious purple object by the door. A warm summer breeze blows through the open kitchen window, rustling the sheet. I'm still slightly intrigued. I'll just take a quick—

A knock at the door stops me.

What the actual heck! No one ever comes to our door.

Mom rushes past me, announcing, "I'll get it!"

Opening the door, she lets out a happy gasp. "Hello, stranger!" I can't make out the voice that quietly responds. "Amber, it's for you!" Mom smiles as I approach the door.

"Hi, Amber. Can we talk? I've missed you."

The caption of her Instagram post flashes through my mind, followed by the words from the Starburst Staff ceremony: "May our thoughts, our actions, and our words always be kind…"

"Hey, Miranda. I've missed you, too."

My Bright Light Playlist

Eye of the Tiger / Survivor

My Heart Will Go On / Celine Dion

Fireworks / Katy Perry

The Flying Theme from E.T. / John Williams

The Raiders March from Indiana Jones / John Williams

The Imperial March from Star Wars / John Williams

Eleanor Rigby / The Beatles

Shine / Collective Soul

Dreams / The Cranberries

Rain / The Beatles

Paperback Writer / The Beatles

Tomorrow / Charles Strouse & Martin Charnin

This Little Light of Mine / Traditional

Hero / Mariah Carey

You've Got a Friend / James Taylor

Candle in the Wind / Elton John

Acknowledgments

This book and its characters may never have reached their full potential without the encouragement and insight of my earliest reader, Lori Greabell. Thank you for believing in this story from the start. Your praise, thoughtful critiques, and genuine excitement gave me the courage to believe in myself and not give up on writing Amber and Mari's story.

A very special and heartfelt thanks to my writing critique partner, Emily Shepherd. Your early suggestions and feedback directly impacted this novel's transformation from draft to final publication. This novel would not be what it is today without you.

I'm also deeply grateful to early readers, Bill Kauffman, Charley Kauffman, David Kirk, Heather Perez, and Sonia Ivette Falú, for their support and thoughtful feedback. Each of you helped me get this story right.

To my parents, Keith Marquart and Paula Marquart, for their unwavering love and support. Dad, you taught me the importance of embracing my individuality and letting my light shine. Mom, you taught me to have grace and kindness, for myself and others. Your insights helped me write this story authentically. Thank you for the hours you spent listening and helping me work through details that were too important to gloss over.

A special thank you to my middle and high school band teacher, Gibs Flock, for fostering my creativity and passion for music, listening patiently to me as a teenager struggling to find hope, and helping me know that I am, in fact, "a good egg."

To my children, thank you for patiently listening to me when all I could talk about was Amber and Mari, and for letting me weave some of your camp memories—and some of our fondest *family* memories—into this story. *And* for schooling me on Instagram—I couldn't have done it without you! Each of you has taught me many of life's greatest lessons, especially that no one is perfect, but that doesn't mean they're unworthy of unconditional love.

To my husband, Richard, for believing in me and encouraging me, even on my darkest days; for pushing me when I wanted to give up or take a step back, and for reminding me how important my dreams are, thank you for not giving up on me.

I'm grateful to Wildebeest Publishing Company and all of my writing colleagues, both in person and through the wonderful *"World Wide Web,"* who shared their experiences and advice, helping me gain knowledge and confidence in the writing and publishing process.

To all the summer camp counselors, too many to name here, who shaped some of my most cherished memories and those of my children, I thank you. Your influence lingers in these pages.

There are so many others whom I have not named here but whose kindness, encouragement, and light have shaped me and this story in big and small ways. Thank you to all the people in my life who let their light shine and helped me see my own. Keep shining, my friends.

Mari's Light Burning Bright
A sequel to the award-winning novel
Amber Luna My Bright Light

Chapter 1

After the two-hour drive home from Camp Evergreen, I'm feeling brave enough to talk to Mom and Dad about getting help because of the nightmares—*memories*—that are taking over my life.

I begin to think about how to bring it up as we pull into our driveway, but my mind spins in circles as I clutch my seatbelt strap. A giant *SOLD* sticker is slashed through the *Coldwell Banker Realty* sign. *Of course*, another decision that affects me has been made, and I don't have a say in it.

"It sold so quickly, Mari, and I wasn't sure how to tell you," Mom says, when she sees me staring down the sign, biting my lip, and holding back tears. "You had such a good time at summer camp, and I was enjoying all the stories you were sharing. I didn't want to spoil it."

You could have prepared me.

Mom parks, wasting no time getting out of the van. She's greeted with a slobbery kiss from our dog, Corky. "Who's a good girl? Did you miss us? Go give kisses to Mari," she says cheerfully, as if a stick of dynamite hasn't just been lit and thrown into my lap.

I open the passenger door partially, and Corky noses it open further, but I'm too distracted and I ignore her.

Laura gets out of the back seat, happy to give Corky the attention I denied her. "Poor puppy. Don't let Mari get you down. She's just crabby."

Crabby isn't the word.

Laura grabs her suitcase and sets it on the ground before reaching for mine. She hands it to me but doesn't let go when I take hold. "What's the magic word?"

I'm not in the mood for games and tug hard, forcing her to release it.

"Ouch!" she cries. "What's your problem?"

I mumble an apology even though I'm sure she's fine, and stomp toward the front porch, where pots of marigolds line the railings. I glance over my shoulder before opening the door and see Laura with her arms crossed in front of her and Corky with her head cocked to one side. They both stare at me with sad eyes.

In the front hall, moving boxes lean against the wall, and four tape guns rest on top of a pile of old newspapers. The air inside the house is void of the usual delicious smells of simmering cinnamon applesauce and slow-cooked beef stew. Instead, it reeks of damp cardboard and foam packing peanuts.

Dust motes, dancing in the sunlight, don't know where to settle now that the items they usually cling to are being ripped from their homes and shoved into boxes. It's difficult to breathe, but it's not the dust that has me feeling like a vice is being tightened around my chest.

After dropping my suitcase inside the laundry room, I slip through the back door unnoticed and then a sudden urgency to get as far away from the house as I can makes me break into a run.

When I come to a stop at the banks of the man-made pond the highway department built five years ago, my lungs are filled with fire, but the burning is nothing compared to the pain in my heart. I look out over the water and immediately I'm transported back to the freshwater pond at Camp Evergreen. Only then can I breathe a little easier.

The memories of camp—nightly bonfires, singing silly camp songs, archery, and conquering the rock-climbing wall with my new friends— it all overwhelms me. Remembering my bunkmate, Amber, and her spunky Christmas in July Grinch outfit with coordinating knee-high candy cane socks, gives me an unexpected but welcome laugh.

But the memory blurs before disappearing. Another one, darker, takes its place: leaving the mess hall at camp, launching a kayak from the beach, paddling my way through a rainstorm to the forbidden island. The voice that haunts my dreams was shouting, *"Now look what you've done!"*

I don't remember shoving my kayak into the dirt or taking the path that led me to the small clearing, sheltered by a grove of trees. It was Amber who found me and pulled me out of the dark living room, where I was stranded, and didn't know that what was happening to me wasn't right—it wasn't normal.

A pair of robins whiz past me, one plunging toward the water, grazing the surface. I watch the ripples multiply and disappear as the intrusive thoughts and images return, barging into my life like the local news interrupting a television show: "We interrupt your regularly scheduled program to bring you this important message…"

They're annoying interruptions, but they're meant to help people. The images that invade my mind don't help me. They only remind me of the monster who hurt me and the monster I've become.

I hurt myself to drown out the memories. But I'm ashamed of the evidence of that hurt, no longer possible to hide, that proves I'm broken.

Amber's voice dances around the edges of my dark thoughts. *You know who you really are is already inside you, right? Remember who you are.*

I wish I could remember who I am, but *remembering* is what got me into this mess. I just want to get back to my regularly scheduled program—

My life.

About the Author

After graduating high school, Kaitlyn attended Ricks College (now BYU-Idaho), where she studied piano. She accompanied both instrumental and vocal performance majors and played for the college's theatre department. She later earned an Associate of Arts in Music Education from Onondaga Community College while pregnant with her second child.

Following a successful 15-year career with a manufacturing company in Syracuse, NY, Kaitlyn faced health challenges, prompting her to leave the industry. However, her disabilities didn't stop her from pursuing her dream of becoming an author.

In November 2024, Kaitlyn's first book, *IDK What to Say: A Guide for Navigating Social Situations*, a reference book that equips readers with confidence-building tools to help them navigate social situations, was published by Wildebeest Publishing Company.

Kaitlyn lives in Central NY.

Discussion Guide:

Describe the book in one sentence.

Discuss the first sentence of the book.

What were the themes of the book?

What was the main point of this book?

Did you uncover any symbols in the book?

What were the characters' biggest struggles?

What are the characters' strengths and weaknesses?

To which character did you most relate or empathize?

Were you able to easily keep track of the characters?

How did the characters influence each other?

What do you think would happen in the characters' lives if the book continued?

What was your favorite part of the book?

Do you believe the book touched upon any broader social issues?

Did any historical or cultural references stand out to you?

Did the book change your opinions or way of thinking at all?

What will you remember most about this book in a few months?

Did you learn anything new by reading this book?

Did reading the book affect anything in your own life?

Were you able to "guess" the ending?

Was the ending satisfying?

How did you want the book to end?